PRAISE FOR *ZIG ZAG*

"A book that starts with an epigraph from D.C. Berman already has me eating out of its hand but then J.D. O'Brien goes and ups the ante. *Zig Zag* is a cosmic American crime odyssey that's reminiscent of Barry Gifford, James Crumley, Charles Portis, Elmore Leonard, and Charles Willeford. Wild, funny, and entertaining as hell. Capri Dall and Harry Robatore are characters I won't soon forget."

-William Boyle, author of *Shoot the Moonlight Out, City of Margins,* and *A Friend is a Gift You Give Yourself*

"An at times funny, at times hard-boiled, at times sweetly sad crime romp set in some of the scuzzier pockets of Southern California. J.D. O'Brien lovingly limns these divey bars, rundown motels, and ticky-tacky apartments and brings to life the stoned and soused oddballs who stumble through them. It's Elmore Leonard meets Warren Zevon with a wry sensibility all its own, and I enjoyed every page of it."

-Richard Lange, author of *Rovers, The Smack,* and *Angel Baby*

"A wry and raucous thriller. Droll humor swirls nicely with serious violence in this madcap adventure. This is his debut novel, but the author comes off as a seasoned pro in *Zig Zag*. He serves up a mesmerizing story with a strong set of characters in this engrossing page-turner."

-*Shelf Awareness*

"Feels like a great 70s movie."

-David Gordon Green, director of *Pineapple Express, Joe*

ZIG ZAG

A Novel

J.D. O'Brien

schaffner
press

TUCSON, ARIZONA

FOR THE EAGLE

Once you zag, you suddenly see how choosing
to zig could legitimize the whole rig.

D.C. BERMAN

GETTIN' BY IN VAN NUYS

1

WHEN HARRY CHECKS in at Reduced Rent-A-Car, Ken from the desk escorts him to the lot and unfurls a rinkydink red carpet leading to the driver's side door of a Ford Fiesta. An added feature of the white-glove service package. The dingy carpet is matted flat and Harry sees the rest of his life laying there in front of him. Thirteen steps to the gallows.

He removes his Stetson Sundowner like it's made out of lead and hunches in behind the wheel. "I think the last guy must've smoked in here," he says.

Ken looks over the inventory sheet.

"Let's see if we have something else for you."

"Don't bother," Harry says. "I just don't want to get bit for it."

He points to a bold line in the rental agreement that threatens a two hundred dollar charge for smoking in the vehicle. Ken makes a note and initials it.

Harry nods. "Appreciate it."

Waiting to make an illegal left out of the lot, he adjusts the rearview and watches Ken roll the carpet like a boulder up a hill, the back of his shirt dark with sweat.

Harry unwraps his Tareytons with a sense of ceremony. Each new pack is a present he gives himself every morning. He lights his first and cuts across Van Nuys Boulevard.

Motoring north toward his office, he passes the pawn shops and car dealerships, the junk boutiques with trampy mannequins out front. Everything in this five-block radius looks sunbaked and secondhand. The Van Nuys Courthouse sits in the middle of it all like a criminal center of gravity.

Harry feels invisible in the Fiesta. Just as well since he doesn't want to be seen in it. His heap breaks down every couple months, which is why he's in this rented roller-skate to begin with, but at least it's got some panache, some heft.

He parks on Erwin and grabs his hat.

Buckaroo Bail Bonds, established 1998, Van Nuys, California, is head-quartered in an office above the Country General Store, a purveyor of time-tested western apparel. Harry Robatore, established 1954, Del Rio, Texas, is its founder, sole proprietor, and only original member.

BAIL BONDS blazes in nondescript neon from a second-story window over Van Nuys Boulevard. The office windows don't catch the kind of California light that looks romantic flooding through dusty venetian blinds. The sign doesn't even blink.

Late summer, everything sticky and slow, Harry doesn't stray far from the window unit. His wardrobe isn't conducive to the higher temperatures. He reaches for his cigarettes and isolates a loose thread over his breast pocket. Something is awry deep in the fabric of this shirt and he expects it will be a slow unraveling from here on out.

Eleven in the morning and his prevailing desire is to call it a day.

Slip back into his house poncho and come in for a landing on the cradle curve of the sectional. Light up an enormo torpedo and pass another glacial afternoon with Hoss and Little Joe.

Lately he's only been working when he needs to. Hitting the snooze. Listening to that lazy golden voice in his head. The *take it slow* voice, the *fuck it* voice. Most days it sounds like George Jones to him.

For stretches at a time, he'll barely go into the office at all. A chunk of change will come in, five-ten grand, and he'll soft-shoe around the apartment until he's down to seeds and stems again. Like those guys you see at Arco putting a few bucks in the tank. Barely enough to get to the next station.

Harry has designs to move past the retirement-on-the-install-ment-plan model and set himself up permanent. He's tired of a lot of things, but mostly he's tired of waking up thinking, "How am I going to get fucked over today?" In the bail bonds business, you assume everybody is lying to you about everything. People will say anything to get out of jail.

His job isn't complicated when it goes right. A bail amount is set. The client puts down ten percent and he covers the rest. The client shows up for court, Harry keeps his ten percent. When it doesn't go right, when the client skips town or doesn't show, Harry is out the whole nut.

The idea is to invest a little extra time upfront to save a lot of extra time later. Running credit history and criminal background checks, looking into assets and assumed identities. The main thing is to make sure they have collateral to cover the bond if things go south. Most of them don't. If they don't, or if they seem like a flight risk, Harry has to rope in a qualified signer. Someone who will stake their house or their diamond ring on this deadbeat.

Harry doesn't believe he's hit rock bottom in terms of what people will do to fuck him, but he doesn't want to find out what that looks like. The routine is getting old. It has been for a while.

His old man always said Harry had a loitering manner about him. That he was born with an ass dipped in flame retardant. It wasn't untrue. For a time, Harry tried to dress it up in Buddhist thinking, but it only made things worse. If we're just grains of sand drifting across the beach, why bother getting out of the house poncho at all?

If he survives until March, Harry will be the same age his old man was when he died. Right as he was about to retire from thirty-five years behind the counter in a Del Rio feed store. The fact that Harry's been more or less retiring for a decade may be tied to a fear of suffering the same fate. It's something he's considered.

Harry resembles the old man physically, cast in the same mold as generations of male Robatores. Texas-tall and thin as a branding iron. And he shares his father's distinctive taste in western couture. But the work ethic was lost somewhere along the line.

Tumbleweeding toward seventy, Harry's starting to see himself as the kind of guy Tom T. Hall might've written a song about. An old pothead trying to turn over a new leaf.

Time to get to work.

A bondsman can't approach a client directly. You have to wait for them to approach you. It's easier for that to happen when you're hanging around the courthouse. You just need to be discreet about it.

Some familiar springers are milling around. Jorge Alvarez paces, pretending to take an important call. Toss Papadapoli, the Ancient Greek, occasionally glances in the direction of a James Michener paperback without turning a page.

Harry's primary competitor, Rick Devlin of Gold Key Bail Bonds, has the bus benches in the vicinity locked up so his smiling face is everywhere. It's the kind of smile that makes you reach back to check that your wallet is still there. Harry doesn't have that kind of advertising budget. He can barely afford the smallest square in the Yellow Pages.

Harry shoots the shit with an older court officer he knows and learns Cal Hensley got picked up this morning for public intoxication. Again.

He skims the report. Cal was found slumped against a concrete planter outside the James C. Corman Federal Building, clutching a half-empty pint of vodka. With another in his coat pocket. Unsteady on his feet and slurring his words, Cal was known to Officer Werner, who took him into custody.

Clients come from all walks of life but Harry's tend to come from the lower staggers. His two most consistent clients are Hensley, a public drunk, and Lenny Disco, a public masturbator.

Both men look the part—Hensley ruddy and bearded with a prizefighter's nose, Disco with a lint-trap mustache that suits his predilection—and in both cases, the crime isn't what they're doing, it's where they're doing it.

Rick Devlin likes to brag about his high-end connections, celebrities he's bailed out and can now claim affiliation with. That's why he's the one with his face on the bus benches and the custom limo.

Harry gets it. The payday cases can be great, if the money is right and the risk is low, but most of the time they're more trouble than they're worth. The guy who can afford the higher bond can also afford to get hid. It's easy to get excited by the big numbers but small potatoes clients are more dependable.

The Cal Hensleys, the Lenny Discos. Guys who aren't going anywhere.

Outside the courthouse, Cal holds up one hand to shield the sunlight and rifles through the pockets of his army coat with the other, patting himself down for a stray nip.

They walk the two blocks up Erwin and Harry clicks the key fob to unlock the Fiesta.

"What happened to the Olds?" Cal says.

"In the shop."

Cal lowers himself into the passenger seat. "Again?"

Harry makes a stop at Louie's Liquor and Check Cashing so Cal can cash a check and buy some liquor. Then he takes him to Tommy's World-Famous Hamburgers on Victory to get something in his stomach. People assume Cal is homeless, but a small inheritance provides him just enough to rent a one-room efficiency, drink, and post bail.

He lets Harry pay for the chili burger.

They pull up in front of Cal's apartment complex and Harry drops him at the curb with their signature sign-off. Two drunks in a midnight choir.

"Hey, Cal, they got Mogen David in heaven?"

"If they don't, who the hell wants to go?"

2

CAPRI DALL WORKS at the Big Smoke dispensary on Hazeltine Avenue. She has an idea to rob the Big Smoke dispensary on Hazeltine Avenue.

The idea came two weeks into the job, the day she realized the security camera didn't work. Two weeks after that was when Eddie, the manager, gave her a key to the place.

Now it's week five and the idea is forming into a plan.

Each shift she's worked has gone by slower than the one before. The constant throb of bass, the stale air overcast with vape clouds. Losers on the beat-up leather sectional, ripping bong hits and playing video games. Carvell the security guard mooning like a mental patient at his gun magazines. Days when she smokes along with everyone else, most days, it drags even more. Her boyfriend Ted acts like it's a dream job she has. Standing there for shit pay while someone else makes all the real money.

Capri watched her mother work shit jobs all her life. Just so they could live in shit apartment complexes, ride around in shit cars, and scrape together enough money to pay the past-due amount on bills to avoid shutoff every month. And where did it ever get them? It's a sucker's game and she'd rather die than live that life.

Dancing was a way to survive for a while, but the cash had a way of disappearing and if she stayed anywhere too long the same guys would start coming around and it would get creepy. Some guys tipped in pills and she'd try to save them to sell but she'd end up taking them more and more.

She thought porn might be an easy exit plan but it's even hard to make money doing that anymore. During webcam shows, she'd get a rush hearing the dinging of the tips coming in, like items being rung up in a supermarket, but it never added up to much. It was like that hopeful second when multiple crosslines light up on a slot machine, before you realize you've only won like ten bucks. But at least all the eyes were out there in the ether, hiding behind lame screen names.

It's only eleven o'clock but it feels like it's at least three. She tries to distract herself by watching the movie everyone's howling at, some hip-hop pot comedy they watch every other day, but the only way she can endure another second here is to spend every one of them plotting her escape.

She has most of it figured out. Carvell the security guard is the only wild card. Something's off about him. He's always staring her down. She's not sure if he's suspicious of her or just another leering pervert. He doesn't say much, but he's an overreactor. The slightest issue with a customer and he's in full defense mode. Like he's looking for an excuse.

She runs it down in her head again. Big Smoke is a strip mall hole in the wall so it's not like it'll be a massive score. And there's no way to take the money. One thing Eddie is strict about is not having a lot of cash on hand. Anytime the register has more than five hundred in it she has to put it in an envelope in the drop safe, not the storage safe. But if she does it on the right day, she could walk away with at least fifty thousand dollars' worth of product.

Thursday afternoon they're finally getting the big Acapulco Gold delivery. It was before her time, but the last batch apparently had a THC count in the high thirties and sold out immediately at sixty an eighth. They had to set limits on how much people could buy.

One of their suppliers, a friend of Eddie's down in Hermosa, has a connection to some old-time grower in Mexico, one of the only people who can match the original strain. A couple times a year if they're lucky, some will make it up the coast and Eddie will grab as much as he can. A large amount is supposed to be coming this time, along with the usual delivery of the supplier's other strains.

It all arrives at the end of the day Thursday, so they won't put it out until the next morning. Fridays and Saturdays are the busiest days so Thursday night would be the time to do it, before it's even unpacked. Today is Wednesday. So that means tomorrow.

3

THE CUSTOM-WRAPPED LIMO for Gold Key Bail Bonds takes up three spots in front of the Blue Grotto Lounge. Rick Devlin's smiling face billboards the evening traffic on Oxnard.

Harry parks the Fiesta and gives the limo a slow pass on his way in, fighting his nightly urge to key it.

Rick is posted at the Megatouch machine at the bend of the bar, under the blue halo of the Molson Canadian clock. He's less handsome in person than he is on the limo and the bus benches but he looks like just as big an asshole. Sunlamped skin, mane of white hair. His fitted peach Polo shirt makes him appear barechested at a distance.

He's playing Erotic Photo Hunt. The object of the game is to identify subtle inconsistencies in side-by-side shots of half-naked women. His finger hovers over the screen on a slow patrol.

"No strap on that brassiere there."

Harry's loping drawl stretches the word brassiere like taffy.

Rick taps the screen and racks up a few points under the handle UNCLE MILTIE'S HORSE in the player box. Harry catches his own gaunt reflection in the curve of the glass and gives Rick a slap on the back.

"Focus, pal. It ain't just a nudie show."

Harry saunters toward his regular stool, his transition lenses undimming in the lounge light. Tall and lanky with a slight hunch, he walks even slower than he talks. The maroon windbreaker is more countrypolitan than his standard western wear. His girlfriend Ruby talked him into it, but he doesn't see it becoming a staple. He does like the new Levi's she picked out, darker with a slimmer fit, so that's a compromise.

Behind the bar, Fuzzy sponges the rim of a rocks glass with lime juice and rolls it through a crunch of kosher salt. He adds ice and a heavy pour of Wolfschmidt vodka and makes his way to an antique juice press.

Harry watches a drizzle of grapefruit pulp cloud the cocktail.

"There stands the glass," he says.

Fuzzy jabs a pink straw in the Salty Dog and sets it on a soggy Heineken coaster.

"There it stands."

"I've been seein' a lot of that shirt lately," Harry says.

"I can't be bothered anymore."

In the Grotto's heyday, Fuzzy fancied himself a nightlife impresario. He wore Panama hats and white sport coats. He smoked long slim cigars. He looked the part.

These days, he cuts a wider figure in orthopedic Velcro sneakers, Sansabelt pants, and roomy guayabera shirts by Bobby Bermuda, a big-box Tommy Bahama knockoff. He's only fifty-nine but they're bar years. He still has the buzzcut, which is why they call him Fuzzy in the first place, but it doesn't make him appear youthful anymore. It just looks patchy, like he cut it himself. Which he has.

"Why don't you take a vacation? I thought the prodigal son was helping out."

"I can't trust him around the booze and the register," Fuzzy says. "It's bad enough he's living with me. I don't need him here."

"Maybe I'll get behind the stick a night or two."

Fuzzy says what he always says when Harry says that.

"You get people out from behind bars."

"Mr. Robatore." Rick sidles up to Harry. "What's with the Larry Gatlin jacket?"

Harry looks Rick up and down.

"You wearin' lifts?"

"Got to keep my cock off the floor."

"Two guys cracking wise," Fuzzy says. "Kings of the zing. Harry, what do you think of Rick's haircut?"

"What is it, Washington's birthday?" Harry says. "Father of our country over here."

"More like Charlie Rich." Rick settles in on his barstool. "The Silver Fox."

"I still say that's a piece," Fuzzy says. "You doing another?"

Rick rattles the ice in his glass. "I could snorkel one down."

A fresh gin and tonic arrives and Rick clinks with Harry. They've been back on speaking terms for a week. They've gone stretches without talking, but neither will ever surrender the Grotto. They'll sit one bondsman on one side, one on the other. Fuzzy running interference. Switzerland with a swizzle stick. The last dust-up was over an off-color remark Rick made about Ruby but Harry decided to let it go.

"I remember when Charlie Rich died," Rick says, salting the coaster so his glass won't stick. "I put on *Behind Closed Doors*, smoked a pack of Kools, drank half a quart of Gilbey's, and cried like a baby boy." He lets that sit a second. "How long's he been gone now?"

"'Ninety-five."

"Shit, ninety-five. Really?"

A solemn nod from Harry. "I took that one hard."

Rick pulls an electronic cigarette from his shirt pocket. "I miss the Kools almost as much as I miss Charlie."

"Careful with that thing, Rick," Harry says. "You drop it in your drink you're liable to give yourself a zap."

Rick takes a long draw on the device. A blue light glows at the tip.

"You eat?"

"No comeback?"

"I chose to fork the conversation in a different direction." Rick rubs invisible lint off his lap. "I'm like a talk show host that way."

"Right."

"Keep it light. Keep it moving."

"You didn't have a comeback."

"Try me. Say it again."

"Careful with that thing, Rick." Harry grins. "You drop it in your drink you're liable to give yourself a zap."

"How's business?"

"Fuck you."

"What I did there was counter a jab with a right hook. The old one-two." Rick makes a float-like-a-butterfly move. "And laugh it up, but this thing is a godsend. Haven't had a cigarette in two weeks. Breathing deep. Increased bloodflow to the penis. I feel robust."

"You look like FDR."

"I thought I looked like ol' Georgie Washington."

From their post, Harry and Rick can size up the whole bar. Harry nods in the direction of a mountain man type sitting alone with a pitcher of beer. He wears two flannel shirts and his beard climbs high on his cheeks. "Who's the beard?"

Rick shifts into his John Wayne.

"A beard that size in a town this size, ya notice it."

"Ya ask me, a man with a beard that size has got somethin' ta hide."

"Your Duke sounds slow," Rick says. "Like he fell off his horse too many times."

"I'll work on it."

Fuzzy comes by and Rick tells him to sprinkle the infield again. "And less ice this time, Fuzzard. I want to drink it, not skate on it."

He turns back to Harry. "Where's the lady?"

"Work. Tomorrow's date night."

"A little lovin', a little turtle-dovin'."

"That's the idea."

Harry lights a Tareyton. The Grotto is one of the few places left in Los Angeles County where he can smoke indoors like a civilized man. There's a loophole in the law that still allows smoking in owner-operated establishments. Other than his pal Gordy, who holds down the fort during occasional Vegas jaunts, Fuzzy is the only miner in the mine.

"Heard you took the Olds off the road," Rick says.

"Should be back in action tomorrow morning. She's under Beryl's care."

"You've got to spruce yourself up. That limo is a golden goose. People get arrested just so they can ride in it. Had some Armenian ape the other day tell me it was classy. You believe that?"

"It's not my style. You're a hot dog. I'm not a hot dog."

"Right. Hopalong Harry. Why don't you pick 'em up in a stagecoach?"

Depending on Harry's mood, engaging with Rick can be heavy lifting. A drill of hoisted laughs and clenched smiles. The drunker Rick gets, the more of a buzzkill he is.

He has two primary conversational modes. There's the macho harangue of the wrestling heel when he's juiced on gin and on the topic of his ex-wives. Then there's the hushed tone of the co-conspirator, leaning in and looking over both shoulders, when he's discussing his current romantic or financial affairs.

He swings between the two when doling out unasked for advice. Harry resents these trade-secret sessions, even if he does reluctantly heed Rick's barroom counsel from time to time.

Tonight, Rick is trying to goad Harry into admitting the new low-baller approach he's been selling him on has been working.

The approach is this: you let clients put down five percent, rather than the standard ten. Then you tack a high interest on the remaining five, with fees that increase with every missed payment.

"A fast nickel is better than a slow dime," Rick said to Harry when he ran it down for him a few weeks ago. "The shitbirds you spring, this could be your bread and butter."

Harry has no illusions about being the last honest man in the bail bonds business—and the strategy has been working—but it feels predatory, since the people who can't afford the ten percent down are more likely to miss the follow-up payments, putting them into a payday loan spiral.

You take it where you can get it. Everybody has their line. For Harry, it's domestic violence cases. Which is a loss since the bail amounts are high and the charges are often dropped before the court date. It's basically free money but it never feels great to cash those checks, especially when it's a woman with a shiner writing them. Which isn't unusual. Rick, of course, has no problem with the domestic cases. Even to the point of practically specializing in them after his second divorce.

Most nights Harry keeps the peace by avoiding these ethical pissing contests. But tonight his silence is enough to torque Rick into delivering his well-rehearsed monologue on the sordid history of the bail bonds profession—from the two Irish bartenders who started the practice to its current status as being illegal everywhere except the Philippines and the United States of America.

"And it's on thin ice here, pal, believe you me," Rick says. "You want to move to the Philippines? Butch and Sundance in Bolivia? We're outlaws. Last of a breed. Now's not the time to get high-handed. Stick to getting high."

Harry signals Fuzzy for another round, his finger hula-hooping over the empty glasses.

4

"IT'S SOME OLD hippie weed," Capri says.

She's topless on the couch, finessing a grape Swisher blunt. "Real zaza shit. Super rare. It'll be gone before the weekend, so Thursday night is the only time if we want to get the whole load. We don't put it out until the next morning."

Her boyfriend Ted is stretched out with his head on her lap looking up at her. He's a scrawny guy with a sunken chest and he doesn't have his shirt on either.

"They just leave it out?"

"It goes straight into the safe."

"Don't they lock it up?"

"It's my job to lock it up."

"So—"

"So, I don't lock it up."

"I don't know, boo. Don't you think they'll know it was you?"

Capri nudges his head off her lap and stands up. Pink terrycloth shorts labeled *PINK* hang low on her wire hanger hip bones. She lights the blunt and turns down the laptop speakers.

"All Eddie talks about is how he's been suspicious of Andre since he fired him and hired me. He says Andre has a chip on his shoulder about the whole situation." Capri takes a hit and speaks in a pinched gasp. "Eddie's been meaning to get the locks changed but he hasn't done it yet. He's so faded."

She exhales and watches Ted sit there and scratch himself under his gym shorts.

"I don't know," he says.

"I'm serious, Ted."

She passes him the blunt. Ted holds it in his hand and stares at the muted TV. *Chain Reaction* is on. His dad always has the Game Show Network playing and he doesn't like it changed, even when he isn't home. She watches him move his lips, trying to link a word beginning with *P* to the word GALLERY listed below it.

"It's *Peanut*," she says.

"I don't think so."

Ted watches, unenlightened, as PEANUT fills the panels letter by letter.

"What about the security guard? Doesn't he close up with you?"

"Carvell's in charge of the cash. I'm the one who sets the alarm and locks up."

Ted takes a deep hit and hands the blunt back. "I'm not sure it's a good idea. You haven't even been there that long. Give it a chance. You're good with the customers."

"Good with the customers? What the fuck is wrong with you?"

"I mean, at least it's a legit job."

"My last check was a little over four hundred. For a week. I'm used to making five hundred a night, close to a thousand on weekends."

"Yeah, but you were—"

Her voice sharpens. "I was what?"

"Forget it. I don't want to fight about it."

When they first met, Ted was all about the dancing and the web-camming. He thought it was hot. Now he's changed his tune on everything. He doesn't like other guys seeing her naked, he says. It makes him feel like a chump.

"What about the cops?"

"The place doesn't even have a legit license, Ted. Eddie's not going to call the cops. He's going to send Carvell to talk to Andre and Andre's going to say he didn't do it and they're not going to believe him."

"And what are you going to do?"

"I'll go back to work like nothing happened. I'll say how fucked up it was that Andre could do something like that. Then I'll quit after another couple days or so, saying I don't feel safe there anymore."

"What about Andre? What happens to him?"

"Are you serious?"

"I still think it's suspicious. What about a different dispensary?"

"I don't have a key to different dispensary."

Ted considers that. "Okay, when are you going to do it?"

She one-eighties the blunt into the shotgun position and Ted leans in to take it. A trail of smoke escapes as she pulls away from him.

"I'm not," she says. "You are."

"What do you mean *you are*? You mean *I am*?"

"Yeah, that's what I mean."

"It's your plan. Why am I the one breaking in, taking the risk?"

"You're not breaking in. You'll have a key."

"Is it breaking and entering if you have a key?"

"No, it's just entering." She knows Ted won't bother to look into that. "And anyway, you're not going to get caught."

"If you're so sure I'm not going to get caught, why don't you do it? I have a record."

"You think I don't?"

Capri watches Ted for a reaction, but he doesn't seem to want to push it. One of the reasons she thought he'd warm to this robbery plan is it would keep her out of the sex stuff for a while. And he's dumb and romantic enough to buy the idea of it being something they can do together as a couple. Just the two of them.

"How about this," Ted says. "I go in when you're working and I rob you, but you know it's me. That way we both—"

"My way works better."

"What about the alarm?"

Capri looks at him.

"Right. You won't set it."

5

HARRY CRANKS THE AC and eases into the house poncho Ruby got him for Christmas. It's alpaca wool with an Aztec print and makes him feel like Clint Eastwood in an opium den. He clicks on American Movie Classics and catches *Hud* after the opening credits.

Hud's nephew Lonnie turns down the little battery-operated radio in his pocket and approaches a barman sweeping up glass in front of a saloon. "Must've had quite a brawl in here last night," Lonnie says.

"I had Hud in here last night is what I had," the barman says.

Harry smiles at the line.

It cuts to commercial after Lonnie follows a breadcrumb trail of high-heel shoes to the door of a married lady and he and Hud run off in Hud's Cadillac. A pink Cadillac in a black and white movie.

Harry likes to watch westerns late at night. It's a comfort to imagine himself bedding down next to a campfire after a day of cantering on horseback, crossing barren landscapes under wide open skies. Ruby calls them country movies, like country music, and only tolerates them because they put her to sleep almost immediately.

Ruby won't be around until tomorrow when her work is done for the week. She lives in La Puente and works as a second-shift nurse at the

Queen of the Valley Hospital in West Covina.

Harry runs the last of his Purple Mountain Kush through the grinder and taps it out on one of the trashy check-out magazines Ruby keeps around. There's enough there for an adequate nighttime jibber. Harry hits toothpick pinners throughout the day, building to the end-of-the-night pinecone. The Big K.O. Some nights he allows himself one whiskey. One. Three fingers of Tullamore Dew. Brown to come down. When it gets low, he tops it with a splash of water to make it last. He swishes it around, buoying the magic in the shallows.

He lights the joint and winces through the roll call of potential side effects on a medication commercial until he can't remember what the pills are supposed to cure anymore.

His phone buzzes with a low lilt of lap steel. Ruby showed him how to make it so a song plays and a picture of her comes up when she calls. The song is "I Love You A Thousand Ways" by Lefty Frizzell. The picture is one he took of her on the Catalina ferry last spring. Squinting into the sun, her hair wild in the wind.

Harry's old grey cat comes out of hiding when she hears him talking. She drags her sandpaper tongue across his palm and Harry tells Ruby that Emmylou says hello.

Ruby tells him about her night. The moon was full and the emergency room was out of control. Harry isn't inclined to believe in the lunar effect but he's seen firsthand proof of it in barrooms and has noticed a spike in calls for his services on occasion. People getting all wound up in a moon frenzy and landing in jail.

She wants to make sure everything is set for tomorrow. Sometimes Harry is scattered on the details. He tells her he's already made reservations at Dan Tana's and that he'll stop off and get the ingredients to make margaritas. She wants the Monte Alban mezcal and he needs to put it in the freezer in case she wants to do shots.

"Straight into the icebox, darlin'. Worm'll be freezin' his ass off."

Ruby says she's tired and can't wait to go to sleep and wake up and have it be tomorrow. He tells her he loves her and that he can't wait either.

He hangs up and unmutes the TV. Hud and Lonnie are eating fresh peach ice cream on the front porch. Then they head down the dark road to town in Hud's Cadillac.

"Lonesome old night, isn't it?" Lonnie says.

Harry and Hud respond in kind. "Ain't they all."

If Ruby were there, she'd have shushed him. That's one of her pet peeves, Harry stepping on movie lines. Especially when it's Paul Newman saying them.

FUZZY PULLS INTO his driveway just before two a.m., hoping his son is out of sight. It's been a long night and he wants to take off his pants as soon as he walks in the door. The kid's been here a couple months and now he has the new girlfriend staying with him.

Fuzzy has lived alone for a long time and this arrangement has thrown his day-to-day routines for a loop. At the beginning, it was nice to be reconnecting. He and his son have mostly been lifelong disappointments to one another, no pretending otherwise, but in the first stretch of having him here, it felt like all wasn't lost. That there was still something to salvage, maybe even build on.

Sometimes they'd catch a late morning breakfast at Norm's or find something they both liked on TV and have a few laughs. Fuzzy even had him taking shifts at the Grotto. He didn't see it becoming a father-son operation, but bartending is a good skill to have. There are worse ways to make a living and Fuzzy thought it might teach him some responsibility. His whole life, the kid hasn't been able to hold onto any job, even on the lowest rungs of the fast-food ladder, for more than a month or two.

Everything changed when the girl showed up. The two of them would stay up all night, make a mess of the place, then sleep all day. Then the Grotto register started coming up short. Now Fuzzy can feel he and his son slowly becoming strangers again.

He walks in and there they are conked out on the couch. Same as the past couple weeks. He claps his hands like he's rousting a couple drunks at last call.

"Get your asses up. I want to watch the *Feud*."

Weeknights from two to three a.m. the Game Show Network shows back-to-back episodes of *Family Feud*. The original, with Richard Dawson. It's something Fuzzy looks forward to.

Ted squints awake and Capri shifts under her blanket. Fuzzy grabs the bag of pot off the coffee table and tosses it on Ted's lap.

"This wouldn't fly at your mother's, Teddy."

Ted snatches the bag and the stubbed-out blunt in the ashtray.

"C'mon, boo."

Capri slides out from under her blanket. She's naked and doesn't hide it. She looks at Fuzzy a second like she's waiting for him to react. He never does. He's taken her in in glimpses over the past couple of weeks. Ladders of tattoos up and down her. Earrings everywhere.

She opens her legs a little getting up and follows Ted down the hallway with her pink shorts in her hand. Straight inked lines like pantyhose seams start at the top of her heels and stop just below her ass. Fuzzy cocks his head, trying to decode the intricate script on her ribcage.

She turns back and he looks away.

He knows she doesn't want to seduce him. He's not that delusional. Probably just wants to taunt him. Mean thing to do to a harmless old bastard pushing sixty like a stalled car.

Fuzzy grabs a can of Bud from the dorm fridge and drapes his pants over the side of the couch before climbing into the cockpit of his recliner. He shifts the lever on the right to put his feet up and the one on the left to set his back at full tilt. Doctor's orders.

He thumbs up the volume as Dawson introduces himself to the Hewetts, a decent-looking family from somewhere down south.

BAD DAY AT BIG SMOKE

6

T HE BUSINESS CARD for Beryl's Automotive advertises glad-to-see-
you service and look-you-in-the-eye prices. Harry sits across from
Beryl at a metal desk piled high with smudged carbon receipts. There's
a girlie calendar on the wall, Coors Banquet empties crushed flat on
the floor.

Beryl runs through some specifics regarding the alternator and
torque convertor and Harry nods like he understands.

With a car like the Olds, you need a mechanic you can trust. Harry
trusts Beryl. He's also sprung more than a few of Beryl's guys. Beryl
hires ex-cons and his ex-cons becoming cons again provides a dependable source of repeat business for Harry.

He signs the bill and Beryl leads him outside. The aging chariot
gleams in the lot.

"She's road-ready." Beryl hands him the keys. "Showroom condition."

Harry's lenses darken in the sun glare. "Maybe if you squint."

The Olds is a 1986 Oldsmobile Cutlass Supreme Brougham sedan. It
has a washed-out gunmetal exterior and a plush burgundy driver's seat
that feels like a Barcalounger.

Harry puts his hat on the dash next to the dancing hula girls. Everything looks good. They vacuumed the floors, hung a tree off the mirror, and went heavy on the Armor All. They even cleaned the plastic gutter in the center console and didn't swipe the roaches.

He fires up the engine, and one of those roaches, and roots through the cassettes in a Tony Lama boot box on the passenger side floor. He pops Hoyt Axton out of the deck and slides in Johnny Bush, the Country Caruso.

Harry and Ruby saw Johnny Bush and the Bandoleros at Don Laughlin's casino last year and spent the night. Won two-fifty on the slots and blew every penny at the Saltgrass Steak House at the Golden Nugget. Bacon-wrapped filets with blue cheese on top. A flock of drinks. Hifalutin desserts. There was a bottle of complimentary champagne and a Whirlpool jacuzzi in the suite and he went down on her for so long he had a crick in his neck for a week.

After the Fiesta, the Olds feels like a luxury liner. When Harry turns onto Van Nuys, he wants to bob and weave down the boulevard. He stops by Yum Yum Donuts for half a dozen and heads to the office.

A CHEESEBURGER AND a Cherry Coke in the morning can carry Capri straight through until dinner. Ted goes with a Breakfast Jack and bacon cheddar wedges and makes his usual commentary on the superiority of Jack in the Box over other fast-food franchises in the San Fernando Valley.

They could be beat on specific items. In-N-Out has a better burger, Chick-Fil-A and Popeye's superior chicken, but overall, considering menu selection, convenience, and hours open, Jack in the Box is in a league of its own. He can't believe it isn't more popular than McDonald's and Burger King combined.

"Tacos, burgers, breakfast," he says. "Normally I say do one thing and do it well, but they manage to do it all without sacrificing quality. Look at the shine on that brioche."

Capri plunges her straw deep in the giant plastic cup and sucks the ice clean.

"I don't think that's brioche."

"Could've fooled me."

They pull into the Big Smoke lot and see Carvell the security guard asleep in his car. Before she gets out, Capri hands Ted a piece of paper. It's a shopping list: vacuum-seal bags, heavy duty contractor trash bags, a hand vac, and rubber gloves.

"You can probably get everything at Walmart," she says. "You should go now so you have it all ready for tonight."

"What do you mean tonight? We're doing the robbery tonight?"

He looks around like someone may have heard him.

"I said Thursday. It's Thursday."

"You didn't say this Thursday. Don't we need to plan this some more?"

"That's what last night was."

On her way out the door Capri reminds Ted to call his friend Max, the one he said might be able to help them move the stuff. Then she tells him to throw away the shopping list when he's done.

Ted feels ambushed. He doesn't know what to say but it doesn't matter. She's already out of the car.

He backs up to the chain-link fence at the edge of the lot and watches Capri knock on the window of Carvell's car to wake him up before she lets herself in the back door.

The smell of the bacon cheddar wedges starts to make him nauseous. He has no appetite when he's nervous. He stuffs them back in the bag and sits there looking at the building like he might learn something.

It's smart to scope a place out before robbing it but he doesn't know what he's looking for exactly. Nothing special about the parking lot. A couple shoppers for the Spanish grocery next door. One of those cars where the hood is a different color than the rest of it.

Then there's Carvell the security guard's car. A silver Honda Crosstour with Storm Trooper rims. Ted watches him step out. A big dude, heavy, wearing a military-style blue uniform.

Carvell stretches then reaches back into the car, coming out with a shoulder holster with a semi-automatic handgun snapped in place. He straps up, scanning the parking lot with an intense expression. They make eye contact for a second and Ted feels like a spotlight hit him. He gives a friendly wave that Carvell doesn't return.

7

"**I** DON'T KNOW what to tell you, Guy," Harry says. "They're probably drinkin' coffee and smokin' big cigars."

He switches the phone to his good ear and rolls his lucky marble around on his desk, half-listening as Guy, his go-to attorney, runs down his latest predicament. Three kids were picked up in a stolen car. Guy's client was sentenced to ninety days, and he wasn't even the driver. The other two went with court-appointed counsel and got off with a conditional discharge.

Harry and Guy traffic in a similar clientele. If Guy gets the call, he's good about recommending Harry to handle the bond. Harry has better lawyers who compensate him on the rare occasion something big comes through, but the lowball stuff goes to Guy.

"You took the arrow on that one, boy," Harry says. "Who was the judge?"

Guy says it was Clements and bellyaches about how he has it out for him. Then he says the kid's father cornered him outside the courtroom and threatened to file an IAC motion.

"That's life on the prairie," Harry says.

He hangs up and puts his lucky marble in his pocket.

Buckaroo is a one-man operation, except for a revolving door of assistants Harry keeps around to work the phone, chase down clients, and keep the paperwork in order.

Manny is the latest.

Like most who fill this position, Manny is working down a debt, not earning a living. Unlike most, the debt is Manny's brother's, not his own. His brother Hector is a petty thief and drug dealer, repeat offender, who is behind on his payments.

Manny isn't covering for his brother so much as he's trying to help their mother, who recently had to put down her car as collateral, a car she relies on to get to work. Harry respects this about Manny, but it makes it harder to fire him.

Manny's a slow learner. The job doesn't take a lot of smarts, but it requires checking in with clients at least once a week to make sure they're staying put. To make sure they have their court date circled on the calendar. To make sure they still have the calendar.

Harry has promotional calendars printed every year, 65-cents a-piece from the same mail-order place that does his business cards. That way when a client leaves, Harry knows they have the court date clearly marked, as well as the due dates on upcoming payments. People are always eager to take anything free but Harry wonders who actually goes home and tacks up a year-long reminder of their legal hassles.

Manny has been somewhat useful in applying more modern methods. He's set up a few shadow profiles to befriend clients on social media, which has proven to be a good way to keep track of the younger ones. He's also working on getting Buckaroo outfitted with a new website. He says he knows how to rig it so the site will come up higher on the list when you do a search on the computer.

Harry shakes a Tareyton loose and walks over to Manny's desk. Manny looks up, taking a break from his third donut.

"I got a new prototype for the website. I was waiting for it to finish rendering."

"Can't sell that stuff to me," Harry says.

"Take a look."

Harry looks over Manny's shoulder. BUCKAROO BAIL BONDS is spelled out in cursive rope lettering over a cartoon cowboy.

"It looks like a loop," Manny says, waving his hand in a circle over his head.

"A lasso?"

"Yeah, like a vaquero. A buckaroo."

"I don't know, man."

"It looks good. Trust me."

Manny scrolls to the bottom of the homepage. "What do you think about a slogan?"

He shows Harry the site of a competing concern.

"This one here says, 'We get to you before your cellmate does.' Something like that. Clever, catchy."

Harry shakes his head.

"I don't like that horseshit. Where are we on the list?"

Manny checks names and numbers on a yellow legal pad.

"Still dialing for dollars."

"We're runnin' out of week."

Harry pats himself down for his lighter.

Manny pulls up a picture on his phone. "I got a good lead on this man."

"Who's that?"

Manny finds his name on the pad. "Tom Willis."

"Who's Tom Willis?"

"He's this man." Manny points at his phone. "The man in the picture."

On busy days, and today qualifies as a busy day, Harry writes himself a to-do list in the morning. It's only ten a.m. and he's already picked up the car and stopped by Amigo Liquors for Ruby's drink requirements. He even remembered to snatch a couple low-hanging limes off his neighbor's tree before he left this morning.

He peruses the rest of the list. Plenty of time to get a quick haircut, grab his boots at Country General, make a Costco run with Fuzzy, and stop off at Big Smoke to pick up some cheeba before he heads home.

There's a satisfaction in checking off each item. It makes his eventual indolence feel earned. When you stretch out on the couch with a torpedo after a day of honest toil, there's a sense of accomplishment that isn't there when you stretch out on the couch with a torpedo after a day of being stretched out on the couch with a torpedo.

He runs his hand through his hair and decides to head over and see if Giovanni has time to take a walk-in. He selects a straw Stetson Rancher from a collection of hats hanging on the wall under a mounted longhorn and a photograph of himself in a buckskin jacket in the 1970s. It was taken at the Palomino Club in North Hollywood, not long after he and his buddy Chris Nederhoffer landed in L.A.

Harry looks young in the picture. He still feels young, maybe because he's always felt old.

The phone rings. Harry points to it on his way out the door.

Half a block from Buckaroo world headquarters, Giovanni's Barbershop is a perfectly preserved time capsule with glimmering mirrors, a checkerboard floor polished to a high gloss, and jet-black combs floating in jars of sky-blue Barbicide.

Harry sits in a bright red chair looking at the autographed headshots on the wall. Vic Tayback, Peter Falk, Val Avery. All dead. He points to a framed glossy of Ernest Borgnine, scrawled with, *To Gio, love ya, kid!* — *Ernie.*

"Give me the Ernie cut," Harry says.

Giovanni looks ancient in his smock. He smells like fresh talc and hair tonic and he circles Harry like a sparrow, peering at his head and mumbling in Italian before getting down to work with the snippers. There's a frail, quiet man, even older than Giovanni, who seems to have the hair swept up before it even hits the floor.

"How's business, Harry?"

"Circlin' the bowl, you?"

"Busy, busy." Giovanni gestures around his crowded shop. Harry assumes these guys hang out there all day looking at old *Playboys*, playing dominoes, and drinking espresso. Some are very thin and sit cross-legged and wave their arms around a lot when they talk. Some are very heavy and sit with their legs far apart and look around a lot when they talk.

"You not busy?" Giovanni says.

"Busy, sure. Also broke. I spend more time chasing these deadbeats. I'm fixin' to pack it in, move down to Baja like Jesse Ventura."

"Not me. I get out of here, I move down the Hawaiian Islands."

"You and Don Ho."

"Big talent. The Hawaiian Elvis, they called him."

"Mexico's more my speed. My baby's from Veracruz. You been there?"

There's a trashy Italian movie on the TV and Harry thinks Giovanni is a little too engaged in it. "Keep your eyes on the prize here, Gio. I need to look good. Big date tonight."

Giovanni gets back to work until a naked woman on the screen nearly animates him into a tap dance. He puts down his scissors and goes to get a closer look.

Harry turns to one of the guys sitting there.

"Horny old goat, ain't he?"

8

CAPRI GETS THE jars of bud from the safe and lines them up under the glass countertop. There isn't much of the Heroijuana OG left so she erases it from the main board and makes it the shake special. She's trying to go about her business and not check the clock every two seconds waiting for the delivery. She sees Reggie standing at the counter and ignores him for as long as she can before going over.

Reggie's a friend of Eddie's, a photographer who is always trying to talk her into doing a shoot for his SexPotz site. Saying he's looking to monetize the thing, take it wide, but he needs hotter girls, girls like Capri, to get there. Today's no different.

"It's not even full-on nude," he says. "It's implied. You got big buds covering your nips and your puss. Or we got this party bong, how about you pose with that?"

His spiel reminds her of Terrence, the first of many wannabe hustlers she's encountered since she left Arizona, changed her name, and moved to Los Angeles three years ago.

Terrence talked good enough game for a 19-year-old desperate to get out of Tempe. Capri had been checking out the L.A. Craigslist postings for a few weeks when she saw an ad for a reality show with a rapper named G-Strang. She responded, attaching a few thong pics her ex-boyfriend Jamey took of her.

Terrence responded right away, saying he was G-Strang's producer and that they both liked what they saw. He said they were filming the making of G-Strang's new album and they needed hot girls to hang around this mansion in the Valley and shoot footage for the show and some music videos.

The pay was a thousand a week for six weeks, cash, plus being put up in a nice house.

Capri had never heard of G-Strang, but she checked out the production company online and it looked legit enough. There were videos on YouTube that looked like the kind of thing Terrence described—Hennessey, blunts, bikinis—and six-grand would be plenty to get her started in L.A.

A week later she got off the Greyhound in Hollywood and a guy in a white Escalade picked her up at the Mel's Drive-In on Highland. This was Terrence.

He said the house in Sherman Oaks was still being prepped and took her to a motel in Studio City where she shared a room with a girl named Riza. She and Riza killed time by the pool and stretched out on the hard motel beds, eating McDonald's and watching *Family Guy*. Capri thought it was weird he took their cellphones away, but she remembered hearing they did the same thing on *The Bachelor*.

One night Terrence packed Capri and Riza into the Escalade and took them out to get their nipples pierced, G-Strang liked pierced nips, then to a club in Hollywood. He said it was part of the shoot but all he did was take some videos on his phone. No crew or lights or anything.

G-Strang finally showed up, fatter than he looked in the videos. He took them to a private table with a bottle of Grey Goose that didn't taste like Grey Goose.

She doesn't remember much about what happened after they got back to the motel, but she remembers how she felt the next morning. And she remembers stealing Terrence's Escalade that next night.

She thought about driving it back to Tempe but there was nothing there to go back to. Her mom was back together with her asshole ex-boyfriend and Jamey, her own asshole ex-boyfriend, was back in jail.

She found some cash in the center console and drove to Venice where she abandoned the Escalade in front of the Davy Jones Liquor Locker and treated herself to a night at a fancy beach hotel she recognized from one of her mom's *Star* magazines.

She'd never fall for it today. Especially not from an amateur like Reggie, still standing there talking her up, not even realizing she hasn't been listening to a single word he's been saying. Eventually he gets the picture, buys a half-ounce of shake, and heads out as a local street dealer is coming in.

The dealer is another pain in the ass who thinks he's charming. Eddie gives him bulk discounts on ounces, but Capri doesn't want the supply diminished. Not tonight. She wants to take the place for all it's worth.

She tells him the real good Acapulco shit will be out tomorrow and he decides to hold out and just buy enough to carry him through the rest of the day.

"Make sure you set plenty of that aside for me," he says on his way out.

"Yeah, sure," she says.

FUZZY REACHES DEEP in the cooler for two cold Buds while Harry stacks the last of the Costco haul on the bar. Every couple weeks, Fuzzy hits the Costco on Sepulveda to load up on supplies. Harry isn't a member, but he'll tag along if he needs a carton of his Tareytons. He always says cartons of cigarettes remind him of Thanksgiving. Plentiful times, surrounded by family and friends. Fuzzy gets them wholesale with his vendor card.

They drink their beers and watch the news on the Magnavox. There's a manhunt for a child molester. A sullen sketch on the screen, dominated by heavy double-bridge glasses. "I don't know why the FBI don't team up with LensCrafters," Harry says. "Flag every guy who buys those frames."

The coverage shifts to a wildfire in Altadena. "Supposed to get some boom-booms the next couple days," Fuzzy says. "Maybe it'll break the heat."

The screen scrambles and blurs.

"I'll bite the bullet and grab one of those Roku smart TVs on the next Costco run," Fuzzy says. "I had them put the dish on the other side of the building but it's still not picking up anything but birdshit. Can't even get my game shows anymore."

Fuzzy knows the afternoon schedule by heart—*Chain Reaction, Card Sharks, $25,000 Pyramid*—and is always aware of what he's missing.

The first paying customers of the day arrive. A ratty guy with a game leg and a lummox in a work shirt with his name on it. Fuzzy takes his time getting over to them.

Nights are bad enough, but afternoons at the Grotto all run together, a record stuck in the same groove forever. At least he stopped opening in the morning. Nothing but third shifters and ironside alcoholics, people on benders and coke jags. He tosses a couple coasters down and asks what they're having, even though he knows.

When it was built in the 1970s, the Grotto was done up to look like an aquarium. Coral castles, sunken ships, treasure chests, neon carpeting pilled to look like perma-glo gravel. A barracuda named Maurice lived in a giant tank behind the bar.

Fuzzy bought the place cheap on a foreclosure deal and kept it hopping for years. Live bands on the weekends. Porn girls in slinky rayon dresses shimmying on the dancefloor with no panties and big bushes. Cocaine out in the open on the tables.

The Grotto eventually fell out of fashion, but karaoke helped keep it afloat during the week and there was still a decent Friday and Saturday night crowd. Things have only really bottomed out recently. Even the kitsch factor is mostly gone. It just looks shabby now, like a theme room in a rundown fuck motel. Something is always leaking or malfunctioning. It's like taking care of an octopus with eight assholes.

Fuzzy surveys his crumbling kingdom. Despite the garish décor, it always feels like a cloudy day in here. The room is bathed in a murky blue light, offset by the yellow haze of the popcorn machine, the slurred neon of the beer signs, and the faded blacklight glow of the sexy mermaid paintings.

It's been years since anyone's ordered a Blue Barracuda, a slush of rum, grenadine, and curaçao that once served as the Grotto's signature cocktail. The original Maurice the Barracuda is long dead. His final replacement was tossed in the dumpster sometime around 9/11. The tank sits empty, grime caked on the sides. Fuzzy doesn't even bother with the karaoke anymore.

Reminders of better days are tacked to the walls. Polaroids from when a night at the Grotto was worth documenting. Postcards from when he had customers who could afford to go on vacation. The only decorative upgrade Fuzzy's made in ages is a sign above the register that reads, "If Assholes Had Wings, This Place Would Be An Airport."

Down the years, Fuzzy has blamed any number of factors for the Grotto's decline: the economy, flair bartending, craft beer, foodies. These days his biggest competition is church basements. Or the Pierce Brothers Cemetery.

In most neighborhoods, the place would be long gone. It could only survive in an outpost like this, between a check-cashing place and a fly-by-night wireless store.

Fuzzy comes back to his beer and Harry nods in the direction of the jukebox, sitting dark in its boggy corner. "Buddy Holly die?"

"Let's enjoy the quiet."

Harry gives him a look and Fuzzy flips a switch behind the counter that brings the machine to life. Harry hunches over the domed glass and punches the buttons. The first note of "I Stepped Over The Line" by Hank Snow plinks through the speakers.

"Heartaches by the number." Fuzzy says it like a catchphrase.

He leans against the back bar. The guy with his name on his shirt signals that he and his buddy want to cash out.

"That's it for us. We've got to go unload the truck so we can load the truck."

TED HASN'T BEEN inside the Army & Navy Surplus store on Van Nuys Boulevard since he and his friend Max got caught trying to shoplift a ninja star there when they were fourteen. He walks the aisles, returning to the scene of one crime while he prepares for a bigger one.

They don't carry ninja shit anymore. Maybe kids aren't into ninjas now. There's more sunglasses and survival gear but otherwise it's pretty much the same. Smells the same. Everything that seemed old back then is still there now.

Ted's been involved in a couple things bigger than the botched ninja star heist but nothing too serious. He was picked up for hawking stolen hearing aids one time. Max was there for that one too. This guy Wayne, who sold them Oxys back then, hired them to work the streets on commission, selling items he'd boosted from a local medical center.

Some stuff went quick, but people were suspicious of the hearing aids. An old guy called it in after they gave him the scripted sales spiel outside the Ralph's on Burbank. His dad's friend Harry got him bailed out.

He racked up another offense when Wayne sent him into a pawn shop on the boulevard to sell a gold bar, the kind they use for fillings, that he'd stolen from a dentist's office. It was a canary in a coal mine mission. Wayne had him go in with a little bit to see if it was safe.

It wasn't.

The shop owner locked the door from the inside and held Ted at gunpoint until the cops arrived. Ted said he found it on the street and wriggled off the hook eventually, but his name was down in the books again. And Fuzzy had to call Harry in to bail him out again.

Tonight is different. He can't fuck this one up. He has to be prepared. There's plenty of camo stuff but that won't help for this. He buys a black tactical backpack, a tight black commando sweater, a pair of black fatigues, and a black watch cap that unrolls into a ski mask.

He grabs some other supplies, including a couple stickers, "Don't Tread On Me" and an angry eagle, to make himself look patriotic to the big bald guy at the counter.

9

BEFORE HEADING UPSTAIRS to the office, Harry stops in at Country General to pay the August rent and pick up a pair of boots from Travis at the repair counter. The two-tone Lamas. He wants to wear them to Dan Tana's with Ruby tonight.

Harry looks at the boots with admiration. "Manly footwear."

"Got some new Rockmounts in," Travis says. "Real beauties."

"Take me to 'em."

Travis leads Harry past a rack of crisp white button-downs. "Got some new George Straits."

"I don't like the Straits."

"C'mon, 'Amarillo By Morning'?"

"Nothing against Strait. Just don't care for his menswear."

They get to the Rockmount display and Harry takes it in. "That an Aloha?"

Travis takes a dark blue shirt emblazoned with bright red flowers off the rack. "Hawaiian Hibiscus. Based on a classic Paniolo design. Look at the arrows embroidered down on the sleeve here. That's chenille."

Harry holds it up. "Little flashy for me. Maybe if I was going on vacation."

He turns it around and looks at the back. "You ought to show this to Gio over at the barbershop. He's got plans to hang up the trimmers and move down to Waikiki. Get his news from the coconut wireless."

"He don't shop here."

Harry briefly considers a shirt based on a design Elvis wore in *Loving You* before zeroing in on a navy-blue gabardine. Shotgun cuffs, smile pockets, barbed wire embroidery pattern along the piping. A good everyday shirt. "How much for this puppy?"

"I think we can work something out," Travis says.

Travis guides him the long way back to the counter, past a second rack of Rockmounts.

"Anybody actually wear them Cavalry Bib numbers?"

"We get the occasional Civil War wingnut come looking for 'em, but they're not a hot seller." Travis slides a few shirts aside on the rack. "We just got these in, though. A real specialty item. Not for everybody, but you'd probably appreciate 'em."

They're the Ranchers Harry remembers his father wearing.

"We got the dobby stripe Hombre model here," Travis says. "They've also brought back the classic denim."

Harry takes a good look at the shirt. He can almost see the old man sitting on the porch with a can of Pearl, tapping his foot and warbling along to Jimmie Rodgers.

"You got the custom yokes and the classic Quarter Horse pocket cut," Travis says. "But what I really like are the black diamonds here." He runs his hand over the triad of snaps at the cuff. "Gilt rimmed."

IT'S ALMOST CLOSING time at Big Smoke. The big delivery came in on schedule, a lot of Acapulco Gold, plus a good supply of Blue Dream, Sour Diesel, and Purple Mountain Kush.

The bales of Acapulco Gold have a sweet, pungent aroma and glow green and orange, even through the plastic wrap. Capri feels a contact high looking at it all. And thinking about how much she'll be able to sell it for.

She puts everything in order, with the Acapulco front and center in the safe, making it as simple as possible for Ted. He ought to be in and out in two minutes.

The last customer of the day is a guy she's seen a few times before. Capri remembers the cowboy get-up and his slow way of talking. He exchanges terse hellos with Carvell and takes a deep breath on his way up to the counter.

"I smell an Acapulco breeze blowin' through here," he says. "It finally come in?"

"Just arrived. But we can't put it out 'til tomorrow."

"Shit, man." Another big breath. "Takes an old nickel-bagger like me back to the days of Maui Wowie and Thai Stick. All the good shit. But the Gold was always the best."

"Yeah, everyone's been waiting for it."

"You sure you can't just pinch me off a little? Tonight's date night."

"It hasn't been unpacked."

He sighs.

"I guess I'll just take some more of that Purple Mountain Kush for now then. That one had me cruisin' at a comfortable altitude."

"You want an eighth?"

"Quarter."

Capri weighs out the buds and watches the guy squint at the display case. He's wearing those glasses with the lenses that slowly get clearer when you come inside. His eyes come into view like Polaroid pictures developing.

"I also need something with some giddy-up-go. My gal likes the giggly kind."

"Try this," she says, setting a jar of fluorescent buds on the counter. "Green Crack."

He takes a whiff and his eyebrows go up.

"Add on a quarter of that. And let me grab one of them fudgy brownies too."

10

HARRY PUTS POMADE in his hair and tries to recreate the Dutch Reagan side-sweep Giovanni had going for him earlier. It's never the same when he does it at home.

His face thinned out in his fifties, giving him that dustbowl photograph look, and he's currently adapting to a trimmer mustache. Ruby said the fuller bandito version looked like a big sad frown on his face.

He shaved it completely, which felt all wrong, before cultivating the little Vincent Price number he wears now. She reluctantly said she'd let him keep it, like it was a stray cat he brought home. He makes a Robert De Niro face in the mirror as he razors its greying coastline.

There are days he thinks he looks alright. And there are days he can't tell himself apart from the sad-eyed Grotto denizens, hollowed by the weak vacuum of the barfly life. Drugs act fast. Booze moves slow. First you puff up, then you waste away. Like a corpse.

He slaps on some aftershave. Overall, one to ten, today's about a seven. Not bad. The shirt Travis sold him goes well with his new dungarees.

The buzzer buzzes and Harry stands on the landing watching Ruby come up the walkway. She's wearing a spangly sequin dress and silver high-heel shoes. He knew she'd be all dressed up, wearing that skimpy underwear he likes, and he knows they'll come back here later and have a hell of a time.

Ruby looks high class but she's low maintenance. She makes her own money. Most nights she prefers a chili-size and a pineapple shake at Four 'N 20 to some fancy sushi place. Then they'll go bowling down in Koreatown, blow the foam off some beers over at Ireland's 32, throw some darts.

Once a month Harry springs for a nice dinner somewhere. They both like the classic old spots like Musso's in Hollywood or Chez Jay out by the beach. Tonight it's Dan Tana's, one of Harry's favorites. Ruby's never been there.

He watches her pass an Armenian kid tooling around on a Big Wheel in the courtyard. She has a confident strut, proud of her curves and swerves without being too show-offy about it. But she knows what she has. She knows Harry knows it too.

He kisses her when she reaches the top of the stairs. Almost two years in and they're still lovey-dovey. Bill and Coo. Sometimes he wishes she lived closer, or even here with him, but it's nice to have Thursdays to look forward to, and after a few days away they can't keep their hands off each other.

"I got you a present, baby," Ruby says when they step inside. "I didn't have time to wrap it. I saw it at the store when I stopped to buy some lip stuff."

She hands him a plastic bag. Harry reaches in and pulls out a device called a Lighter Leash.

"You hook this part to your belt and the lighter goes in here," she says. "That way you won't lose your lighters anymore."

Harry looks around for his lighter and Ruby hands him a fresh Bic.

It's an unusual gift coming from her since she's always trying to get him to quit smoking. But Harry's stubborn on that issue. He touts his genetics, points to ancestral Robatores, smokers who lived into their upper eighties and died of natural causes. He also believes the day he quits is the day he'll be hit by a school bus. A big yellow possum-squasher.

He slides the new Bic into the holster and mimes a gunslinger quick-draw.

CAPRI DOESN'T THINK it's a good idea to bring the haul back to Fuzzy's house, so she books them a room at Le Rendezvous Motel on Sepulveda. The plan is to weigh it out here and pack it tight so they can stash it at Fuzzy's without stinking the place up too much.

"I love fucking in hotels." Ted looks at himself in the mirror, pacing back and forth in his all-black military garb. "I look legit, right?"

"How much was all this shit?"

"Super cheap. Army Navy store."

He creeps behind her like a cat burglar. She pushes him away.

"Those clothes smell."

"Some soldier probably got shot in them. This sweater has a guy's name in it. Steven something." Ted pulls at the collar to show Capri where the name is stenciled in silver marker.

She isn't interested.

"Might be a good thing to throw people off. I leave this sweater behind and they go looking for this Steven guy."

"Don't leave the sweater there, Ted."

"Right. DNA."

Capri runs down the operation one more time, step by step so he understands it. Ted nods at all the right places.

"Got it, boo."

He roots around in his new backpack.

"What's in the bag?" she says.

"Reinforcements."

11

HARRY AND RUBY are seated in a red leather horseshoe booth facing the bar. Harry scans the wine list. "Let's get a bottle of something."

"Couple of shots first."

"You're a rowdy broad, you know that?"

He's been planning to take her to Dan Tana's for a while. She likes this kind of thing. Red checkered tablecloths. Professional waiters with napkins draped over their arms.

"What looks good to you, baby?" Ruby says.

"Chicken parm. I get it every time. Big as a battleship."

Harry's been coming here since a night in 1973 when he and his buddy Chris Nederhoffer stumbled in after a Doug Sahm show at the Troubadour and saw Warren Oates and Harry Dean Stanton, their two favorite movie actors, posted at the bar.

He likes that it hasn't changed much since then, except for the prices. Same Croatian bartender with the thick mustache. Oates is long gone, but until Harry Dean finally died a few years ago, you could still find him here most nights. Playing the mouth harp and singing songs in Spanish, drinking cranberry juice spiked with tequila.

Ruby dips her bread in olive oil and peruses the menu. "The Dabney Coleman steak is sixty-five dollars."

"And it don't even come with potatoes. You have to pay extra."

"Ala Carte."

"Ala Something."

"So expensive."

"Order whatever you like, darlin'. We'll split it down the middle."

Harry grins.

"Hardy-har," Ruby says.

The waiter comes by and Harry orders two mezcals and the calamari to start.

TED'S SEBRING IDLES in the dim lot behind Big Smoke. The Spanish grocery next door is closed. No other cars around. He kills the headlights and backs up to the back door. He surveys the scene and pops the trunk. His stomach is jumpy.

In movies, the getaway driver always leaves the car running, so that's what Ted decides to do. He grabs the backpack out of the trunk and slings it over his shoulder. Scanning the street again for any activity, he lowers the trunk just above the hitch and unrolls the ski mask.

The key to the back door is clenched in his right hand. Part of him, a big part of him, hopes the key doesn't work. That would abort this mission. Or at least postpone it. But the key works. Of course it does.

Inside everything is set up like Capri said. No alarm. The safe is open and the bales of weed are neatly arranged, like the pictures cops take after a big bust.

He sets the backpack down and removes a roll of heavy duty 50-gallon contractor bags. He double-bags and fills two of them, then two more, and sets them by the back door. He grabs the scale last, resting it on top of everything.

Out at the front counter area, he scans the room with the small flashlight from the Army Navy store. It's only been a couple minutes since he's been inside, but it feels longer.

He looks under the empty display cases. Everything has been packed up and put away. He pans the flashlight around one last time. The air conditioning clicks on and Ted spooks like it's a rifle shot. He needs to load up the car and get out of here.

Driving down Victory, Ted is careful to keep it under the limit, but not too far under. He doesn't usually smoke but Capri's Camel Crushes are in the console and he lights one, his hands still shaking.

He checks the rearview and pats his pocket to make sure he didn't leave the key in the door. There's a cop car in the parking lot of Tommy's World-Famous Hamburgers. Ted makes sure he doesn't look too intently in its direction.

The smoke burns down fast. Ted puts it out in a Jack in the Box cup. He's heard about traffic stops set off by a lit cigarette being flicked out the window. No taking chances. He's pretty sure his registration is revoked anyway.

He stops at one last light, Victory is rigged for long reds, and takes the left at Sepulveda.

Le Rendezvous Motel is a few blocks down on the right. Ted pulls into the lot and backs up to Room Two.

"I LIKE A walk after a meal," Harry says.

Ruby grabs the cigarette out of his mouth and takes a long drag.

"You're just too cheap to valet."

"You see that bill?"

"You made sure I saw it."

"Now's not the time to call me cheap, darlin'."

She hands his cigarette back. "El Cheapo."

This stretch of Santa Monica Boulevard brings back memories. The Raincheck Room. The Tropicana. Duke's. Places long gone. There's a line of young people outside the Troubadour, a name on the marquee Harry doesn't recognize.

"I saw Kristofferson here in seventy-four."

"Kris is sexy."

"You should've seen him back then. And you should've seen me."

"I was a baby."

He holds his cigarette at a distance and kisses her on the forehead.

Harry played the Troubadour twice. When he and his buddy Chris Nederhoffer arrived in L.A., they put together a cosmic cowboy outfit they called The Lusty Men, after a Robert Mitchum movie about rodeo riders. Four hippies in knockoff Nudie suits playing psychedelic covers of country classics.

The two of them went by long-haul trucker handles—Nederhoffer was Panama Red and Harry was Captain Zig Zag—and co-wrote a handful of originals, "Nowhere Slow" and "Chasin' My Dreams With Whiskey" being the best of them. They also wrote a song called "Rodeo Romeo" long before Moe Bandy did.

Number zero with a bullet.

Nederhoffer didn't live to hear Bandy's version. He fancied himself a mescaline-addled Webb Pierce, with that high lonesome voice, but his life went more the Gram Parsons route. The drugs got harder. The spacey desert trips turned to solo junk binges and he was fully off the rails by the end of 1976.

Chris was found in a room at the Tropicana a few days before he and Harry were supposed to drive back to Texas for Christmas. Harry's music career, if you could call it that, fizzled quick. Nederhoffer had most of the ambition there.

The Lusty Men were playing regular slots at the Topanga Corral and the Palomino Club and after Nederhoffer died Harry fell into a bartending gig at the Palomino that sustained him for more than a decade. He met Willie, Don Everly, Jerry Lee Lewis. Got drunk with the stuntmen and the cowboy actors. Shook hands with Elvis Presley one time.

Ruby has heard all these stories. He may have even told her about the Kristofferson show before but she's too polite to say. Harry doesn't like to catch himself getting too sentimental.

Don't look back. Like that Dylan movie from fifty years ago.

They walk arm in arm up Doheny. The Olds is parked on Elevado, below Sunset. They get in the car and Harry navigates the traffic and bright lights on the Strip.

"Careful driving. You had a few drinks."

"It's a can of corn, darlin'."

He passes the Chateau Marmont, another cavern of acid-tinged memories, and takes the left on Laurel Canyon back to the Valley.

"Let's stop in and see Fuzzy," Harry says.

"I want tonight to be you and me."

"Okey-doke."

"Plus, I want your margaritas."

"The Mad Dogs."

"Strong ones."

"You boozehound."

"I hate when you say booze. It's a stupid word, Harry."

"Boooooze."

"You talk so slow, baby."

"It's called a drawl. You used to like it."

"Maybe it's getting old. Like you."

TED BURSTS INTO the room with a bag over each shoulder, expecting more of a hero's welcome than he gets. Capri closes the heavy curtains and grabs both bags.

"Where's the rest?"

"There's two more bags in the car."

Unloading the trunk, Ted gets that feeling again, one he gets with her more and more. Like he works for her. He wonders what would've happened if he'd refused to go in on this plan.

When he walks in, Capri is bent over the bed sorting through the bundles. Her shorts are riding up and Ted's a puppet on a string again. He'd go commit another robbery right now if she asked him to. And Jesus that weed smells like a hundred gallons of honey.

"You believe all this? I did good. I was in and out."

"Did you close the safe behind you?"

"Yup. Spun the dial. Kept my gloves on."

"Is it better to keep this in your dad's basement or garage?"

"Attic is better. He can't climb the ladder to get up there."

"Let's get it packed up and bring it there tonight while he's at the bar. Did you talk to Max?"

"I'll text him tomorrow."

"You should text him now."

Ted pulls at her shorts.

"Take a shower with me."

"Not now, Ted. Text him. If we can set it up so he buys—"

"I told you he sells edibles. For that-guy-he-know's company."

"What do you think the guy makes the edibles with, Ted?"

"I know. I told you. I'll text him. He'll be down for this, I'm sure. I wanted to wait until we had the stuff."

Capri looks at the bed. "We have the stuff. Text him."

"Can we fuck in the shower after?"

"Maybe."

"Take pics of you all wet and naked and shit?"

She just looks at him. That smoky eyeshadow alone gets him going.

Ted reaches in his pocket for his phone. Then he fumbles through the pockets on the fatigues. He puts the flashlight on the nightstand. He pats himself up and down again.

"My phone."

"What do you mean *your phone*? Where is it?"

"In the backpack. I wanted to make sure it was secure."

"Where's the backpack?"

He's having trouble breathing. It feels like a rabbit is hopping around in his chest.

"Are you kidding me?"

"I set it down by the safe when I went in."

"And your phone is in it?"

Ted feels his head bob up and down.

"What else?"

"Some extra stuff I thought I might need. And my wallet."

"Your wallet. With your ID in it."

"I think I need to go back."

"You think?"

Capri has already put the key back on her keyring. She takes it off and throws it at him.

It hits the wall and Ted scrambles to get it.

He looks up at her. "You still love me?"

"Go get the fucking bag, Ted."

12

OFFICERS WARD AND Higgins are finishing things up at Tommy's World-Famous Hamburgers on Victory. Ward pulls up slow alongside the trashcan and Higgins tosses the cardboard boats. Ward dips a napkin in his Sprite and dabs at a chili stain on his shirt.

Ward is in his late fifties, with the small mustache that was standard issue when he joined the force. The mustache is grey now, mustard-smeared at the moment. Only a couple more years till he puts in his papers and kicks around Rancho Mirage in golf pants the rest of his days.

He's been partnered with Higgins, still baby-faced under a tight crewcut, for more than a year but they've never developed much of a rapport. They mostly patrol in silence, except when it concerns eating or pissing.

They head east on Victory, Ward driving, and turn down Hazeltine.

"You think's going on here?" Higgins says.

Ward slows the car and shines the light on a Chrysler Sebring backed tight against the rear door of the Big Smoke dispensary.

"Looks like it's running."

"Let's take a look-see," Higgins says, unsnapping his holster strap.

Inside, Ward sweeps his flashlight and freezes on a skinny kid desperately trying to roll down a ski mask. Both officers identify themselves and raise their weapons.

Higgins finds the wall switch and snaps on the light. He elbows Ward and points through the glass countertop where the shithead is clearly visible, doing a boot-camp style crawl before wedging himself against a modem tower like it's a barricade of sandbags.

The kid removes the tactical backpack he's wearing and roots around in it. Ward and Higgins train their guns and raise their voices, instructing him not to move. Ward doesn't think he seems dangerous, but he does seem stupid. Which can be dangerous.

They slowly approach, guns still up, until the kid is lying flat on his stomach. Higgins reaches for his cuffs and there's sudden motion before a hand grenade comes sailing over the counter. It hits the wall with a thud and slides across the floor, spinning to a stop at the feet of the two officers.

Ward looks down at it. Then he looks at Higgins.

13

RUBY KNOWS HARRY is sozzled when he starts in talking about Mexico. The two of them are slow dancing in the living room, Conway and Loretta playing, and Harry's mumbling about Veracruz, bringing her home to be near momma, his slow drawl drawling even slower.

Harry's bareass under his poncho. Ruby thinks it gives him the raw sex appeal of a Scotsman with nothing between him and the rough tartan of his kilt. She's an avid reader of a subgenre of romance novels devoted to this. The kilts, not the ponchos.

The room is lit only by Harry's year-round Christmas lights and a neon cactus glowing green next to the turntable. Ruby stumbles and the record skips.

"Take your heels off, baby," Harry says.

She puts her shoes under the coffee table and re-lights the joint that's resting on the lip of the ashtray. She takes a hit and comes back to Harry, dancing like one of his dashboard hula girls.

"You know how Arnold Schwarzenegger's getting older now?" she says.

Harry nods.

"Now he says, '*Ow, my back.*'"

"That may be your worst one yet."

Ruby slaps his shoulder. "He says it instead of, '*I'll be back.*'"

"I got that part figured, darlin'."

"I heard it at work. I thought you'd laugh."

He kisses her. "I wish I thought of it myself."

Ruby reaches up the back of Harry's poncho and holds her hands there, waltzing to "I'd Rather Have What We Had," him singing softly to her.

She smacks his ass. "I'm thirsty."

"You say I'm the drunk in this relationship."

Ruby disregards that, grabbing the glasses off the table and striding into the kitchen. Harry follows close behind, taunting her. "No, listen to me, you say I'm the drunk in this relationship. But it's you, darlin'. It's you."

Ruby sets the glasses down and smiles at the various mixers and fixins—sour mix, a sombrero of margarita salt, limes sliced and notched—Harry has set up on the kitchen counter in preparation. She appreciates the trimmings. Umbrellas. Fresh fruit. Proper glassware.

Harry has it all on hand.

He pulls the mezcal out of the freezer. "We're makin' this bottle look stupid."

The bag of ice they've been dipping into is frozen solid again. Harry keeps a hammer on top of the fridge for that very reason.

"Why don't you ask your landlord to put in a modern-day fridge, Harry? With an ice maker."

"I don't want to make waves." Harry breaks up the block and scoops the cubes into the glasses. "We have an unspoken agreement. I don't ask much of him and he don't ask much of me."

The sound of ice clinking in a cocktail glass always makes Ruby think of Harry. Even when he isn't around. Like it's a bell she can ring and he'll magically appear.

She takes another hit on the jib. "Do you think there's not a light when you open the freezer because the bulb would freeze?"

"You ponder that while I fix us another couple of drinks." Harry grins. "Though there weren't nothin' wrong with the last two."

"How many times are you going to say that?"

IT'S BEEN ALMOST an hour since Ted left. Capri paces the floor and sends a couple where-are-you texts. Nothing too specific. Someone might be checking his phone.

She's not that worried. She has all the stuff. And if he gets caught, she'll say he stole her key. That he's been talking about doing something like this, but she never thought he'd go through with it.

And she knows Ted will take all the blame, even feel honorable doing it.

Other than his doglike loyalty, Ted isn't the ideal accomplice. Jamey, her ex, would be better. But he'd insist on running the show. Capri likes being in charge. She just wishes Ted was smarter. But if he were smarter, he probably wouldn't have gone along with this as easy.

She thinks about texting Jamey. She's going to need help if Ted ends up getting stuck in jail.

Their only real lead is his friend Max. They're counting on Max to not only buy a decent amount of product himself but also point them in the direction of other potential buyers.

No Ted, no Max.

Jamey is out of jail, she knows that. He texted her from a new number when he was released, but she never replied. She was already in L.A. when he got sent away this last time, for aggravated assault, but she was the reason he went away before.

His neighbors called with a noise complaint and the police found the two of them drunk and high, drugs out in the open. She had bruises all over her arms and legs and she told the cops Jamey had abused her. She was seventeen. He was twenty-eight and had a record.

She remembers thanking the cops for saving her, feeling like she was playing a role, really selling it. With his priors, Jamey was sentenced to forty months and served sixteen.

They were back together as soon as he got out. He told her he never stopped thinking about her. She thought about him too. Visiting days, she pressed her tongue against the dirty glass between them.

They settled on a revised version of the story. Too much rum, too much coke. Rough sex gone too far. Capri glossing over the whole hitting her thing, Jamey the whole sending him to jail thing.

They were on and off again for a year until Capri found out he got another girl pregnant. He denied it but she didn't believe him. She had to leave town before she did something to the girl. Assault on a pregnant woman would be hard to talk her way out of.

There's something there between her and Jamey, though. A criminal chemistry she sometimes recognized in couples they'd see on *COPS*, Jamey's favorite show.

As pervy as Ted is, he's relatively gentle. He likes to talk dirty but he sounds like a teenage boy when he does. He's wide-eyed with amazement at some of the things she does with him. Things Jamey expected of her. Or grabbed her by the hair and demanded of her.

She sends Jamey a text and waits for three blinking dots that don't come.

She packs a bowl of Acapulco Gold and takes two deep hits. Once the initial headrush passes, she feels an energy that's both floaty and focused. She works the scale for a couple hours, breaking the haul into pounds and half-pounds, ounces and half-ounces. The vacuum-sealed bags are stacked in the heavy-duty contractor bags which are then packed securely in two large duffel bags.

She runs out of her Camel Crushes and walks to 7-Eleven to get two more packs and a couple Icehouse tallboys. She switches to a heavy indica. That, combined with the beers and three Xanax, calms her enough to stop checking her phone every two seconds and start thinking about sleep.

Worst case, she'll go to Max herself. Explain what happened. They met once before, that day at the Santa Monica Pier. She doesn't have his number but knows he lives at that motel in Malibu. Tomorrow morning she'll get herself out there and touch base. Maybe he'll buy more if he thinks she needs to raise bail or pay court fees for Ted. Either way, she can unload some product on him and figure out a plan.

Now there's only the matter of getting there. She used to have access to this one guy's Uber account, but he changed the login. Her credit cards are all revoked. On the rare occasion she actually pays for something, it's in cash.

She sends a few texts but it's late. The only person to respond is Derrick, a DJ from the Golden Banana, the club where she used to work.

He says he can come by around eight in the morning.

It's almost three now, which means he's coked up, probably still at the club. He always stays and parties late with the dancers. There's a good chance he'll pass out or forget about it. But he's all she has. She gives him the address and room number.

Ted never texts back. Neither does Jamey. She checks one last time before passing out in front of *Family Feud*.

THE ARM ON Harry's turntable doesn't go back automatically. A Sammi Smith record crackles on the runout groove while Harry and Ruby make out on the couch. Ruby climbs on his lap. He says something dirty to her and slides her dress off.

She stands up and bends over slow in front of him in her matching bra and thong set. Hot pink. He watches her strap herself back into her heels then follows her into the bedroom. She does a slow, twerky kind of dance for him in front of the bed and he takes off his poncho, a lopsided grin on his face.

Harry grabs the shower curtain liner from under the bed and sets it on the mattress with a couple heavy beach towels over it. Ruby has been drinking which means she'll be spraying all over the place once they get going. The squirting thing started after she took those kundalini yoga classes. He'd seen it in pornos but Ruby was his first time up close. He heard somewhere it's mostly whiz but it drives him wild all the same.

They play around with their trucker and lot lizard scenario. Harry hauling freight in a Peterbilt, Ruby lingering by the diesel pumps. It's a fun one for them. They can laugh at it but it works.

He says the things she wants to hear and she responds vocally, wind-milling around with the *ay, papi*, the *si, papi*, geysering all over the bed. After, Harry wipes them both down with a hot cloth and tosses the drenched towels and shower curtain liner in the bathtub.

They lay there a while with the sheets pulled up around them. Ruby kisses Harry's neck and rakes her nails down his chest while he rolls another joint. He sets it in her mouth and lights it for her. She takes a deep hit and hands it back to him.

"What are we going to have for breakfast?"

"I could make you one of my sandwiches," he says. "I got the thick bacon. Or we could go over to Du-par's and get some pancakes."

"I get so hungry before bed, but I don't want to get chubby. Mami used to tell me sleep was a time machine to breakfast. I never remember my dreams, but I think they're probably about food."

Harry clicks on the TV and thumbs the volume down low. They're coming in late on a John Wayne double feature on the Encore Western channel. *True Grit* is over and it's already into *Rooster Cogburn*.

"Who's that guy?" Ruby says, resting her head on Harry's shoulder. "He was in the other one we watched."

"That's Strother Martin," Harry says. "Ol' Shanghai McCoy."

THE LAW IN
THIS TOWN

14

SIX-THIRTY A.M. AND Harry's phone buzzes on the nightstand. Fuzzy doesn't have a personalized ringtone like Ruby. Harry silences it and it buzzes again.

He squints awake and picks up.

Ruby rolls over. "You're rocking my dreamboat, baby."

Harry shushes her and moves the phone to his good ear.

"Alright, sorry Fuzz. Go ahead."

Fuzzy tells Harry the circumstances of Ted's arrest and where he's being held. Harry has been through similar things with Ted in the past, but this sounds more serious.

"I'll be down there." Harry listens another second. "Yeah, I've got a guy."

He hangs up and stares at the ceiling. Last thing he needs first thing this morning.

Ruby stretches and yawns. "I slept like a little baby rock."

"You up now?"

"Awake as a bedbug."

Harry lights the roach from the ashtray on the nightstand. The smoke hangs in the air over the bed, shot through with new sun. He swings his legs over and puts his feet on the floor.

"Gettin' out of bed just ruins my whole day," he says.

"What was the call about?"

He says he has to go spring Fuzzy's son, that he'll be back later. "And a baby rock is a big rock, by the way," he says. "An old rock is a little rock."

"What are you talking about, Harry?"

"Erosion."

"You sound like a fortune cookie."

"Your lucky numbers are—"

"Shhhh." She takes the joint out of his hand.

"Let me get one more toke, darlin'. I've got to light a shuck here."

GUY DONLEAVY, ATTORNEY-AT-LAW, comes to in the courtyard of the Casa Royale Apartments, still in the rented tux he wore to the wedding last night.

Even when Guy drinks to blackout depths, he usually surfaces with a decent recollection of the night before. Half-awake, his memory unblurs and a vague timeline clicks into place.

The open bar was only beer and wine and only for the first hour. He remembers spending most of the reception in the parking lot behind the Knights of Columbus Hall, drinking from a wet bar in the trunk of his buddy Greg's RAV4. A handle of Pepe Lopez and a cooler stocked with Bud Lime-A-Rita cans.

Someone offered to drive him home, but Guy couldn't remember the name or address of the apartment complex where he's lived for the past seven years. The driver circled the neighborhood while Guy tried to explain it was the place with the "king hat" on the sign. The driver finally realized he was talking about the big gold crown outside the Casa Royale on Saticoy.

Guy made it through the gate but didn't attempt the flight of stairs to his apartment. He crawled into a poolside deck chair where he slept like a bear, clutching the near-empty jug of tequila in his paws.

The temperature dropped in the night, but the sun rose early and strong, roasting him. His mouth is so dry the swimming pool looks like something he could gulp down. He looks at his phone and decides to close his eyes for a couple more minutes.

He wakes again after seven, cooled by a shadow hovering over him.

The shadow has a cowboy hat.

"COUNSELOR," HARRY SAYS.

Guy's eyes slit. He jerks awake and the jug of Pepe Lopez rolls off his lap. Luckily it's plastic. It just bounces a little.

"I musta fell asleep."

"You *musta.*"

Harry follows him upstairs to his apartment. Guy's thatch of hair is tangled and the deck chair has pleated the back of his baggy tuxedo. He looks off-center.

Harry hasn't been over here since Guy's ex-girlfriend Amanda moved out. Empty tequila and vodka bottles are lined up like bowling pins on the counter. What's left of a Hungry Man dinner sits shipwrecked in the sink. It looks like a dog has been at it.

"They still make those?"

"They've gotten better. The turkey dinner is my favorite."

Guy points to a bong the size of a fire hydrant on the coffee table.

"You want a toot on the trombone?"

"Let's shag ass, Guy. We've got to get down to the courthouse."

"Let me change real quick."

"No time."

Guy goes into the bathroom to freshen up. He talks to Harry through the open door. "I got a new toilet seat last week. Wood. You ever get that brown rainbow on the back rim of your toilet seat? You don't get that with the wood."

"It's still there, Guy. You just don't see it."

Harry sifts through a few issues of *The Watchtower*, the Jehovah's Witness newsletter, on the coffee table. He knows Guy has been depressed about the break-up, but he didn't realize things had gotten this bad. Each headline is bleaker than the next. *Is Life All There Is? Does God Care About You?*

"What's this about?"

Guy steps out of the doorway to look.

"Sometimes I let those guys in and talk to them."

"The guys with the briefcases?"

"Yeah, the Witnesses."

Guy squeezes a sloppy stripe of Aquafresh out on the brush and goes back to the sink. Harry sparks the ashy remains in the bowl of the bong. He pulls the pin and gets a wispy hit. The water tastes rusty.

"Don't you know Jehovah was a fuckin' shoe salesman?"

15

OUTSIDE THE COURTHOUSE, Harry has a quick pow-wow with Guy and Fuzzy before the bail hearing. He's still confused about how everything went down.

"He was arrested empty-handed on the premises?"

"That's what I'm told."

"Where's the weed?"

"The new girlfriend is obviously the missing piece here," Fuzzy says. "She works there. He had a key to the place on him when he was arrested. Must've gotten it from her."

"You think he stole it?"

"I wouldn't put it past him but the fact that she never came back to the house last night tells me she was in on it with him and somehow managed to run out the door with the goods when the cops arrived. Left him high and dry."

"How long has she been staying with you?"

"A few weeks. I told him she was trouble, but she's got him wrapped. Ted's too soft for this world. Given his criminal nature, you'd think he'd be a little more streetwise, but he's the most trusting thief you've ever met."

Harry remembers the girl from Big Smoke. Black hair, skin and bones, with a dead-behind-the-eyes look. Kind of scary-sexy. Not his type, but he can see the appeal.

"This whole ordeal with him staying with me has been a fucking mess," Fuzzy says. "First he's dipping into the register, then he drags her in off the street. Now this. I ought to let him sit in there."

"Why don't you?"

"He'll just call his mother and I'll never hear the end of it. It's better this way."

"Maybe the two of you can work something out."

"That ship has sunk, Harry. You know that."

"I mean financially. I hate to bring it up, but I'm not in the position to do one on the arm here. This isn't like his other shenanigans. It could be a substantial bail."

"I'll put the bar down against the bond. If push comes to shit, that dump is your problem."

"I may have to change the name."

"Cut the shit, Harry, will you for once?"

"Call it the Buck and Doe Lounge. Get more couples in there. A little line dancin', some sawdust on the floor."

Guy laughs a little harder than he should. Fuzzy shoots him an aggravated look, then turns to Harry.

"This is the representation you bring? For my only son? He looks like he has a fucking baloney sandwich in his pocket."

Guy has never been to the Grotto, so he and Fuzzy haven't crossed paths. By the end of a workday with Guy, Harry wants to unwind away from Guy. Sometimes they'll have one at Ireland's 32, or the

Legion Hall up by Guy's office, but the Grotto is Harry's sanctuary.

"Just get this taken care of," Fuzzy says. "Come up later and tell me what's what."

"Will do. If the girl's out there somewhere with all the merchandise, I'll put a guy on Teddy."

"I don't think he'll run. Besides, his car was impounded. The girl has no car. I'm betting she ran off and left Teddy in the lurch."

"Still might be good to keep an eye on him," Harry says. "I'll bring the paperwork by the bar later."

CHECKOUT AT LE Rendezvous isn't until eleven but Capri plans to be long gone by then.

She's surprised when Derrick the DJ rolls up close to on time. Her phone buzzes and she looks outside. A familiar Mazda is idling in the lot. He helps her lift the bags into the trunk and she's surprised again when he doesn't ask any questions.

She isn't surprised he expects her to suck him off on the drive out to Malibu. It's what he always wanted in exchange for giving her coke or doing her other favors at the club.

He'd give her a ride home and talk about how driving the empty freeways in the middle of the night felt like a video game. Sometimes they'd go back to his loft in North Hollywood and fuck. Or they'd get something to eat at Western Bagel, the only thing open at that hour.

Derrick has a satanic goatee, ink black, and all the gauges and piercings that come with the rocker identity he's glommed onto. His hair is an identical black and looks painted on, same as his leather pants.

Capri has a similar look but she doesn't like it on guys. Strippers seem to go for it, though, so she gets his motivation. At least he's young. A lot of guys use that look to mask that they're well into their fifties. She gets depressed by the sight of L.A. eyeliner on a leathery old man face.

It's over with by the time he pulls off the 101 at the Kanan Road exit. She re-straps her seatbelt and drinks a flat Monster drink from the cup holder to wash away the taste. Derrick tells her he isn't working at the Banana anymore. He's downtown at the Spearmint Rhino. But he still lives up in Van Nuys. He asks why she never hits him up anymore and she says she's been busy.

They light cigarettes. She scrolls through her phone as he navigates the sharp curves and drops of the canyon roads down to Pacific Coast Highway.

16

"**W**HO IS REPRESENTING the defendant in this case?"

"Good morning, Your Honor." Guy stands before the court, Judge Lawrence Clements presiding. "Guy Donleavy, appearing on behalf of Theodore Ryan."

"I appreciate the formality, Mr. Donleavy," Clements says. "But our proceedings this morning aren't black tie."

That gets a laugh in the courtroom. Harry sits in the back, embarrassed for Guy, bright red in his flammable tux. Maybe Clements does have it in for him.

"I came directly from an affair, Your Honor."

Clements consults Ted's sheet and peers sleepy-eyed over his reading glasses. "Mr. Ryan is being charged with the following: Count one, second-degree burglary, a felony. Count two, possession of burglary tools, a misdemeanor. Count three, assault on a police officer with a deadly weapon." Clements adjusts his glasses. "In this case, a fragmentation hand grenade."

"It wasn't a live grenade, Your Honor. For the record."

"And thank God for that, Counselor."

Another wave of laughter from the lawyers, officers, and chained defendants in the gallery.

"And I submit that the tire iron was strictly for automotive use, in light of the fact that my client had a key to the establishment. The fact that he had a key also complicates the notion of forced entry—"

"Nothing complicated about it, Mr. Donleavy. He used an instrument to gain entry. The instrument in this case was the key. You know this. I *hope* you know this. As for the unnecessary burglary tools, I'm sorry if Mr. Ryan was having tire trouble, but the charge stands."

Every time Harry watches Guy in court, it's clear he inherited none of his old man's lawyerly talent.

Terry Donleavy, Guy's father, was a charismatic defense attorney, Massachusetts bred, with a shock of white hair and a face like a slab of rare roast beef. In the eighties, when Guy was a kid, Terry took the Boston lawyer swagger west to L.A., where he played the part of a displaced Kennedy, even feigning a slight Hyannis accent during closing arguments.

Terry worked courtrooms and barrooms like a stage Irishman, a master of the patter. The Battleship of Bullshit, he called it, sailed right over from the Ould Sod. "Back home I'm a nickel-a-dime," he told Harry several times. "Out here I'm a fuckin' novelty."

His enemies used to say he was one of the snakes St. Patrick drove out of Ireland.

Terry was the guy who set Harry on the bondsman path. They met when Harry tended bar at the Palomino Club. Terry wasn't a fan of country music, except for Big Tom, but he liked being the only suit and tie in a room full of denim and cowboy boots. He always wanted Harry's take on things. Thought he might make a good investigator because he picked up on the little details.

Most investigators don't look like Sam Spade, Terry told him. They look like what they are—cops who can't cut it. People see them coming a mile away. A shaggy dog like Harry could snoop around much easier.

Harry took to tracking people down, first as an unofficial defense investigator and process server. Then he got his P.I. ticket and worked that way for years. It was cool. He always dug *The Rockford Files*. The wisecracks, the car chases, the trailer on PCH. The job wasn't anything like that, but he liked the image.

Then he got his bondsman's license with the express purpose of sitting on his ass. Slowing down a bit.

For years Harry only knew Guy as Terry's son, a doughy dunce who got into trouble with drinking early. Terry didn't mention him much, mostly headshaking anecdotes of disappointment over some under-achievement or other.

Harry was surprised when he heard Guy followed his father into the practice of law. They saw each other at Terry's funeral then Harry ran into him in the metal detector line at the courthouse. He's been throwing cases his way here and there ever since. Harry wouldn't recommend Guy in the event of a trial, but he can handle a simple bail hearing.

Clements continues down the list of Ted's charges.

"As regards the vehicle, the 2008 Chrysler Sebring is currently in impound until such time as the defendant has addressed the several outstanding violations and gotten it properly registered."

Guy raises his eyebrows at Ted, a sign of weakness Terry never would've shown.

Terry had a commanding demeanor. Big drinker, big eater, big everything. Guy has similar appetites, but Terry carried them effortlessly. They just seem to weigh Guy down.

Same with the white-shoe furnishings crowded around Guy's dumpy office in Panorama City. When Terry died, Guy inherited the leather chairs and U-shaped executive's desk, along with the leather-bound tomes, the Colonial globe. Guy even has Terry's designations and awards hung on the wall in ornate frames. Impressive if you don't look too close at the first name. These things gave Terry's office gravitas. In Guy's, they only amplify the shabbiness of their surroundings.

Clements leans into the microphone. "Have you had the opportunity to review these issues with Mr. Ryan such that he's ready to be arraigned?"

"Yes, Your Honor."

"And how do you plead, Mr. Ryan?"

"Not guilty," Ted says. "Your Honor."

When given a chance to speak, Ted gives a convoluted explanation that his girlfriend had forgotten her key in the door and when he went to retrieve it for her, he found the place had been robbed. No explanation of the ski mask, the grenade, the burglary tools.

Another fuck-up on Guy's part, Harry thinks to himself. Never should have let the kid open his mouth. Maybe a bail hearing is out of his depths too.

"All right, thank you very much," Clements says, sighing. "We'll get you on the docket for a preliminary hearing. As for the matter of the bond—"

Guy clears his throat. "Your Honor—"

"Mr. Ryan's sheet includes three previous offenses. Albeit all misdemeanors, but he does have a history in this court. Taking that into account alongside the burglary, the tools, and the assault on the officers, I'm going to set the bond at fifty-thousand."

The number gets Harry's attention. A little higher than he expected, but he can swing it. Through his underwriter, Harry is approved to cover bail up to $150,000.

"Assuming there is nothing further, I think we can move on until the date is set." Clements looks at Guy. "You know you're supposed to say yes, right?"

"Yes, Your Honor."

"YOU'VE GOT THE flag on you, boy." Harry eyes Ted in the rearview. "And lobbin' that paperweight grenade at the arresting officers? That added a tidy sum to the bail. What were you thinkin'?"

"I wasn't thinking, Harry. I just—"

"Your old man wanted to leave you in there. You're lucky to be out."

"I know, Harry. Thanks."

Ted sulks and looks out the window.

Fuzzy probably should've left him in there, at least for a day or two. Let him suffer some consequences and see where he'll end up if he doesn't straighten out. Fuzzy puts it on his ex-wife, but Harry knows the old crank has a soft spot for the kid and has been trying to rebuild the relationship. He doesn't need another loss on the board in that department. As a wayward son himself, Harry has some understanding of Ted's predicament as well.

"The big mystery here is the whereabouts of the cheeba," Harry says. "I hope you're not thinkin' about pullin' some jackrabbit stunt and going to look for your girlfriend."

Harry watches Ted's face for a reaction and gets one.

"That's right. I'll be comin' after your ass with a net. Nowhere behind a goddamn marshmallow you can hide."

They pull up in front of Fuzzy's house.

"Thanks for getting me out, Harry. And for the ride."

Harry watches him look both ways and back at the car before going
inside. Something feels off. Harry calls the office.

"Yeah, Manny. I've got a job for you."

17

HARRY AND GUY sit in a booth at Golden Sky Fine Chinese Cuisine, housed in a pagoda on Victory Boulevard. Guy reads the drink menu. "You want to get a Scorpion Bowl, Harry? To share?"

"No, I don't."

"How long are you going to keep Manny out there?"

"I'll let him twist a bit."

"Has he been on a stakeout before?"

"A couple minor jobs, but he needs more field experience. Teddy's no Houdini. Manny just needs to watch the house and see who comes and goes." Harry turns the menu over and reads the specials on the back. "I'll check in later but I'm sure as shit not sitting out there all day in this heat."

"You think Ted will stay put?"

"The girlfriend is at large, presumably with the missing cheeba. So, either she comes to him, which is unlikely, or he goes to where she is."

"Then you grab him?"

Harry sets the menu down. "We'll see what happens. If it looks like he's going make a break for it, I'll tie a tin can to his tail and slap a bracelet on him. But I'm thinkin' once he leads us to her, I swoop in and grab both him and the contraband."

A waitress appears and stands silent with her pad and pen.

"I'll have the Kung Pao," Guy says. He checks the drink menu again. "And a Fog Cutter."

"Cashew Chicken," Harry says. "And a Coke. You got the Mexican kind?"

She nods and walks away.

Harry mentions something offhand about when you could still smoke in the lounge area, but they mostly wait for their food in silence. They smoked half a joint on the way in and Guy is lost in thought, following the intricate tree patterns in the woodblock print above the booth.

He works with Harry on a fairly regular basis, but they don't hang out much. The fact that he's high—he doesn't usually smoke during the day—makes the silence feel longer and more strained.

This is the first time he's been out to lunch with someone in months. He and Amanda were together for so long that she became pretty much the totality of his social life. It's nice to have some company to share a meal with. Thinking back on his order, though, Guy wishes he'd gone with the garlic chicken and brown rice. He told himself he was going to be good this week. Blame that on the weed too.

He's always been heavy but since Amanda left in March, he's been steadily increasing in size as his life snowballs downhill. Amanda, on the other hand, has bloomed to life post-break-up. Going to L.A. Fitness every day. She looks incredible.

The two of them used to love to order in. Binge-eating take-out and binge-watching TV shows. Those lazy weekends were his favorite.

Amanda probably doesn't even eat Chinese food anymore.

He doesn't blame Amanda for jumping ship. Some days he wishes he could too. It's so hard to climb out of the rut. No matter how promising a day begins, most nights grand-finale with him bong-struck on the couch, grease-stained fast food bags balled up around him like used jizz wipes. He knows what he has to do—eat better, drink less, and exercise more—but it's just so damn hard to do it. Pretty much everything he likes is bad for him.

At least he knows he needs to change. That's a start. The real goners are the ones who don't even see it. As long as he keeps getting up and trying again, he can still turn things around. Just because Amanda gave up on him doesn't mean he needs to give up on himself.

The drinks come and Guy's mood improves a bit. His eyes widen at his first sip of the Fog Cutter. "That's the stuff. Try it, Harry."

"That's okay."

"Just what I needed. A nip of the tail."

Harry removes the straw from the long glass neck and takes a pull from the Coke bottle.

"Would you own Fuzzy's bar if Ted skips bail? Sounds like a win-win."

"I wouldn't call it a win." Harry wipes his mouth. "Fuzzy's a pal and ownin' that honkytonk lagoon would be like taking possession of his leaky boat. What does interest me is potentially taking possession of several pounds of that reefer. An Acapulco retirement plan."

IN SPANISH, THE Amazing Spider-Man comics are called El Sorprendente Hombre Araña. Manny is staked out across from Fuzzy's house, a squat adobe ranch on Costello Avenue, reading a story in which Hombre Araña is careening through alternate Earths in a time warp, discovering multiple corpses of himself.

Harry has posted Manny to stake out different locations a couple times but only to ascertain if someone was home. This time he's supposed to make sure someone doesn't leave.

He's been given instructions to watch out for a scrawny dark-haired kid and to follow him if he leaves the house. He even has a picture. He's also been told to look out for a girl who may come by, but the focus is on the kid and where he goes.

Manny is prepared to settle in for the long haul. He stopped by his mother's house to get a Tupperware container of snacks and a few bottles of Gatorade. He also took Harry's advice and brought along an empty gallon jug to pee in.

He makes a point to look up every two minutes from the comic book to survey the house and the street. He fans himself with the comic and has a look around. There's plenty of gas in the tank but his shitty Celica barely runs. No way it could stand idling for long stretches of time. Even if the AC worked well, which it doesn't.

He doesn't like this part of the job and doesn't get why Harry has him doing it. He has no idea who this kid is, what he did, or where he may or may not run off to. It would be much easier to track his phone. He could have set that up in two seconds. But maybe Harry wants to show him the old-school way of doing things. Maybe it's a test.

An hour in, Manny looks up right as a skinny young dark-haired guy, his subject, crosses the street and walks by the car with his hands in his pockets.

Manny starts the car and follows him down Costello, slow like he's looking for an address. The kid makes a right and heads toward the shopping plaza on the corner of Victory and Hazeltine. He stands on the corner looking down the road. It takes Manny a second to realize it's a bus stop.

Manny turns right on Hazeltine and backs into a spot in front of Angela's Hair Studio. He watches Ted get on a 164 bus headed west.

TED GETS OFF the bus at Sepulveda and walks south toward Le Rendez-vous Motel.

He's afraid to use his cell phone. Hopefully Capri is waiting in the room. They can have Max come get them and figure out where to go from there. If Max buys a decent amount, they might have enough money to get the car out of impound.

It's hard to believe twelve hours ago he was driving toward the motel victorious with a trunk full of weed and his girl waiting for him. It's always the small details that trip you up.

He knocks on the door of Room Two with caution, looking around to make sure he hasn't been followed. He smoked before heading out but it did the opposite of taking the edge off.

A woman who looks like a prostitute answers the door and Ted stares for a second. She has a hard look and Ted can smell stale menthol and pot smoke in the room. Ted looks around her like Capri might be in there. The woman folds her arms and blocks his view.

"Are you with law enforcement? I haven't done shit and you know it."

Ted apologizes and says he has the wrong room. He skulks away, looking back at the door a couple times. You could see her nipples through her lacy top and he can't help himself.

He finds a working payphone outside a Winchell's Donuts and reads Capri's number off the contacts in his cell phone. He has to call twice in a row before she picks up.

"Why are you calling me from a payphone?" she says.

"Just being careful."

She tells him her friend Ami dropped her off at the motel in Malibu with Max. She didn't know where else to go. Ted hears Max say something in the background. And yes, she has all the stuff with her. She tells him Max can't buy much stuff himself, but he knows someone who can. She tells him to get out there now so they can get moving.

He's about to explain that the car's impounded but just says he'll see her soon. Now he has to get out there.

He thinks about the dealerships on Van Nuys Boulevard. Then he's in the lot of Keyes Toyota, getting the sell from Russ Haxby, a salesman in shiny black pants and a red-tie-on-red-shirt combo that makes him look like the devil.

They make a slow circle around a silver Highlander SUV and Ted says he's thinking about taking a test drive.

"I can make that happen for you, son. Let's go on inside, make a copy of your license, have you fill out some paperwork and we'll go tool around in her. Whaddya say?"

Ted says something about not liking the color, maybe needing something smaller anyway. Gas mileage. Haxby tells him to take all the time he needs. He hands Ted a business card and says to give him a ring-dang-doo when he's ready to talk turkey.

Ted lets the card fall from his hand and wanders over by the service area where a few cars are lined up for oil changes. A set of car keys dangles from the ignition of a Yaris.

He looks left and right like he's about to cross the street.

18

HARRY SAYS TO Guy, "Why don't you hand that back to me?"
Guy is sprawled out on the office couch with one of Harry's
Stetsons tilted over his eyes, like a napping ranch hand. Harry returns
it to the rack and goes back to drawing up Fuzzy's bail agreement.

Harry's phone buzzes and Ruby's song comes up. She's still in her pa-
jamas back at the Sylvan Shores, sounding fresh from her meditation.
"Cleaning up some of the damage, baby. Looks like a bomb dropped
on this place."

Harry can hear her loading the dishwasher.

"Don't worry about it, baby. I'll get to it."

"No, you won't. And I can't relax in a mess. Last night was so fun.
Too bad you had to go so early. You Don Juan-ed me."

"That's my move, darlin'."

"All my cats are meowing for you, Harry. You know how I get."

"You have some breakfast?"

"I had some toast. Your bread is a little stale."

"I just bought it."

"You need to check the color of the twistys before you buy."

"Twistys?"

"On the bag. They tell you what day the bread was made. Tuesday,
green. Thursday, red. Your twisty is blue, which means the bread was
made on Monday."

"Huh."

"It's okay. I put on butter and jam. It tasted good."

Harry fills her in on Fuzzy and Ted and says he'll tell her more later.

"I'll be here. Feed Emmylou and watch my shows."

They sign off. Harry looks at Guy sweating all over his couch.

"I need to get Fuzzy up to speed," he says. "Let's go up to the Grotto
for a short one."

That gets Guy on his feet.

Driving past the AutoZone on Victory, Harry hits the signal and waits
for a break in traffic to turn left on Costello.

"Let's make a pit stop and check on the palace guard. See if he's
standin' sentry."

They pull up in front of Fuzzy's house, directly across from Manny's
post. Manny sits content in the car reading a comic book.

Guy waves at him. No reaction.

"He hasn't noticed us."

"I wonder what else he hasn't noticed." Harry kills the engine. "Let's
check the house."

Harry raps on the front door. No answer. Guy stands on the porch
and surveys the street. They go around back, looking in all the windows.

"I don't think there's anyone here, Harry."

Harry crosses the street. Manny sees him this time and gives him a
wave.

"He's on the move, boss."

"Then why aren't you?"

"I followed him until he got on the bus. Then I followed the bus."

"What bus?"

"I don't know. I lost it."

"How do you lose a bus?"

"It came up next to another bus and I got confused. I couldn't tell which one."

Harry sighs. "What the Christ are you doing here then?"

"See if he comes back."

"Manny—"

"Yeah, boss?"

"I think this is the end of the road for you and me."

THE MALIBU RIVIERA MOTEL

19

TED IS LESS nervous since he changed the plates on the stolen Yaris. He did it in the outer reaches of a Walmart lot, using a quarter as a screwdriver, and he's pretty sure no one saw him. The service engine light keeps turning on and off but traffic is moving on the 101. It only takes an hour to get out to Malibu.

There's tension at the motel. Ted doesn't think Max would try anything with Capri, and she made fun of Max after that day at the pier, saying he looked like a sunburned He-Man doll, but you never know. Something feels off.

Ted watches Max pace. He's different since he quit drinking and taking pills. Now it's all steroids and supplements and working out. Most of the muscle seems to be in his bald head. He does seem to be getting his shit together, though. He's living out here by the beach and says the edibles business is about to pop.

"This isn't what I expected when you called," Max says. "I told you I needed to set the groundwork with my boss and next thing I know some dude drops your girlfriend off here and she starts laying some plan on me."

A dude dropped her off? Ted looks at Capri. "I thought you said

Ami dropped you off."

"Her boyfriend drove."

Ted turns to Max to verify but Max looks like he has other things on his mind.

"I told you," Capri says. "Just set up a meeting with your distributor and we'll handle the rest."

"I am the distributor," Max says. "He's the CEO. I can't just send anyone his way. He can't afford to get caught up in criminal shit."

"CEO?" Capri says.

"Dude, how long have we known each other?" Ted says.

"This is bigger than shit we've done together, bro. This is legitimate business."

"This is a big deal, *bro*," Capri says. "That's why you should call him. You'll probably get a promotion."

"I'll think about it."

Capri gives him a hard stare. "We don't have time for you to think about it. Ted said you were a player. He said you were a guy who could set up a deal." She shoots the stare at Ted. "Bullshit as usual."

Ted watches Max for a reaction. He knows Capri is one step away from making a threat and he doesn't want it to come to that. It's hard to tell if Max is frustrated or pissed or both. A long second ticks by and he says he'll do it. Ted's surprised at first then realizes he shouldn't be. He's never seen Capri not get what she wants.

Out in the parking lot, Ted loads the car with the supply, stashing as much as he can around the spare tire and under the rear seat cushions. Capri sizes up the stolen sedan. "Only you would steal a Toyota Yaris."

"Inconspicuous," Ted says. "And good gas mileage."

He opens the passenger door for her before getting in behind the wheel. Capri lights a cigarette and rolls her window down. "Doesn't even have power windows."

"We're on the run, baby. We don't need to be weighed down by bells and whistles."

Ted keys the ignition and the service engine light is gone.

Maybe it's a good omen.

FUZZY HAS WORKED in a bar long enough to read his customers. He can tell right off if someone is looking for a fight or looking to get laid. If they're having their first post-shift beer or if they've been drinking all day. When he puts his pencil behind his ear and looks up at Harry and Guy, he can tell by their faces that Teddy's done the skedaddle.

"Teddy's in the wind." Harry mounts the stool and slumps over his elbows. "I had a guy on him, but he slipped through his fingers."

"Should've left him in there."

Harry lights a Tareyton. "Too late now."

Fuzzy reaches into the cooler and grabs a Bud for Harry and one for himself. He looks at Guy. "You having something?"

"You know how to make a Fog Cutter?"

"Just have a beer," Harry says.

"No, no." Fuzzy looks Guy in the eye. "Whatever suits you fine."

Fuzzy puts on his reading glasses and flips through an old Trader Vic's recipe book. He takes his time making the drink and tells Harry he might have some luck with Teddy's buddy Max Waddell. Harry jots the name on a napkin.

Fuzzy delivers the drink to Guy. "Didn't have any orgeat syrup handy. Not much call for it the past fifty years. I hope this will suffice."

He plants a collapsed umbrella in the glass, bobs a dry maraschino on the surface. Guy takes a sip and tells him it's delicious.

The review gives Fuzzy no sense of pride or satisfaction.

"Listen, Fuzz, I apologize for having to go through the official motions here." Harry sets a manila folder on the bar and opens to the bail agreement. "But it's probably better we take care of it now."

"You got a pen?"

Harry fumbles around in his pockets.

"Forget it. I got one."

"I filled out most of it. You just need to initial here and here and sign there."

Fuzzy grabs a Bic from a pint glass next to the register and hovers over the document.

"I hit every goddamn pothole in the road," he says.

20

FIRST STOP FOR Ted and Capri is a Pilot Travel Center next to a Little Sister's Truck Wash.

On trips to Vegas when Ted was a kid, Fuzzy would stop at the Little Sister's in Barstow so Ted could watch the big dusty trucks roll through and come out clean on the other side.

They're fully baked from passing a bowl back and forth on the drive. Capri heads into the store to load up on Red Bull and snacks. She's wearing short denim cutoffs and a thin tank-top with no bra. Posted at the gas pump, Ted can see truckers' necks craning out of high cab windows.

Back on the road, Capri searches for local dispensaries on her phone. She says maybe they can unload a little product that way and make some quick cash while they try to orchestrate a bigger sale. Eddie at Big Smoke doesn't have much reach outside the Valley. She's not worried about anyone being on the lookout for them here.

Higher-end places would never consider buying from someone off the street, so they try a couple of the less reputable-looking dispensaries in the Chino area, saying they're growers from Ventura. No one's buying. Even with the Acapulco Gold. No one seems to believe it's the real thing.

Only one guy is remotely interested but he says there's such an abundance of product now it isn't worth the risk, no matter how low the price is. He suggests getting further away from L.A. Capri seems agitated but leaves without an incident. For a second Ted was worried she was going to hurt the guy.

They continue east on 60 and Capri wants to stop off to visit her friend Daniela in Fontana. She says she hasn't seen her since the two of them danced together at the Golden Banana and shared a condo at the beach for a couple months. Daniela got pregnant sometime after that and moved out here to be closer to her mother. Ted's never met her.

"Welcome to Fontucky," Daniela says when she answers the door. Platinum blonde in gold yoga pants. Same hard edge as Capri, same uncut sex appeal.

Daniela's boy Javi comes running into the room and wraps himself around her legs. He has pierced ears and wears a Batman shirt and a diaper. He looks down at the floor when he's introduced. Ted says he'll hang with him so Capri and Daniela can go outside to smoke.

CAPRI AND DANIELA pack a bowl and light cigarettes on a balcony over-looking the parking lot. The stolen Yaris bakes in the afternoon sun.

Daniela tells her about Javi and the baby daddy. She's also dancing again, this time at the Fantasy Topless Theatre in Colton. The clientele is worse than L.A. but so are the girls, so she's one of the hotter ones.

Capri and Daniela used to talk about that all the time. How L.A. was full of girls like them who were hot shit where they came from. Who thought they'd roll into town and bag some rapper or producer.

Everyone says it's all makeup and airbrushing but then you see real models and celebrities in person and it's like they're a different species.

Capri and Daniela were hot enough to score a ticket deep in the cheap seats, but the VIPs were never interested in anything more than fucking them. Marrying them? Never.

They got a small taste of the big life, a few perks to wow them and keep them on the hook, but they mostly saw the worst of these men. They would never get the big door prize. The brass ring of the fancy house and the expensive divorce.

When she was dancing at the Golden Banana, Capri was trying to meet rich guys on sugar baby sites but most of them turned out to be full of shit. Daniela got her into what she called freestyling. They'd get dressed up and hang out at places like Bar Marmont or the Polo Lounge and zero in on guys who were rich looking but not good looking.

The guys would be expecting a hooker come-on but when it never came, they'd think they lucked out. When it worked, it was better than escorting or the sugar baby stuff. No money upfront led to more money and other benefits later if you put the time in and played it right.

Tourists were one thing but what you wanted was someone who lived in L.A. or was in town for business a lot. You could sink your hooks into someone like that, especially if they were married. That's how Capri met a guy named Ben at the rooftop bar at the Thompson Hotel in Beverly Hills.

She asks Daniela if she remembers him.

"Oh fuck. Ben," Daniela says. "How could I forget?"

Ben was forty-five but looked older. His hair was dyed brown with a reddish tint. He had chronic indigestion and was always burpy and wincing, like he'd just washed down a chili dog with Dr. Pepper.

Capri and Ben had a wild midweek run and met up every time he was in town over the next couple months. He showered her with jewelry and shoes. Called her princess, daddy's little cumslut. He made a lot of money selling insurance or something. Enough for a country club membership and a nice condo in a quiet complex in Marina Del Rey where he docked a boat and garaged a black Lexus.

Capri was also kept there for a period. Then she invited Daniela in. The arrangement was cool for coked-up threesomes, but things went south when they got in trouble with the neighbors for partying too much when Ben was out of town. He told her he had some business partners coming in and she and Daniela had to find another place to stay for a while.

Daniela split and Capri never told her what happened next. Which was that she faked a pregnancy and threatened to contact Ben's wife. She even pulled her phone out to show she'd found his wife on Facebook and could send her a message right then if she wanted.

Ben didn't react like she thought he would. He smashed the phone and kneed her in the stomach. Then he dragged her down the hallway to the office he always kept locked. There was a gun in his desk and he put it in her mouth as deep as it would go. She admitted she wasn't pregnant and she swore she'd never come anywhere near him again and she didn't.

Capri never told Daniela that part either. And she doesn't say anything about the robbery at Big Smoke or the real reason they're out here. She just says they're taking a road trip to Vegas.

Daniela asks if she and Ted are getting married and Capri says no fucking way. That would hurt Ted's feelings if he heard it, but he's inside oblivious, chasing the kid around the living room with a broken lightsaber.

Daniela asks if she's been talking to Jamey at all.

"Not really."

The last time Capri saw Daniela, Jamey had just gotten out of jail and was trying to get her to come back to Tempe for a few months until he was free to leave the state and come to L.A. with her.

"Is he back in jail?"

Capri shakes her head.

"So, you're still talking to him?"

"Once in a while." Capri drags on her cigarette.

"Does this guy know about him?"

Daniela looks inside at Ted, doing karate moves for her son in the living room.

"Not much."

"What does he do?"

Capri tells her Ted sells weed and asks if she needs any. Daniela says she has plenty, but she'll take two ounces anyway. She has extra cash from this customer she's fucking who owns a chain of Jiffy Lubes throughout Inland Empire.

SUNLIGHT POURS INTO the Grotto and Harry squints toward the door where Rick stands in silhouette, holding two paper bags.

"Look at you sorry sons of bitches." Rick enters the darkness of the bar, the closing door bum-rushing the light out behind him. "You can tell a man who boozes by the company he chooses."

He sets the bags down on the bar.

"If I knew you were here, Har, I would've grabbed you some bird. It's Church's."

"That's good bird," Harry says.

Harry's no stranger to the Church's Chicken franchise on Sherman Way. Some Saturdays he and Ruby have a late afternoon cocktail or two at the Clipper Club Lounge at the Van Nuys Airport and grab some Church's before stopping at the Redbox to pick out a couple movies.

Harry always felt like he was cheating on the Grotto when he drank at the Clipper Club until one day he ran into Fuzzy himself at the bar, wearing a Hawaiian shirt and looking like he got caught fucking the dog.

Rick tucks his purple and black striped necktie into his breast pocket away from the grease and gravy.

"Nice tie," Harry says.

"I'm hoping it'll round the edges off this king-hell hangover I'm wrestling with."

"Big night last night?"

"Had me a time with a poor man's lady."

"You certainly keep it damp," Fuzzy says.

"If I laid any more pipe, I'd have to join the plumbers' union."

Harry does Melvyn Douglas in *Hud*. "You're an unprincipled man, Rick."

"You watch it the other night too? I caught the end when I got home. Still a killer."

"All them cows," Harry says.

Fuzzy rifles through the bags, doling out the condiments and sides. "Am I pouring you one?"

Rick checks his watch. "Just to be polite."

Fuzzy reaches for the gin bottle and Rick stops him.

"Just a CL Smoothie, Fuzzard. I need to keep my head screwed on."

Rick looks at Guy. "The fuck are you drinking?"

"Fog Cutter," Guy says. "Take a sip."

Rick dips a cocktail straw in the drink and sticks his finger over the top to extract a sample. "Fuzzard made this?"

"I haven't made one since the war," Fuzzy says.

"What war?" Guy says.

Rick cracks his Coors Light and pours white gravy over a golden biscuit. "What's with the pow-wow?"

"Teddy robbed a pot dispensary last night," Fuzzy says. "Harry boosted him this morning—"

"And now he's in the wind," Rick says.

Fuzzy shrugs, deflated.

"Kid's a shitheel," Rick says, biting into a drumstick. "No offense, Fuzzard."

Fuzzy moves his mashed potatoes around. "I get it."

"Any idea where he went?"

"I haven't the foggiest."

"Turns out Teddy's girlfriend worked at the dispensary," Harry says. "So we're goin' on the assumption she was in on it with him."

"She's trouble," Fuzzy says. "Used to work at that jiggle joint by the one-seventy."

"Show N' Tail?" Rick says.

"Golden Banana."

"Right. They're full nude over there. Kind of a Persian theme."

"From what I've been told, she got into a he said, she said kerfuf-fle during a lap dance," Fuzzy says. "The guy claims she went for his wallet. She claims he slipped a finger in or plunked his magic twanger or some such infraction. Either way, she did some real damage with a broken champagne flute. Used it like a goddamn yard shiv."

"Teddy told you this?" Harry says.

"I've asked around about her," Fuzzy says. "I like to know who's staying in my house."

"I've got to whiz." Rick descends from his stool and stretches. He presses his hand into the small of his back. "Goddamn Kama Sutra."

He heads to the Gents and Fuzzy clears the take-out containers.

"You think the Waddell kid might know something?" Harry says.

"Yeah, Malibu Max. One of Teddy's old pals. He's from Reseda but he mentions Malibu more than the Beach Boys. Lives in a motel on PCH, up around Zuma Beach."

"You know the name of it?"

"The Malibu Riviera."

"Sounds like a swanky place," Guy says.

21

THE MALIBU RIVIERA is a row of rooms perched on the ocean side of Pacific Coast Highway, not far from where the Zuma/Trancas Canyon road bottoms out. There's a gravel lot with beat-up *M-O-T-E-L* letters propped up against a gate.

"Swanky as you thought it'd be?" Harry noses the Olds at an angle next to the dumpster. "May as well park here. I don't see no valet."

Guy surveys the line-up of rooms. "Which one's he in, you think?"

"Let's make the rounds."

After a couple of knocks with no answer, Harry hears the Grateful Dead leaking out of a unit at the far end. "Wharf Rat," he says.

Harry raps on the door frame and sizes up the guy who answers. He looks more meathead than Deadhead. Chrome dome with a shadow goatee. One of those juicers scattered like birdshit around the Gold's Gym on the Venice boardwalk. Muscle-bound, jail-bound. He wears an old T-shirt emblazoned with Mel Gibson's face and the line *I OWN MALIBU*. Rick has the same one.

"Hey, Sugartits," Harry says.

One lesson Harry's picked up over the years is the way to deal with an asshole is to act like an asshole. This guy's an asshole.

The guy steps outside and puffs himself up. His bald head looks like a dented soup can. Harry cranes his neck and peers through the crack in the door. "They in there?"

"Who?"

"You know who. Let's skip the rigamarole. I'm tired."

"I don't know what you're talking about, man."

"You're Max, right? Malibu Max?"

He doesn't say anything.

Harry raises his voice. "I have it on good authority that you're a known criminal associate of a shitbird named Teddy Ryan and—"

An old lady in a housecoat comes out of the front office and shoots a look in their direction.

"Alright," Max says. "Let's talk inside."

Harry turns to Guy. "Wait here. Keep an eye out."

"An eye out for what?"

"Comanche."

Max's bluster deflates once they're inside. He sits at the edge of the bed, hunched over like a palooka. "I don't know where they went, honestly."

"Glad we're being honest." Harry puts a Tareyton in his mouth and scans the room.

"You're not supposed to smoke in here."

"You tryin' to kill the theatrics, kid?" Harry lights up and slides the Bic back in the Lighter Leash holster. He's enjoying trotting out his old P.I. hard guy act. Hasn't done it in a while. "How do you know Ted?"

"We grew up together. I've known him since we were seven. He stole my bike but then he gave it back. He felt bad."

"And Capri?"

"Only through Ted. I told him I thought she was trouble." Max fiddles with his shark tooth necklace. "It was a feeling I got from her."

"A feeling like what?"

"Like she was sizing me up. I felt it again today. Like maybe we cut Ted out of this thing and me and you go in on it, you know what I mean? Or maybe she was testing me, seeing what kind of friend I was. Head games."

"You met her before today?"

"Once. They were at the pier a couple months ago and Ted bugged me to come down. Wanted to show her off, I guess."

"You try to fuck her?"

"Fuck no, man."

"You think about it?"

"I thought about it." Max fiddles with the necklace again. "Ted says she's got a pussy ornament."

"That a fact?" Harry looks at him. "What other tidbits you got for me?"

"Look, man, Capri showed up here unannounced. Like you. Trying to unload a bunch of weed. A bunch. Then Ted showed up."

"They showed up separately?"

Max nods. "I couldn't really help them. I don't move pounds of weed and shit. I distribute edibles to dispensaries. Strictly that. Totally legal. I have a license."

"So you told them to hit the road and that was that? Legitimate businessman like you can't be involved with stolen merchandise. You could lose that license."

Max doesn't say anything.

"This sounds like a police deal," Harry says. "I'll let them run this down and save myself the hassle."

"Listen. Elmer, that's my boss, he buys in bulk. He makes the edibles himself. I told them he might be interested in buying some stuff as long as they didn't let on it was stolen."

"Right. So where do I find Elmer?"

"He lives out in the desert. Johnson Valley. But he knows people all over the place. I pointed them in that direction. Gave them his business card and called ahead to let him know they were coming. That was the extent of it."

"You got another one of those around? I'd like to take a squint at it."

"What?"

"The card. I'd like to take a squint at it."

Max gets one from the top drawer of his desk.

Harry takes a squint at it. Elmer's Eatables.

"The guy must be legitimate," Harry says. "He's got business cards."

The Olds rambles south on a wide open PCH. Harry lights a pinner and rolls down the windows to let the sweet smoke mix with the Pacific Ocean breeze, a distinctly Californian pleasure that takes the edge off the other hassles.

One thing he still loves about L.A. is you can take a vacation without leaving town. He swears he's even crashed at the Malibu Riviera before. Probably after a day of too much sun at El Matador and too much beer and fried fish at Neptune's Net.

He fills Guy in on what he learned from Max.

"He looked like a seedy character," Guy says.

"What'd you think he was going to look like, Hugh Beaumont?"
Harry takes another deep drag and passes the joint.

22

HARRY LIKES COMING home to the Sylvan Shores when Ruby's there. Twelve years of Tareyton smoke and bare-minimum upkeep has given the place a sort of fossilized stagnation. She brings warmth and energy and light. It's like opening the windows on a spring day.

When he and Guy walk in, she's putting a pot of coffee on, adding some Café Bustelo to Harry's Kona blend, giving it some extra zip.

"You're all dressed up, Guy."

"I went to a wedding last night."

"That's fun."

Guy moves at a good clip toward the bathroom and Harry hears the combined whoosh of the sink and the exhaust fan. It does little to muffle the rifle crack of Guy's first release.

Ruby laughs. She has a middle school sense of humor. Farts and boners. Guys getting hit in the nuts. That's the kind of thing that tickles her. Another quality Harry appreciates. He can rip one and she thinks it's a hoot.

He comes up behind her and rubs her shoulders. She turns to the side and leans into him. "What's your plan, baby?"

"I don't know, what do you think?" Harry says. "You want to order in? Or we could make some quesadillas. I got some green chiles."

"I mean about Fuzzy's son."

"He'll turn up one way or another."

Ruby walks to the fridge for some cream.

"Why did he run away?"

Harry shrugs. "Who knows why people do what they do."

"What if he's in trouble?"

"He is in trouble."

"What are you planning on doing?"

Harry leans against the counter.

"I thought I'd drop back twenty and punt."

"No idea where he went?"

"We went to see a friend of his in Malibu and he said Teddy and the girl went to some guy out in Johnson Valley to unload some of the cheeba."

"Didn't he get caught in the robbery? How did he keep what he took?"

"The way his buddy Max tells it, Teddy got out of there clean the first time then went back for more. That's when he got caught."

"Greedy greedy."

"Stupid stupid."

Harry sits on the couch and puts his boots on the coffee table. He fishes a fresh pinner out of his cigarette pack and gets it going. Guy comes shuffling out of the bathroom and plants himself on the other end of the couch.

"Why don't you go out there and talk to the man?" Ruby says. "How far is Johnson Valley?"

"Far enough. The desert."

"I know the desert," Guy says.

"What are you, an Indian?"

Ruby looks at him. "Harry—"

She brings Harry his coffee and hits the pinner. She asks Guy if he wants any coffee and he shakes his head no.

"I think you should take a look, baby. It's Fuzzy's son. And you say you can track anyone down. A single bee to the hive, you said."

He's been debating whether he ought to go, but he really isn't in the mood. And he and Ruby have a date to go dancing at the Cowboy Palace on Sunday. Now he's getting the sense she'll be more disappointed if he stays home.

Maybe he'll be back by Sunday anyway. Teddy shouldn't be too hard to catch up to. Not sure about the girl though. She sounds like a wild card.

"Why don't you come along with me, darlin'? See the old man in action."

"I'll watch things here," Ruby says. "And take care of Emmylou. Why don't you take Guy?"

Harry gives her a look. She smiles and looks away.

"Amanda loved the desert," Guy says. "We used to go camping in Joshua Tree."

"This is a quick run, Guy. No time for camping or anything like that. Probably easier if I go it alone."

Harry catches Ruby eyeing him again. She has a big heart for the down and out. Not that he should complain. It accounts for her affection for him.

"Do you know the desert?" Guy says.

"Cosmically I do." Harry pauses. "Psychically."

Ruby gives him a weird look and Guy sits there with a sulk on. Harry feels like his kindliness is being taken advantage of here. This is a skip trace, not a Make-A-Wish vacation.

"Christ," Harry says. "Quit lookin' like the cheese fell off your cracker."

"It's okay, Harry."

Guy sounds sad saying it.

Ruby gives Harry another take-him-with-you look and he sighs.

"Looks like we're lightin' out for the territory, Counselor. Let's at least see what this Elmer has to say."

Ruby says she'll pack them some snacks for the road and Harry heads into the bedroom to throw some clothes in a bag.

It's been a spell, but when Harry's out on a chase he likes to be properly attired. He changes into a fresh shirt, a lightweight arrow print, chocolate brown, with embroidered lassos on both shoulders. He puts on the crisp dark Levi's Ruby likes and a pair of brown Lama ropers that match the shirt. No need for a jacket in this heat.

He packs a few similar ensembles in his duffel, including the new Rancher from Country General, then stands before his gallery of hats. No question about what to go with. The straw Open Road. He kisses Ruby goodbye and tells Guy they need to stop by the office to grab a couple things.

The garage door sensors are on the blink. Harry has to nudge the gate with the bumper to make its rusty bars rattle to life and clang aside. The sun is bright on the hood of the car, inching toward street level like a submarine surfacing. Harry's lenses darken to cut the glare.

Outside the Casa Royale, Harry waits in the car while Guy goes inside to pack a bag. Fifteen minutes later, he comes shambling out in shorts and flip-flops.

"Decided to ditch the evening wear?"

"It's hot in the desert."

When they get to the office, Harry grabs some pot and papers out of his desk drawer and puts them in the side pocket of his duffel. He packs some extra Tareytons, happy he'd picked up the carton at Costco. They aren't easy to find at gas stations and convenience stores anymore. His second choice, Benson & Hedges 100s, are getting scarce as hen's teeth too.

He trusted Benson & Hedges because of all the old people he'd see smoking them. Those geezers must finally be croaking. He turns off the desk lamp and stuffs a half-joint from the ashtray in the cellophane of the pack he has going.

He opens the office safe to grab some petty cash. His gun is in there too, the Gary Reeder Texas Ranger Classic revolver his dad taught him on. His name engraved on the side. Same embroidered gunslinger's holster from when he was a boy. He hefts it in his hand, deciding if it's necessary.

Harry renews his carry license and keeps the Ranger oiled and in good repair, but he hasn't had much need for it over the years, even when he was doing investigation work. Still, it's extra security.

"You think you're going to need a gun?"

"A precaution, Counselor."

Guy points to a rifle on the wall.

"You taking that one?"

"That's my daddy's old Henry. Just for show." Harry shows him the Ranger. "This one here's what I'm bringin'."

Harry packs it in the duffel along with a box of .45 caliber ammo. He also grabs a pair of handcuffs. He hasn't used them on anyone other than Ruby in a couple years.

"How about this one?" Guy unsheathes an air rifle from an umbrella stand in the corner.

"The Remington? That's a varmint gun. A peashooter."

Guy raises the rifle and peers through the scope. He has it pointed at the door when Manny walks in. Manny doesn't notice right away. Then he hits the deck.

Guy lowers the rifle, his hands still shaky as Harry snatches it away from him.

Manny climbs to his feet. "I just came by to get a couple things."

He fills a box with a few keepsakes: a travel mug, a take-out menu from Emperor Express, and a framed picture of his mother. With a sense of gravity, he returns a brass bullhead paperweight to Harry.

"I'm sorry he flew the coop on you, boss. That's my bad. I'm no good at stakeouts. But if you need me for anything else let me know. I'd like another shot."

Harry holds the paperweight in his hand and feels taken advantage of again. Fuck it, he's not paying the kid anyway. Maybe he'll turn something up.

"Tell you what, see what you can do technology-wise. We're hittin' the road but get on your computer and put a couple bobbers in the water. You know how to reach me."

Manny looks down at the box. "Should I take my stuff?"

"You can leave it here for now."

He hands back the paperweight and Manny returns it to his desk, along with his other items. Harry asks him to type a short note on Buckaroo Bail Bonds letterhead:

I will be out of town for a couple days. - Harry S. Robatore.

Harry tapes it to the door on the way out.

FAR OUT

23

CAPRI DOESN'T GET why anyone would choose to live this far out in the desert.

Barren backlit mountains loom in the distance. The clouds look sketched in chalk and all you can hear is the wind. Her thoughts rush inward and that's never a good thing for her.

Growing up in Arizona, the desert was always out there, surrounding, threatening, but she and her mother rarely strayed far from the strip malls and Walmarts around the various offramp apartment complexes they lived in.

Right now she wishes she had Jamey to handle some aspects of the plan. She has no idea how things are going to go with the guy they're going to see. And it all depends on her. Ted is pretty much along for the ride. His main asset is he's harmless. People let their guard down around him. That's useful in a deal. She can be the bad cop, the arsenic in his cookie.

Ted also took the fall for her when it came down to it. And it could come down to that again. If things went sideways, she couldn't trust Jamey not to hightail and cover his own ass.

Getting closer to this guy Elmer's place, it feels more and more like

another planet. Everything looks scorched. Pavement surrenders to
sand, radio to static. There are dune buggies in driveways. They pass a
fortified compound flying a foreign flag.

Ted looks at the map on his phone and says it's only a little further.

They turn off Ocotillo Road onto a narrow path of sand and gravel.
Then up a long weedy driveway leading to a doublewide trailer. They
park the car and look around. A couple junk cars on blocks. Some wire
fence pens with pigs, ostriches, and skinny goats. An old donkey tied
to a post. Capri fills a duffel with some sample product and Ted goes
over to take a look at the donkey.

EVEN WHEN ELMER isn't expecting anyone, he sits on his porch in a
meditative state, drawing on his pipe and looking down the driveway
that leads to his square of land. Few cars pass by on Ocotillo let alone
turn off in the direction of his compound.

He watches a young guy and girl, the kids Max told him about, get
out of a Toyota Yaris and look around like they aren't sure they're in
the right place. He sits there a few seconds before he reveals himself,
standing tall in his Stetson, plaid robe, and cowboy boots.

He takes a slow draw on his pipe and descends the stairs. "Careful of
the jackass, son. He ain't exactly friendly."

"I love donkeys," the kid says. "You never see them anywhere."

"He's a real beauty but he don't like strangers. Keeps us safe, right,
pal?" Elmer scratches the donkey roughly behind the ears. "I can pet
him, of course. He's known me a long time."

"What's his name?"

"He never told me. How about you two? What do you go by?"

The two introduce themselves and Elmer sizes them up. The girl doesn't have much on. A real kitten-with-a-whip type. The kid with her seems like he's head over heels but in over his head.

Elmer gets down to business.

"Maxie says you guys got some rarified goods," he says. "Let's tip-toe inside the mobile estate here and take a look-see."

The trailer is cluttered with knickknacks, cooking supplies, and stacks of business and entrepreneurial advice books. Elmer makes room on the kitchen table and Capri pulls four wrapped packages out of the duffel, each one roughly the size of a football. "This is all high-test, medical-grade stuff, really powerful," she says. "But this stuff is next level."

Max had told him they had genuine Acapulco Gold, but Elmer was skeptical. He'd never come across it. When the girl opens the bundle, though, Elmer almost senses a light beaming from it. And the smell is appetizing. But he keeps his poker face. Never appear too interested.

Capri continues. "This strain is very hard to—"

Elmer holds up his hand like a traffic cop. "Let me stop you right there, sweetheart. I'm a huckster myself so I appreciate the spiel, but I'm what you might call a quantity-over-quality man. Fact of the matter is, I cook the stuff down in butter to make my candies."

She doesn't appear to care for the interruption, but Elmer pushes on. Better to keep the upper hand. He recently finished a book by an author named M. Stuart Peck about the art of persuasion and mental manipulation. There's negotiation and compromise but Peck's school of thought puts you on track to getting what you want without giving up anything in return. Doing the deal exactly on your terms.

Rule number one is to control the conversation.

"Maxie told you about the candies, I assume?" Elmer says. "That's my business. Elmer's Eatables. Been working on a new logo for my stickers here, if you'd like to get a sneak peek."

He unveils a large sketch pad with a few similar versions of a logo, each featuring a likeness of Elmer himself, with the calabash pipe and cowboy hat, drawn out in pencil. "These are prototypes, of course. But in business it's important to brand oneself."

Ted cocks his head at the sketches. "You ever worry about getting confused with Elmer's Glue?"

"I wish you were the first person to say that, son." Elmer grimaces. "Good Christ, I wish you were the first."

"I'm sorry, Elmer. What's the best thing you make?"

"Specialty is chocolates, but I make a quality lollipop too. Once our business here is taken care of, I'll fix you kids a goodie bag to go."

Elmer reaches into a yellow pouch and fills the deep bowl of his pipe.

"I don't smoke anything stronger than Sail pipe tobacco myself, but I find my chocolates and lollipops to be relaxing on occasion. Particularly in the bathtub after a trying day. And they were a great comfort to my wife when she was unwell. It's a long, sad tale but it's how this business of mine got started."

Elmer shakes off the memory.

"And damn it, the market's wide open. Once this shebang becomes a legal enterprise nationwide, I'll be in a position to be the Ben and Jerry's of eatables."

"Are you Ben or Jerry?" Ted says.

"I'm a bit more like Ben. Ben's the businessman."

Elmer strikes a wooden match and lowers it over the bowl of his pipe. A large plume of smoke escapes from the side of his mouth.

"Speaking of, let's get transacting here."

24

CAPRI WATCHES ELMER stack $1,800 in hundreds and twenties, counting it out twice, on the kitchen table. The fucker haggled the price of a pound down from $2,500. Talking to her like she was an idiot the whole time, satisfied with himself. He wanted to buy even more but the price he offered was insulting and he said it would have required a trip to the bank anyway. She just wants to be done with this guy.

While he was getting the money together, she noticed there was more in the safe. Not sure how much, but more. And he left it open. It's all she's thinking about it on the walk back to the car. The old bastard giving her the short end of the stick. Then handing them a bag of candy on the way out like they were kids on Halloween.

When they get to the car, Ted gets in the driver seat and roots through the bag of edibles. Capri grabs the tire iron out of the trunk and walks back toward the trailer.

It's only a couple seconds before Ted is out of the car and jogging up beside her. A nervous look on his face. His voice cracking.

"Boo, where are you going?"

She ignores him, rage swelling up inside her. In the kitchen, Elmer

is stacking the bales inside the seat of an old wooden workbench. He
looks up with that phony grandpa smile and walks toward her.

"Forget something, sweetheart?"

She raises the tire iron and clubs him above the knee. His leg gives
out with a crack and he drags himself toward the wall and upends the
kitchen table, trying to give himself an extra second to reach the safe
before she does.

She pushes the table aside and is stopped short when he pulls a gun
from the safe. She nails him hard in the shoulder with the tire iron and
his gun falls from his hand before he can get his arm up.

She raises the tire iron, higher this time, aiming to hit him in the
stomach. Ted clasps a hand on her shoulder and pulls her back. She
breaks free and gets Elmer twice more, once in the ribs and once in the
lower back. His hat comes off and he curls into a crouch. She threatens
the tire iron again and Elmer flinches, covering his face with his hands.

Capri picks up Elmer's gun, then grabs his cowboy hat and puts it
on. Holding the gun on Elmer she instructs Ted to load the stuff they
sold him back into the bag they handed it to him in. He hesitates for a
second then does what he's told. Next she tells him to go into the safe
and grab the box of ammo and all the cash that's left. He does it.

Outside the animals are riled up. Capri thinks about shooting one of
the ostriches for fun, to see how the big dumb thing would go down
and how the other ones would react, but Ted already looks like he's
about to double over.

He throws the bag in the trunk and gets in behind the wheel. Capri
sets the cowboy hat on the dashboard and tells him to get moving. The
animals are still raising a ruckus.

Capri lights a cigarette and rolls the window down. Her phone buzzes in her pocket and she looks the screen. Jamey.

Hey, babe. Got your text. What's up?

FROM VAN NUYS, Harry and Guy take the 170 to the 134 East through Pasadena. Guy is at the helm, careening past the San Gabriel Mountains on the Foothill Freeway. Traffic slows at the big red Miller Beer sign at the Irwindale exit but breaks up soon after.

"I'm a little hungry."

"We'll stop later," Harry says. "We need to keep the wind in our sails."

"What's in the bag Ruby packed?"

Harry rummages through it. "Couple sandwiches, some crackers."

"Is that a brownie?"

Harry holds up the brownie from the dispensary. "Pot brownie."

He unwraps the cellophane and pops a corner of the brownie in his mouth.

"Can I get some?"

"You're drivin'."

"Just a little. I need something sweet."

Harry breaks off a section and hands it to him.

Guy chews with his mouth open. "Are you a Burt Reynolds fan?"

"I like Burt alright," Harry says. "He's not my favorite."

A few seconds of silence.

"Any particular reason for the question?" Harry says.

"About Burt?"

"About Burt."

"The brownie," Guy says. "Loni Anderson tells a story in her autobiography about Burt eating a whole tray of pot brownies."

"You read that in law school?"

"I had a crush on her from when she was on *WKRP*."

"I never cared for the blonde bombshell type."

"I love her," Guy says. "She's still pretty."

"You ask me, Burt didn't have great taste in women. Dinah Shore, Sally Field, Loni. No thanks."

"In the book, she talks about how she came home one time and Burt was curled up naked in the bed with fudge all over his mustache. From the pot brownies."

Harry doesn't have much to say about that.

"It's interesting, though. You read that and then you read Burt's book and you get the other side of the coin. No matter which way you slice it, that was a troubled marriage."

Harry doesn't have much to say about that either. The traffic comes to a dead stop approaching Alta Loma.

"Watch the road, Guy. And quit ridin' the brakes."

An hour later the Olds is still inching through traffic, on the 15 now. Guy irritated Harry a few exits back by cutting a run of car-clouders and referring to San Bernardino, twice, as San Berdoo. They've been driving in silence since. Now the brownie is kicking in a bit and Harry is looking for some levity.

"You got any jokes?"

Guy thinks a second. "I'm not too good with remembering jokes."

More miles drag by. Traffic lightens and tightens. The brownie buzz is more conducive to desert cruising than this rush hour stop-and-start. It's making everything slower and Harry laments it.

"I got one," Guy says.

"What?"

"A joke. I got one."

"Let's hear it."

Guy shifts in his seat.

"Keep your eyes on the road there in front of you, Guy."

Guy faces forward. "How is a plum like a rabbit?"

A plum and a rabbit. Harry puts a boot on the dash. "I don't know. How?"

"You're not going to guess?"

"No."

"They're both purple except for the rabbit."

Guy repeats the punchline and Harry feels doubly cheated.

"You asked me to tell you a joke," Guy says.

Harry already regrets taking him along. He knew he would. Knew it before they even got in the car.

Over the next few miles, Guy remarks on the light, how it seems to be shifting dramatically in the sky. He also mentions the gas pedal feels loose under his foot.

"I'm having trouble driving, Harry. Everything feels slippery. I think it's that brownie."

Harry feels similarly disoriented but he thought it was just him. He holds his hand in front of his face. "I'm feeling a little atypical myself."

They stop at the New Corral Motel in Victorville. There's a sign with a rearing horse and neon promises of an *air-cooled* room with cable TV and a fridge. Forty-nine dollars and ninety-nine cents.

In the parking lot, Harry and Guy stretch their legs and try to appear lucid.

"What's your motel alias?" Harry says.

"I don't have one."

"Every man needs a motel alias. What's your bowling handle?"

He thinks a second. "Yug."

"Yug?"

"It's Guy backwards."

"That's amateur. What's your favorite movie?"

They check in as John T. Chance and Buford T. Justice. Guy skims a rack of brochures while Harry signs the paperwork and gets a glimpse of the dim, carpeted living room adjacent to the lobby. An empty recliner bathes in the glow of what must be a 70-inch flatscreen TV. It looks like a nice place to get back to and the old woman looks eager to get back to it. The only question Harry has is whether the ice machine works.

The room looks like forty-nine dollars and ninety-nine cents. Not a penny more. Two full-size beds with lurid spreads stare down an outdated TV, nowhere near as nice as the one the lady at the desk has. The remote is bolted to the nightstand.

"We missed *Gunsmoke*."

"I'm sorry, Harry."

"Probably a re-run anyway."

Harry's idea of a joke. Guy doesn't get it.

The minifridge needs to be plugged in and the air cooler is off. Harry sets it to high and walks a few blocks to Quick Pick Liquors.

25

SOMEWHERE ON HIGHWAY 15, Capri points at a roadside sign that says *EAT*, like a 1950s postcard, and Ted edges through two lanes of traffic to the exit.

They arrive at a shuttered stand in the shape of a Dairy Queen. Sun faded menus are taped to the windows. Burgers and fries and soft-serve cones. The parking lot looks quaked.

There's nothing else in sight so they go to an ampm and pick up Icehouse tallboys, Andy Capp Hot Fries, and a shrink-wrapped sub to split. Ted isn't hungry. He keeps flashing back on Elmer. His big soft eyes looking up at him like a scared animal. Silently pleading with him to do something. He feels sick to his stomach but he needs to try to get something down. He tried to puke in the bathroom just now and nothing came up but bile.

The old man ahead of them in line is taking too long with his scratch tickets, ensuring every scratch-away surface is scratched away and making the clerk check and double-check that the losers are losers. His stack finally nets him a twenty-six-dollar jackpot which he parlays into six or seven more low-roller tickets and a soft pack of Maverick menthols.

He staggers away and the fat kid behind the counter, miserable in a maroon shirt that manages to be too big for him, makes a show of spraying Febreze in the poor guy's wake before he's even out the door.

Walking to the car, they pass the old man hunched on a bus bench, scratching a ticket with a dirty thumbnail, his long cigarette ash about to avalanche. Capri tells Ted she wants to squat down and piss on the guy's shoes.

"Why?"

"He's wasted space. Look at him."

Ted doesn't get why she would want to make the guy's life even worse. Between this dude and Elmer, he's really starting to think she's got an anger problem.

They drive the empty road beside the clogged freeway and look for a clearing where they can pull off. Ted spots an old water park he remembers from Vegas trips when he was a kid. Fuzzy always promised they'd stop on the way back but then he'd get late check-out at the Flamingo and Ted would be asleep, his face pressed against the cold window glass as they crossed back across the desert at night.

The water park looks like it's been closed for years. Drifting sands have taken over the parking lot. THE WORLD IS SHIT is tagged in pink spray paint underneath the hollowed-out lettering of the sign.

They smoke a bowl and eat. Then they crack beers and scope the grounds. A monument to the slog of time and the destructive impulses of bored, fucked-up teenagers.

Capri says she needs to make a phone call.

Ted wanders the bone-dry bed of the lazy river, passing under the small bridges that cross it, some still threaded with nautical netting, snaking his way toward the grand downward incline of what must have been the wave pool.

Imagining the place flooded with bright blue water makes everything seem doubly dry. The fallen fronds of parched palms look flammable in the sun glare.

Skateboarders have utilized some of the wreckage. Ted remembers when he was a skater and every curb, embankment, and handrail was something to conquer. It's been years since he's looked at the world through that filter. Now part of him wishes he had a board in the trunk.

He climbs the concrete stairs where the waterslides used to be. The pillars remain bolted in place, now holding up nothing but sky. He takes a big swig off the can and steps over a fiberglass segment of slide emblazoned with the word *MUFFDIVER*. The hill feels man-made and unnatural in the flat landscape.

He sits on a top step and takes another deep hit on the bowl. Flared by the sunset, it isn't hard to remember the place the way he always used to imagine it in his mind. Down the hill he sees the severed base of the splash pad fountain and pictures kids running in the spray of the oscillating sprinkler.

Maybe the park will be rehabbed. Everything leveled and rejuvenated. Traffic returned to the unpopular freeway exit. Or maybe the desert will swallow it whole.

Weed usually kills his anxiety and helps him bob along the surface of things, above all the bullshit, but sometimes when he's alone it makes him tunnel into the darkest parts of himself, the parts haunted by thoughts of his parents' divorce, of people he loves getting sick and dying.

He gets especially sad thinking about Fuzzy, waiting out his days in that dark bar, looking older every time he sees him. He feels guilty about stealing from him. And now putting him through this.

He looks down the hill. Capri has been in the car for almost twenty minutes now. She's talking to Jamey. He knows it. Ted has never even seen a picture of him, but Jamey has been lurking in the shadows the whole time he's known Capri. Whenever she tells a story, it seems like he's in it somewhere, even if she doesn't mention him. And even when she says bad shit about him, it still sounds like there's deep feeling there. Something he'll never be able to compete with.

He's about to walk down to check on her when he sees her crossing the grounds with a can of beer in each hand. She climbs the stairs two at a time. Elmer's cowboy hat is on her head. His gun is in the waistband of her shorts.

"Who were you talking to for so long?"

"Jamey."

The name sticks him like a knife in the ribs even though he knew it was coming. He tries not to let it show.

"I thought he was in jail."

"Prison. He's out now. He's trying to help us, Ted. He says he knows people in Barstow who might be down for buying in bulk."

Ted doesn't know what to say so he doesn't say anything. He stands up and starts kicking at something in the sand.

"You're going to fuck up your sneakers."

"I don't give a shit."

"You think if there was anything going on I would have told you who it was? I'm trying to move this shit. It's not like we have a ton of options."

She wanders down the hill and he follows. She sets Elmer's hat on a short cactus, making a prickly cowboy statue, and he watches her walk slowly back to him, pulling Elmer's gun out of her waistband. She hands him the gun and guides him back twenty paces.

"Target practice," she says.

Practice means something real is coming and that scares him. He hefts it in his hand and looks around. All jacked up and nervous. The rush of trouble. The way it always is with her.

"Let's see what you've got, fucker."

Ted takes aim. The gun is heavy and he winces and jerks at every kickback.

Capri drinks her beer and watches him miss.

He lowers the gun to his side and stares into the endless expanse. Wondering how far bullets can go before they lose momentum and fall.

"Lousy shot," he says.

Capri sets her beer down and takes the gun. The cactus is chunked when she's done but Elmer's Stetson is unharmed. Ted removes some sharp spines from the brim and puts it back on her head.

They make their way down to the car, cutting through the old snack bar and changing rooms. Every structure is stripped to the studs, the drop ceilings dropped out. Everything is covered in graffiti. Cocks, boobs, swastikas, and the names of young couples in love.

Capri says she wants to break something, but everything is already broken.

26

THE MOTEL POOL reflects the motel sign.

Harry and Guy sit in sagging chairs, drinking tequila on ice and Tecate cans with salt on the rim, the Espolon bottle in the ice bucket between them like a magnum of champagne. They have the whole scenario to themselves. The only other vehicle in the lot is an eighteen-wheeler with Iowa plates but there's no sign of the driver.

Harry rests his hat on his knee and considers Guy in the deck chair.

"Not too different from how you started your day, Counselor."

"Once that nighttime breeze hits me, I'm done for."

Harry watches the daylight fade on the surface of the pool.

"I feel bad," Guy says. "We're not even that far out of L.A."

"It's alright." Harry slides a half-smoked pinner out of his cigarette pack and gets it lit. "Long day. We'll bunk down early and listen to the wisdom of the pillow. Better to roll up on this Elmer in the a.m. anyway."

He passes the joint to Guy and they take in the bloodshot sunset.

"What happens if we don't get 'em?"

"We'll get 'em," Harry says.

"How do you know?"

"Because it's what I do, man."

"I thought this was a bounty hunter's job," Guy says.

"It falls within my purview as well."

"How do you do it?"

Harry takes a sip of tequila and cites the Gospel of Waylon. Chapter and verse.

"You wanna get the rabbit out the *l-o-g*, you gotta make a commotion like a *d-o-g*."

"A dog?"

"A *d-o-g*."

Guy considers that, taking another hit and handing the joint back.

"We're kind of like a couple basset hounds on the hunt, you and me."

"Basset hounds?" Harry says.

"The basset hound's nose is second to the bloodhound."

"Then why aren't we a couple of bloodhounds? We're second best?"

"Basset hounds are better trackers. They're lower. Their ears waft the scent up to the nose and the folds under the neck keep the scent in." Guy sips his tequila and chases it with a swig of beer. "Thanks for asking me to come along, Harry. I know you didn't want me to."

"I didn't mean anything personal by it." Harry passes the joint back to Guy. "Just easier to go it alone sometimes."

"I've been going it alone too much lately. The apartment feels so empty with Amanda gone. I don't even like being there, but I don't really have anywhere else to go. I'm trying not to hit the bars as much."

Harry's been dreading this. Guy having a couple drinks, a couple of tokes, and starting in with the what-becomes-of-the-broken-hearted routine.

Guy takes a deep hit and holds it in a while before exhaling.

"I was thinking the other day," Guy says. "All the things we used to say to each other, Amanda and me. Our nicknames and private jokes. It's like a lost language now. Never to be spoken again. You know what I mean?"

Harry knows what he means, and he can tell Guy's really hurting. He's no stranger to that state of loneliness himself, but he still doesn't know how to respond to it, at least not in any way he's comfortable with at the moment. "At least you weren't married," he says.

"I wish I'd asked her back when she still would've said yes," Guy says. "Maybe it would have been harder for her to leave."

Harry shakes his head.

"Would've just made this harder for you to accept. The only happily married man I know is my buddy Slick. His wife brings home the bacon. Then she cooks it for him. He hasn't worked in eleven years. Drinks a case of Coors every day and that's about all he does."

"How does he get away with that arrangement?"

"She's a pretty good-sized gal," Harry says.

Guy pats his stomach.

"I need to lose some weight myself. That was another thing Amanda was always on me about. She said it was because of my health, but I think it made her less attracted to me too. I might try the Keto diet again."

"Which one's that? No starch?"

"Yeah, pretty much all protein. You lose weight quick."

"Then you eat one fuckin' cracker and you're right back where you started," Harry says.

"That's what happens to me every time."

Guy rims a new beer can with salt and cracks it open.

"You know what I can't get enough of lately? Chili."

"I made Ruby my Frito Chili Pie last weekend," Harry says. "Texas thing. Fritos on the bottom, chili and cheese on top. Chop up some onions in there." Harry stubs out the roach and lights a Tareyton. "As for the chili itself, it was my auntie Susanna's recipe. Earned her second prize in one of the first Terlingua Chili Cook-Offs."

"We should make some."

"We ain't got the ingredients handy here at the moment, Guy."

Guy drinks his beer. "You put beer in your chili?"

Harry nods and takes a sip of his tequila. "Tequila too."

"So, we got a couple ingredients."

Harry grins. "Still a few shy."

They drink their drinks and follow the last red line of the sunset.

"Cowboys make chili," Guy says.

"Cowboys?"

He points at Harry. "You think you're a cowboy."

"You think I think I'm a cowboy?"

"You wear a cowboy hat. Cowboy shirt. Cowboy boots."

"It's western wear, Guy. And look around. That's where we are. The west."

"Let's go get some chili then."

Harry dumps the watery dregs from his cup and scoops some fresh ice. Then more tequila, more lime.

"After this drink."

27

RICK SITS AT the Grotto solo. Looks down the bar at a guy wearing a hardhat. Looks up to see if there's something that could fall on his head.

He scans the room and remembers the days of cannon-breasted barmaids and round-heeled good-time gals lined up for karaoke nights and beer-and-a-shot happy hours.

Fuzzy finally comes by and gives him an audience.

"There's the guard," Rick says. "There's the sad old padre."

Rick scrolls through his Tinder. "Listen to this. I match with this girl and all day long she's sending me pictures of her dog. So I say, 'I know what the dog looks like. How about sending me a picture of you?' She asks me if I mean naked and I say, 'Sure. Why don't you show me a nipple or two?'"

"They just do that?"

"Some do. She didn't. I got a raft of shit for it."

"Getting the horns and you didn't even get to mess with the bull."

Fuzzy rolls a keg of Michelob off a wobbly hand truck and finagles it into the old tap system. Rick can see the syrupy puddle at the bottom of the wheezing cooler. Fruit flies. Beer flies. The bar is slow for a Friday and Rick listens to Fuzzy grumble about it. The only time he grumbles more is when it's busy.

"Almost bought a new sport coat today, Fuzzard. Camelhair."

"That a fact?"

"Beautiful jacket. If it wasn't for the hump."

Fuzzy looks at him.

"Had a big hump on the back."

"That a new routine?"

"What do you think?"

"Save it for Harry."

"Right. Gadabout Gaddis. Any word from him?"

"He called a little while ago to check in."

"And?"

"He wanted to know if there was a reputable chili parlor in the Victorville area." Fuzzy raises his eyebrows. "I think the old boy may be losing his fastball."

"He had a fastball?"

"He could get it over the plate."

"Why didn't you call me on this?"

"He knows Teddy better than you do. Went with my gut, I guess."

"I don't trust my gut. It's too close to my cock."

"That's Teddy's problem too. He's been after it since he was a boy." Fuzzy makes a jerk-off motion. "Always frisking the inmate."

"Learned behavior," Rick says.

"I'm not denying my culpability. While he was growing up, I was carousing around, chasing after every piece of tail that came in here." Fuzzy scopes the drunks at the bar like they're tin cans lined up on a fence. "I tanked the marriage and wasn't a good father. But he's not getting along with his mother too good these days, so when he came to me, I saw an opportunity to maybe make up for lost time."

Rick shrugs. He believes in the bartender as silent confessor. He doesn't need Fuzzy stirring his own sadness into the cocktail. Half the time, when Rick is bitching and moaning, he knows Fuzzy's just waiting to chime in with a woe of his own.

"You don't have a kid, you wouldn't understand," Fuzzy says. "Anyway, I didn't realize this was going to be such a production. And I thought Harry might put some of his commission toward his tab."

"Between you and me, I need all the commission I can get. Ex-wife is beating the cork out of me."

"Which one?"

"Number two. It's like she hired a goddamn forensic accountant. Squeezing me for every last gilder."

In the past decade, Rick has gotten divorced, married, and divorced again. He also purchased and surrendered the house in Glendale he shared with his second wife. His relationship with Sun Surety, his business underwriter, is on thin ice after a couple of bonds went south. They've lowered his bond approval from $500,000 to $200,000 and set him up on a punitive monthly payment plan.

He canned a couple agents and the girl he had answering phones and invested in the limo to keep up appearances and promote the brand. And he's been pushing more and more five-percent-down deals to keep cashflow moving

He's had it with the alimony, the hounding of the underwriter, the credit card rotisserie system, the constant catch-up. It feels like he's tap-dancing on a rubber raft.

"Time to time, I think about staging my own death," Rick says. "They say faking a drowning is the best way."

"I read about a guy who pushed a boat out into Lake Champlain with a few personal effects, a rod and reel," Fuzzy says. "They found him down in Florida dressed in a gorilla suit. Delivering balloons to birthday parties, hospitals. It's hard to disappear today."

Fuzzy leans against the back bar and props his right foot up on the beer cooler. He massages his calf and adjusts the Velcro on his sneaker.

"Those the new orthopedics?" Rick says.

"Not cheap. Seventy-five bucks a pair."

"Seventy-five bucks wouldn't even buy you one of these babies, let alone a pair," Rick says, looking down at his Italian loafers, shiny against the dirty brass rail.

"You know it could turn out Harry ends up owning this place?" Fuzzy says. "The Buck and Doe he says he'll call it. You believe that?"

"You put the bar down against the bond?"

"I had to."

Rick whistles.

"You fell for that one, Fuzzard. Hook, line, and banana peel."

"Fell for what?"

"Look at the set-up. Teddy stays gone, this place is Harry's. He brings him back, he's the honkytonk hero. Either way, Harry Robatore never pays for another drink in here again. If he had half a brain in his head, I'd say he designed it that way. The prick."

Fuzzy leans back, putting his left foot up this time.

"You know what, option one is fine by me. Wash my hands of all of it. Pack my Samsonite and hit the wind."

"You could try your luck in the gorilla suit," Rick says.

28

AFTER A LATE start, one sidetrack, and two wrong turns, Harry navigates the Olds up a long narrow driveway off Ocotillo Road.

He's never been this deep into Johnson Valley. It could be a hundred years in the past or a hundred years in the future. Most of the residences look like someone's last stand. Elmer's doublewide looks almost stately in comparison.

In front of the trailer, an old man in a bathrobe is leaning on a hospital crutch, using his right foot to nudge an enormous egg up the front walk. It doesn't seem like any way for a man in his condition to be fetching breakfast. He turns when he hears the car pull up. One eye is concealed by a patch. The dome of his bald head shines bright in a beam of sun.

Harry and Guy step out of the car.

"Elmer?" Harry says.

"I don't want no more trouble."

"No trouble," Harry says, handing him a business card. "We're tryin' to track down a couple that may have come through. Dark-haired kid with a skinny girl in tow."

Elmer nods cautiously. "More like the other way around."

Harry takes in the menagerie of animals on the property. Goats, pigs, a jackass. Three towering ostriches strut in a dusty circle, penned in by chicken wire. Must be where the egg came from.

Elmer examines Harry's business card. "Bail bonds. How'd you get mixed up in this? Hired you to go the bail and then they run off on you?"

"That cracks it."

Elmer rubs the card between his fingers and weighs it in his palm.

"Where'd you get this done?"

"Catalog," Harry says. "I sent away."

"I'm looking to get new cards made myself, but it's the least of my worries at present." Elmer puts the card in the pocket of his robe and produces his own. "Here's mine. As I said, I've been meaning to—"

"Already got one," Harry says. "Max gave it to me."

"Right. Max sent you. Well, I've got a business I'm trying to get off the ground here but those kids you're looking for cleaned me out. Inventory, pistol, petty cash. Even my John B. Stetson hat."

Elmer removes his pipe from his pocket and points it at Harry's hat.

"You must understand the seriousness of that."

Harry tips his brim. "Open Road."

"I know what it is. LBJ wore that hat. What'd it run you, couple hunnerd?"

"Thereabouts."

Elmer fixes his eye on Guy.

"Who are you now?"

"Guy Donleavy. Attorney."

"You got a card?"

"Not on me."

"I apologize if I'm a little wary," Elmer says. "I'm on edge after those kids rolled me. Can't believe she pounced on me like that. If my shotgun was at the ready, I can assure you things would've gone another way."

Elmer adjusts his crutch with a wince.

"I normally never do business with strangers, but they came with Max's recommendation. And I admit I was lured by their product."

"The Acapulco Gold?" Harry says.

Elmer nods. "I've been developing a butterscotch lozenge and thought it'd be a good hook if they were made with genuine Acapulco Gold, at least partly. I could just use the name and no one would be the wiser, but I believe in truth in advertising."

Elmer points his pipe at Harry's belt. "What's that thing you're wearing there?"

"It's called a Lighter Leash. I'm always losin' my lighters."

"What'd it run you?"

"I don't know. My gal bought it for me."

"QVC?"

"She got it at the store."

"Must be a patent on it." Elmer leans in to get a better look. "You ever watch *Shark Tank*? One thing they harp on is cost of production versus price of product. Seems like a winner right there. I'm not the target market, though. I don't have much need to carry a lighter on my person."

"Pipe just for show?"

"I smoke Sail pipe tobacco." Elmer removes a yellow pouch from his robe pocket. "But I'm of the opinion that quality tobacco should only be lit with a wooden match."

Harry watches him fish around in that bathrobe pocket again, wondering what the hell else he has in there. Elmer's hand emerges with a box of matches. "Paper match ain't good for much of anything," he says. "There's a reason they give 'em away free."

Harry reaches for his cigarettes.

"Tareytons?" Elmer says. "*Rather fight than switch.* That was a hell of a campaign."

Harry takes one of Elmer's wooden matches and drags it across the strike strip.

"Hold it a second so you're getting the flame, not the sulfur."

It does have a nice feel. Shaking the flame out, the black smudge on the wood.

"Those cigarettes aren't doing you any good but I'm not one to preach at you," Elmer says. "I used to smoke 'em by the dozen when I was driving truck."

"You know what I like are them strike-anywhere matches," Harry says. "Light one up off the heel of your boot."

"You're like me. Seen too many cowboy movies."

Elmer reminds Harry of someone out of a cowboy movie. The Walter Brennan character. The excitable oddball who walks with a limp. That puts Guy in the Andy Devine role. Most people would deputize themselves the John Wayne of this scenario, but Harry sees himself more in the mold of Randolph Scott. Long and lean, cool under pressure.

"Can we ask you a couple of questions about what happened?" Harry says. "We're tryin' to get an idea of what their next move might be."

"I've been doing some figuring myself. You two coming by may turn out to be fortuitous." Elmer taps his leg with the cane. "Seeing as this old vessel ain't exactly seaworthy."

"Looks like they did some damage," Guy says.

"They made a gimp of me. And I don't think I need to tell you I don't normally walk around with this patch."

Elmer indicates his left eye.

"What happened there?" Guy says.

"Burst vessel. Thing like that'll blind the occasional man. Good thing I ain't no occasional man." Elmer kicks a rock across the lot. "Tell you what, you hoist that egg up the stairs and I'll cook us some breakfast."

Harry looks at Guy and nods in the direction of the giant egg. Guy picks it up like a fragile vase and they follow Elmer inside.

"I'm from Junction City, Arkansas." Elmer is seated at the head of the table. "But when I was driving long-haul this was my favorite part of the trip. Out here with nothing around. Time came to retire I thought I'd sit in on the porch with my shotgun on my lap, pinging lizards. But I've got a restless, searching mind by nature. Sometimes being around nothing makes you think of something."

"Open country," Harry says.

"My dog likes it. He can roam about freely."

"You have a dog?" Guy says, looking around. "Where is he?"

"He's roaming about freely. He'll be back around sundown."

"What's his name?"

"Fred. He's a very serious dog. Like a surgeon with the squeaker toys. Isolates and extracts the noisemaking device in a matter of minutes. Seconds sometimes. I used to have a macaw too. Smarter than a chimpanzee."

"Smartest bird in the world," Guy says to Harry.

Elmer shakes his head.

"Crow is the smartest. They can count to five."

Harry struggles with the heaping portion of eggs. No matter how much he chokes down, the pile never seems to diminish. Elmer points his fork at him. "How about you, Tex? San Antone, right? Thereabouts?"

That takes Harry by surprise.

"Del Rio," he says. "How'd you know that?"

"The way you said *sit* before, like it was *set*. Texas English is interesting. West Texas, in particular. Driving around the country I developed an ear for that kind of thing. Always wished there was a way to make a buck off it. Gets me the occasional cup of Arbuckle's on the house." Elmer raises his coffee mug. "Or a bottle of beer back when I hit the paint regularly."

"Do me," Guy says.

"Doesn't work on everybody." Elmer stands up to fetch seconds. "What's the matter? You guys got something against eggs?"

Guy points at the ostrich eggshell, cracked in half on Elmer's stovetop.

"How many regular eggs fit in that big egg?"

"What do you mean by regular eggs?"

"Chicken eggs."

"Roughly twenty-five chicken eggs to an ostrich egg. Give or take."

Harry adds a drop of Cholula and stabs another forkful.

"Everything's great, Elmer."

"Got any ketchup?" Guy says.

Elmer returns to the table like a sommelier, holding a bottle of Heinz for Guy's inspection. "Read that."

"*Insist on Heinz*," Guy says.

"That's good marketing. You see French's is doing ketchup now? Big push behind it, but they have no place in the ketchup business. Of course, Heinz dabbles in mustard too. Tit for tat."

"I'm a Gulden's guy," Harry says.

"That's a horse of another color."

Harry studies the logos on Elmer's sketch pad. Elmer with the pipe and cowboy hat. It looks just like him. The eyepatch must be recently applied.

"Those are prototypes, of course. But in business it's important to brand oneself."

"You have a slogan?" Guy says.

"I'm toying with a couple. I'd like something along the lines of, *It takes a tough man to make a tender chicken*. That's Frank Purdue."

"It takes a man who looks like a chicken to make good chicken," Harry says.

"He did look like a chicken." Elmer nods in agreement. "Poultry was in that man's blood."

Elmer polishes off his second helping of eggs.

"Speaking of, who's plucking this chicken, you or him?"

Harry doesn't follow.

Elmer rephrases the question. "Who's the hammer?"

"The hammer?" Harry says.

"On this mission you two are on. Who's in charge? Who's the hammer?"

"Harry," Guy says. "Harry's the hammer."

"Good." Elmer zeroes in on Harry. "So how are you going to go about it? From what I understand, skip tracing is done mostly by computer now, like everything else."

Harry puts his fork down, relieved to take a break from the eggs.

"It's one thing if they're in hiding. Can usually nail down phone records, credit card bills. It's harder if they're on the move." Harry wipes his mouth with a napkin. "But I've got a couple irons in the fire. There's a guy back at the office workin' the digital angle."

He makes a mental note to check in with Manny, for whatever that's worth.

"Not long before they won't need guys like you flat-footing around," Elmer says. "It's happening with trucking right now. I got out at the right time. There will be a primarily automated workforce on the road within my lifetime. But as I said before, you two following the breadcrumb trail to my door may be fortuitous. For me and for you."

"Meanin'?"

Elmer flips past the logos to the next page of his sketch pad. It features an old-fashioned Wanted poster with detailed illustrations of Ted and Capri.

"Meaning I emailed this out to my network first thing this morning. If these two are trying to unload product within a hundred miles of here, there's a good chance I know who they're going to try to unload it on."

Harry and Guy look at the poster.

"How are the likenesses? I drew 'em from memory. People have told me I could have been a police sketch artist."

"Almost as good as a photo," Guy says.

"Must be. I already got a nibble from the Dank of America dispensary over in San Berdoo. They came sniffing around there yesterday looking to sell some stuff. Must've been on the way out to me."

Harry grabs a pencil and jots the name on a scrap of paper. "They buy anything?"

"No, they don't operate that way."

Harry thinks a second.

"You got a map?"

"I got a globe."

A globe. Christ. Harry thought he'd met everybody. This guy is something else entirely.

Harry goes outside and gets his road map from the glove box. He comes back in and spreads the expanse of Southern California out on Elmer's kitchen table.

"Where'd you send the poster? What places?"

Elmer grabs a Sharpie and marks an X over the San Bernardino area. "The one from yesterday is right here."

Elmer hovers over the map with the marker in his hand, marking Xs where other dispensaries in the surrounding areas are located. Harry tries to map a pattern but there are Xs in all directions. Ontario. Riverside. Palmdale. Temecula. Barstow. Desert Hot Springs. Elmer has quite the network.

"I don't think they'll go back toward L.A. Head toward Barstow and that leads to Baker and then onto Vegas." Harry points to a cluster of Xs south of Elmer's compound. "Or they swoop down toward Palm Springs and Joshua Tree."

"There are a quite a few outlets down that way where I move a fair amount of product," Elmer says. "It was me, I might head in that direction."

"We'll head that way then," Harry says. "And you put the feelers out."

"So the idea is they come in peddling their wares and I have my people stall the sale until you get there."

"That about does it," Harry says.

Elmer starts stacking plates. "You sure you want to hit the trail?" he says. "Could bunk down here until we get the go sign."

Harry stands up. "I think we need to keep movin'."

"All I ask is I can trust you return whatever you're able to retrieve of my money and inventory. And my Stetson. My wife gave me that hat."

"You got it, Elmer," Guy says.

Elmer deposits the plates in the sink. "Before you go, either of you know how to fix a leaky faucet? I've been tinkering with this damn thing to no avail. I'm afraid I may have to say uncle and call the plumber but—"

Harry signals Guy to get up.

"We've got to light a shuck here, Elmy," Harry says. "The sooner we get on the road, the sooner we get your goods back."

"Good enough," Elmer says. "Time to put the chairs in the wagon. Take a couple boxes of matches at least."

Harry puts the matches in his pocket and thanks him.

Elmer walks them to the door. A shotgun leans against the window that looks out on the compound lot. Elmer posts himself beside it and they say their goodbyes.

29

A T YUM YUM Donuts, Carvell King scans the display case and looks down the row of stools at the counter. Only one is occupied. A guy with white hair and a gold golf shirt. The guy with his face on the limo outside. The guy he's looking for.

He orders two bearclaws and a Sierra Mist from the fountain and posts himself two stools down.

"You're Rick, right? Bail bonds? I see the benches and the limo and shit. Pretty slick."

Rick looks up from his coffee. "Thanks."

Carvell takes a bite of his bearclaw and wipes his chin.

"You know a bail bonds guy named Harry Robatore?"

"Harry's a friend of mine."

"You know where he's at?"

"Who's asking?"

"Carvell King." He gives him a power-move shake. "I work security over at Big Smoke, that dispensary that got robbed. I do some independent contracting as well. VIP bodyguard, bounty hunter, black ops. Whatever you need. Anyway, I heard Harry's out looking for Capri and her boyfriend. The guy that pulled the robbery."

"And?"

"I got the same assignment. Good chunk of change depending on how much they're still carrying. Which could be a lot. You tell me where Harry's headed and I get there first, I give you a taste."

"I take it the inventory wasn't covered by Allstate."

"Something to that effect."

"I wouldn't worry too much about Harry getting in your way."

"I'm not worried about anybody getting in my way." Carvell digs deeper into the bearclaw. "Look at it like you're helping yourself and your friend. I don't think he can handle what happens if he catches up to them. Her, more specifically."

This is partly true. Eddie told him what he'd heard about the incident at the strip club. Originally, they thought that was an asset. Not only was she hot, she was a badass who could handle herself if there was trouble at the shop. They weren't expecting her to pull this.

"How much are we talking here?" Rick says.

"Say around five Gs. They took a lot of shit."

"Five each, or we split it?"

"Each."

Carvell is planning to pull in a whole lot more but this asshole doesn't need to know that. The cops don't even know how much was taken. Stan Lemke, the owner, didn't report anything stolen. He wanted to handle it internally. Eddie took most of the blame for what happened—he was the one who hired Capri in the first place—but he was only the manager.

There's always someone above an Eddie. Eddie answers to Lemke.

Big Smoke isn't the first illegal dispensary Lemke bankrolled that's been shut down. He came in at the end of the wild west days, right when everything was getting legitimized. Bad timing. But he's starting to retool. He has a couple others in operation and he and Carvell worked out a percentage deal on however much inventory he's able to recover. Real money, he says. Could be as much as fifty grand, depending on whether they slow-sell it or move it in bulk. Plus a partnership stake in a legal place he's looking to open in Panorama City.

Long run, Carvell can see himself running the entire enterprise. But he's been benched since the fuck-up in Tonopah. He pulls this off, gets the shit back, it will go a long way toward getting out of the guard post and into some real action again.

It looks like this guy's interested. Why wouldn't he be? Five grand for making a couple calls, pointing a man in the right direction. If he balks, Carvell has other ways of getting the information out of him, but he's trying to keep to the script. He can't afford another Tonopah.

"Take my card," Rick says, standing up to go. "Check with me in an hour or so."

Carvell slurps his soda and examines Rick's business card. Gold on black with a glamour shot of Rick holding the keys to a giant pair of handcuffs. Pretty classy.

He takes the first bite of his second bearclaw.

30

"**I** BELIEVE **ELMER'S** connections have put us in the catbird seat," Harry says.

"A little game of cat and mouse."

"Man and mouse, Counselor. Cat chases the mouse. Man sets a trap, lets the mouse come to him."

"You said catbird."

"I mean it in the sense that we've got the upper hand here." Harry sparks a fresh pinner. "Once we locate Teddy and the girl—"

"The weed is the cheese?"

"They have the weed, Guy. Goddamn it. We're the men, they're the mice."

"So the money's the cheese."

"The idea of the money. They show up thinkin' they're going to make a big sale. That's when we swoop in."

Harry thinks maybe they get this whole business over by Sunday and head home. Go dancing with Ruby at the Cowboy Palace on Sunday night and take Monday and Tuesday to decompress.

"Peanut butter works better than cheese," Guy says. "When you're dealing with real mice."

"I got a cat. No mouse in my house."

"If I were a mouse, I'd be more tempted by peanut butter than a hunk of cheese."

Harry passes him the jib.

"What if you were a man?"

The Olds floats south toward Joshua Tree.

Old Woman Springs Road is riddled with roadside crosses. The crosses make Harry nervous, like the places they mark are portals, rips in the fabric that souls have been sucked through.

He remembers years ago, driving west from Texas, a diner waitress in Las Cruces asked him where he was headed and when he said California, she told him to honk his horn at mile-marker 94 for her son who died in a wreck there. Harry promised he would but by the time he got there he forgot.

Marty Robbins balladeers on the tape deck and the road unscrolls in front of them. Bright black with fresh yellow lines. It has dips you can feel in your stomach but stays on a straight course for miles and miles. Harry is stunned by the panorama, the big empty, and wonders if there's such a thing as a sand globe.

"I keep thinkin' Robert Blake is going to pull us over on a motorcycle."

"For going too slow?" Guy says.

Car after car has been passing them, pulling around wide and speeding up. Sometimes when Harry's stoned, he doesn't realize how fast he isn't going.

There's a sign for something called the 247 Cafe. He thinks maybe some coffee will help but when they get there, the 247 Cafe is closed.

Like they're existing outside of the realms of time.

A sunburned young man walks in a slow circle out front, picking notes on a junk guitar. He approaches Harry and Guy.

"It's two-forty-seven, not twenty-four-seven," he says.

Harry gets the feeling the man has imparted this information many times before, that he feels duty-bound to clarify this confusion for people. He turns a tuning knob, plucks a string. He looks at Harry like he wants a dollar for his trouble.

"It's my first day playing the guitar."

"Keep at it. Anywhere to get coffee around here?"

The man points to a gas station down the road and Harry gives him the dollar he's looking for.

There's no fresh coffee at the Valero station. Harry fans himself with his hat and watches Guy squeegee the stubborn smudges of dead bugs off the windshield.

"Hotter'n a depot stove out here."

"Tires are soft," Guy says.

"This blacktop ain't doing 'em no favors."

Harry gives Guy quarters for the air pump. His phone buzzes in his pocket. Rick. He picks up.

"Hey, Mohair Sam. How's the old road dog?" Rick says. "Goin' down the road feelin' bad?"

"Truckin'," Harry says. "Like the doo-dah man."

"Just checking in, good buddy. Where you guys at?"

Harry sets his hat on the roof of the car and watches Guy put air in a front tire.

"At this very moment, Guy and I—" Harry looks at the desolate landscape. "We just rolled into Reno. Turns out the kids came up here to get married."

"Reno? You shittin' me?"

"I wouldn't shit you, Rick—"

"Yeah, yeah. I'm your favorite turd. You serious about Reno?"

"I got it on good authority," Harry says. "We're going to play some craps, have a few drinks and check the wedding chapels. They'll turn up. I mean, it's the biggest little city in the world but it's still a little city, am I right?"

"When you're right, you're right."

"Shit, Rick. I've got to go. Guy wandered into a place with a neon cowgirl on the sign. Big light-up jugs on her. Looks like a cathouse."

"Why don't you head on over there and get your bell rung, Har," Rick says. "Best of luck to you both."

Harry hangs up. Guy wipes the dust off his knees and fumbles with the air hose putting it back.

"Who was that?"

"You ain't quite ready to make detective, are you?"

"I know who it was. Just didn't want you to think I was listening."

"You should always be listenin', Guy. Keep the antennae up."

"Why'd you tell him we were in Reno?"

"Rick's always tryin' to dog my tracks. And he's a big mouth. Lesson for today is this: Don't let the camel's nose under the tent."

"Is Rick some kind of big shot?"

"He'd like you to think so. Stake him to a gin and tonic and he'll tell you about the time he sprung Treat Williams. Or save yourself a few bucks and he'll tell you anyway."

"You don't like him?"

"We go back. But Rick's a hot dog. I'm not a hot dog."

Harry puts his hat on and catches Guy sneaking around to the passenger side.

"Where you goin'? You're drivin'. It's your leg."

"You only drove for like a half-hour, Harry."

"You lazy sonofabitch."

31

THE VALUE INN is ten dollars cheaper than the Economy Suites. So of course Ted takes a left and pulls in there. The Economy Suites is hardly a palace, but at least the sign says HBO, air conditioning, and California King beds.

She waits in the car while he goes in to book the room.

One thing Capri hates about Ted is how cheap he is. It's a major turn-off in a man. Like the piece of shit Toyota Yaris he stole. Because it's good on gas, he says. Good on gas shouldn't factor into a lovers-on-the-run scenario. She should be flashing truckers from a speeding convertible. Checking into penthouse suites and ordering room service that comes on a cart. That's the life she wants. One she'll never have with Ted.

If she wants that life, she needs to make it on her own. She's not going to make the same mistake her mother made, thinking every new boyfriend was the answer to all their problems. Most of the time they only ended up making things worse.

She doesn't know how she got in so deep with him anyway. He was supposed to be a quick fix in a bad situation. A place to land while she planned her next move. Then it turned out the next move was robbing

Big Smoke. Ted was in the right place at the right time. But she's not sure how much longer she can ride it out with him.

On cue, Ted grovels and begs for sex as soon as they set their bags down. She's not in the mood, but she eventually caves. Then Ted can't even get it up. He stands next to one of the shitty full-size beds, tugging at his skinny dick.

"Jesus Christ, Ted." Capri stands on the bed. "What's your problem?"

"I don't know, boo. C'mere, let me try it again. Say something dirty." He paws at her leg and she kicks him away.

"I don't need that thing pressing against me. Put it away."

"I'm freaked out, okay?" Ted steps into his boxers and shimmies them up. "You're not worried at all?"

"About what?"

"About everything. I don't know where we're going. How we're going to sell this shit. Who is out there looking for us. The one time we did sell something, you beat the guy up and took it right back. You could've killed him and you don't even give a fuck."

"Fuck him."

"Fuck him. Right. Fuck Eddie too? At the dispensary? You don't think he's going to want his weed back? You don't think Carvell may be coming after us. You told me—"

"Carvell doesn't realize he's a security guy at a weed store. Not a fucking mercenary."

"What about my bail bonds guy? He said if I took off he'd come looking for me."

"Who?"

"Harry. The guy who bailed me out. How long before he realizes I'm gone? He probably has bounty hunters and shit he can call."

Sounds like bullshit to her.

"Sounds like bullshit to me. Plus, even if he does, he's looking for you, not me."

"Fuck that, boo. Fuck that. You're in this just as much as me. More."

"More? You're trying to turn this on me? You're the fucking idiot who got caught."

"You're the one that fucked Elmer up. He probably called the cops."

"And told them what? He got fucked over on a drug deal? He was trying to rip us off. You don't understand the business side of things, Ted. He low-balled us and I let him do it because I knew I was going to take it all anyway."

"He would've bought the whole thing if you could have just waited—"

"Yeah, for next to nothing. If he was willing to buy it, then other people are willing to buy it. We don't have to settle for the first shitty offer."

"You didn't have to beat him. He's an old man."

"I can't believe you're taking his side."

"Sometimes you take things too far is all I'm saying."

That sets a fire under her.

"Oh yeah, like when?"

"Forget it."

"No, tell me. When else? Are you talking about the club? When that pig fucking attacked me?"

"No. Listen, I'm sorry. C'mere."

"Get the fuck out of here."

"I just get the feeling you're about to, I don't know what you're about to do, boo. You've got a hot temper is all I'm saying."

She shoves him away and storms into the bathroom, slamming the door behind her.

Time to tag in Jamey to finish things out.

TED IS LOST in town. Capri is messing with his head again. Sometimes she's the moonlight in his canoe and other times he thinks she'll sink his ship. In clearer moments, when his mind is unclouded by lust, the sway of her slutty sorcery, he knows she's a bad apple. That he should get away from her. Run away from her. But every time he gets close, something turns him back around.

It's not always the fuck urge flooding back, though there is that. For someone as sex crazed as he is, Ted isn't that experienced. And definitely not with anyone like Capri.

But there's another side to her. A side that can dig its hooks in even deeper. When she says she trusts him. That he makes her feel safe. Some nights she gets sad and tells him he's the only person in the world who has ever cared about her. But even then, there's always the feeling like she's trying to hustle something. That it all comes at a cost. He has no idea how she really feels about him.

Maybe it's like his dad says. Sometimes you need a mean woman to keep you in line. Whatever it is, right now he's stuck and scared. He feels like they're tied to the train tracks together.

He remembers the night they matched on Tinder. When she was dancing at the Golden Banana she used to drum up business by meeting guys on dating apps and talking them into coming in to see her dance.

Ted showed up with eighty dollars he stole from the register at the Grotto. It was early afternoon and he was one of only a few solitary men scattered at various vantage points around the stage, putting down small bills.

Two dazed dancers lazed against the poles. Others worked the bar area, peddling lap dances and sponging drinks. He was going to turn around and go home. Then he saw her come out of a back room, followed by a businessman who made a beeline for the door.

She wore a pink tube dress slitted on the sides and recognized him from his photo. He could make out her pierced nipples as she walked toward him and saw the white mesh crotch of her G-string when she climbed the stool to sit down next to him at the bar.

She smelled like a candy cane and leaned in for a short jab of a kiss. Cigarettes and lip gloss. It tasted like a mentholated cough drop.

"Let's do a shot," she said. Her eyes swam. She called the bartender over and ordered two Sambucas. Ted recognized the licorice smell from her breath and barely flinched when the bartender asked for twenty-four dollars. He even tipped her.

Capri raked her nails down Ted's thighs and said the shot must have made her horny. "Let's do a private dance." She clicked her tongue ring. "It'll be fun, I promise."

Ted went to the ATM and got a two-hundred-dollar—two-ten with the surcharge—cash advance on his Discover card.

Over the next couple of weeks, Capri became an expensive habit. Ted took extra nights at the Grotto to steal whatever he could. He felt sick and guilty, but he went ahead and did it anyway. Fuzzy never kept good track of the books but he must've figured something was going on because it wasn't long before he didn't want him covering shifts anymore.

A couple weeks later Capri told him she passed out with a cigarette and burned herself out of the place where she was staying. She also had the confrontation at the club that got her fired. That's when he invited her to move into Fuzzy's.

Roaming around Walmart, Ted checks out a bleaching kit in the hair aisle and thinks about stopping in a gas station bathroom, dyeing his hair, and going back to the motel a different man. He decides against it. A disguise is supposed to hide you, not make you stand out. He knows that much.

32

GOLD KEY BAIL Bonds sits on the ground floor of a yellow building on Sylvan Street. A giant neon arrow points to a picture of Rick on the front door. Rick sits at his desk with Carvell King standing before him, in full uniform, reporting for duty.

Carvell makes a show of removing his hat. Solemn. Like Rick is about to sing the national anthem. There's an extra-large military duffel bag slung over his shoulder.

"What's in there, your toothbrush?"

Carvell drops the bag onto Rick's desk.

Rick looks inside at a couple heavy-duty assault rifles and some ammunition. "This is a bounty hunt," he says. "Not a search and destroy mission. I feel like Sam Trautman over here."

Carvell rubs his nose.

"You on something?"

Rick has a bad feeling about this guy. And what he's potentially setting in motion here. Sure, he could use the five grand. Hell, he needs it. But he doesn't want to be carrying Harry's casket next week. And he doesn't want the blood on his hands if that piss ant Teddy walks into a hail of bullets.

"Listen, I understand if you need to bring a piece for protection but leave the bazookas and bullet belts behind," Rick says.

"Never know when you're going to have to go full condor."

Rick doesn't want to think about what that entails. "Just check in with me when you get to Reno."

Carvell grabs a handful of business cards off Rick's desk.

"Can I use your printer? I need to print out the directions."

"To Reno?"

"That's right."

"You don't even know where the Christ you're headed? Maybe pack one less Uzi and bring a GPS. A fucking Thomas Guide."

"GPS drains my phone. And I don't like that bitch's voice."

Rick gestures for him to come behind the desk. The map shows two possible routes from Van Nuys to Reno. One is up the 5 to Sacramento where it connects with the 80. The more inland route would take Carvell up 395 through Death Valley.

"You know Reno is west of L.A.?" Rick says. "Interesting tidbit."

"I heard that somewhere before." Carvell runs his finger up the inland route. "I usually like to stay off the main roads, but in this case I'll take the straight shot up the 5. Small towns have low speed limits and bored cops. Or I'll get stuck behind some hick in a truck."

Rick clicks print.

Carvell rolls up the paper and taps it on Rick's desk.

He heaves the bag of artillery over his shoulder and heads out the door.

33

CAPRI SITS INDIAN style on the motel bed with Ted's Wu-Tang shirt tented over her knees, smoking one cigarette after another.

The Value Inn induces the same blank déjà vu of all cheap motels. Tiny towels bleached stiff, plastic cups wrapped in plastic, a cloudy mirror, a damp carpet. Being here reminds her of being holed up with her mother, hiding out from some boyfriend or another, sharing one bed even though there were two, waiting for something to blow over. When it was time to leave, they'd always take whatever was left of the mini shampoos and conditioners and paper-thin bars of soap that dissolved like pads of butter in the shower.

Her mother brought home every kind of guy. Garage mechanics, bartenders, insurance salesmen, car dealers. They blurred together. Each one a drunk, each one a hothead. Another bloom of bastard. Lots of them named Glenn. They'd go away and Capri would be relieved. Sometimes they'd come back, saying, "You miss me?" in a tone that said they knew she didn't.

As her mother hit her forties, Capri watched her go down the ladder from losers who at least had money to losers whose bills she had to pay. Capri's still young. But her kind of sexy, the kind that plays well in strip bars, can harden into something ugly real quick. If her mother taught her anything, it's that what she's eventually going to have to settle for will only get worse. She doesn't have a lot of time to fuck around.

It's only been three days, but it feels like they've been on the road for weeks. Now they're fighting in a balmy motel with no air-conditioning, only a swamp cooler.

She lied to him about the conversation she and Jamey had when she was in the car at the waterpark yesterday. What the two of them really talked about was ditching Ted and she and Jamey going to Florida together.

Jamey's uncle is an airboat captain in Everglades City. He says high-grade West Coast weed will go quick down there and at a good price. Capri likes the idea of putting three thousand miles between her and her current situation. Especially if it means ultimately landing in Miami.

Jamey said he could drive up to meet her in the next day or two. FedEx the weed and get a flight out of Vegas. Or make the drive if they don't want to take that risk.

It sounds like a good plan but she's not sure she wants to let Jamey back in. He's useful in a different way than Ted, but more unpredictable. And he's a serious criminal, not some guy who's along for the ride.

She gets frustrated with Ted but there's something about him she's drawn to. He seems to genuinely care about her. She feels that from him in a way she hasn't with anyone before. It's also what she hates about him. Because those feelings she has are weaknesses. Her edges soften around him. She almost trusts him.

She feels guilty when he walks in, all sheepish and hesitant, eyes on the floor, a bag over his shoulder like the night he came in with the first haul from the robbery.

He bought everything remotely romantic the local 7-Eleven had to offer. One at a time, he removes items from the bag and lays them out on the bed. A cheap rose, a heart-shaped chocolate, a lighter with a rabbit on it, a bag of her favorite chili cheese Bugles.

Capri tears into the bag and holds her cigarette at a distance while she eats the Bugles off the fingertips of her left hand. Ted crawls into bed and rests his head on her lap. He takes a hit off her bowl and gets a mouthful of ash.

"This thing fucking sucks."

"Let's go buy a vaporizer," Capri says. "An expensive one. Is there a head shop out here?"

Ted searches on his phone and finds a place called High Desert Wellness about fourteen miles east. It's also a dispensary and he says maybe they can talk to them about selling some stuff.

"Let's go." She slides on her shorts and grabs a roll of bills from the bible drawer.

Outside the smoke shop, three hippies are standing around a Joshua tree taking pictures. The hippies walk away and Ted and Capri go over to look. Two wide eyes look down from the branches.

"Great Horned Owl," Capri says.

"Do they attack people?"

"They swoop, but their diet is mostly mice. You ever hear of owl pellets?"

"Is that what you feed them?"

"It's the undigested bones of the rodents all mashed together, like a fur ball the owl coughs up."

Ted mentions something he heard once about owls' heads being able to turn 360 degrees.

"I believe it's only two-hundred-and-seventy degrees," Capri says.

"Let's go get that vaporizer."

The AC hits them as soon as they walk in. The place looks brand new. All delivery systems for THC or CBD are on display. Plus a good selection of bud. Capri notices they carry Elmer's Eatables.

The guy at the counter sees them eyeing the bongs and bowls and pounces immediately, launching into pitch mode. His nametag says his name is Kevin and that he's a team player.

"Check out these sweet new glass pieces we got in," he says. "Totally unbreakable."

Kevin has a crewcut with a strange part in the middle, like he's been grazed by a bullet. He looks like he should be hawking cell phones in a mall kiosk.

He hurls a small pipe against the counter. The pipe shatters like a breakaway prop and a spidercrack slowly expands on the glass counter-top. Kevin is embarrassed and confused. He looks under the counter like he grabbed the wrong one.

"Shit, dude," Ted says. "You going to have to pay for that?"

Capri hisses a mean laugh.

"We're looking for a vaporizer anyway."

The crack expands in jump cuts across the countertop. Capri points to a Volcano.

"We'll take one of those."

"That one's six-hundred bucks."

"You guys do trade?"

"Trade?" Kevin looks at her weird. "What kind of trade?"

The countertop shatters and Kevin ducks.

"Holy fuck," Ted says.

Kevin runs in the back to grab a broom and he's back there a little too long. Capri sees him pacing and talking on the phone, looking at a piece of paper he grabbed off a desk. It makes her nervous for a second but then he comes back out with the broom. Capri runs down her sales pitch while he sweeps.

"We're definitely stocking up," Kevin says. "And if you're talking about that level of quality at that price point, I don't see why my boss wouldn't be interested. I can't do the trade, you'll have to buy the vaporizer, but I can give you a deal on it."

He's the one who sounds nervous now, Capri thinks, but maybe he's just jumpy after the glass breaking. "Are you guys local?" he says.

"We're around."

"Let me take your number. I'll have my boss call you."

Capri hesitates then goes ahead and writes the number down. Kevin hands her a High Desert Wellness business card and says she'll be hearing from his boss.

"His name's Gerry," he says. "With a G."

34

AFTER A LONG stretch of nothing but scrub and sagebrush, Harry and Guy coast down the main drag of a tumbledown town.

They pass a Travelodge.

"Travelodge," Guy says.

They pass an Arco station.

"Arco," Guy says.

They pass a 7-Eleven.

"Seven-eleven," Guy says.

"You wearin' a wire?" Harry says.

"What?"

"Seems like you're trying to alert someone to our location."

Guy lets the next couple signs glide by without comment.

A few miles later, the town behind them, Harry breaks the silence.

"You know what Willie Nelson's middle name is?"

"No, what is it?"

"Hugh."

Guy nods.

Harry adjusts his hands on the wheel. "Not what you'd expect."

DRIVING THROUGH MODESTO, Carvell thinks about John Rambo, adrift in civilian life. Maybe it was Rick mentioning Sam Trautman earlier.

Carvell's military career was unremarkable, but it was his whole life, his whole identity, for a few years there. Stickers all over the old truck he had. Decked out in camo even in downtime. His ambition in those days was to be a ribbon-chested general.

He outgrew it. The sense of valor was gone once he realized most people were only there because they had no other choice. And the older guys, the lifers, were just clocking time. Waiting it out because they didn't know what else to do.

Carvell was a peacetime soldier and didn't see any real action until he went to work for Stan Lemke. Lemke gave Carvell the security guard post at Big Smoke as a holdover position between the real work he does for him. Stuff Carvell isn't supposed to talk about.

Being hired muscle, an enforcer, suits Carvell more than the military bullshit. No trumpeting and marching around. Just settling scores face-to-face. Hard and fast. It's the only time he feels like he's doing what he's truly equipped to do.

Within a year of working for Lemke, Carvell had developed a reputation. It got to the point where, in most cases, Lemke only had to threaten to send him. If Carvell did have to show up, his presence alone was usually enough to get people to cave.

Until the fiasco in Tonopah.

Lemke had sent Carvell out to an associate in Las Vegas who needed help collecting a gambling debt. The man who owed the money had fled to a motel outside Tonopah. The guy was only supposed to be threatened, maybe roughed up a little. But Carvell got cranked up and went too far. He killed the guy, plus a girl who was holed up in the room with him. Plus a cleaning woman who came to see what was happening.

He also failed to collect the money.

This generated some blowback from a biker gang the guys were connected to out there. Carvell killed two of them too.

He was somehow able to get out of town without getting killed or caught, but none of this was good. To Lemke, it demonstrated poor impulse control and a lack of foresight on Carvell's part.

So he's been laying low with the Big Smoke security detail for almost a year. It's an easy gig. Sit there and smoke free smoke, read his gun magazines. But he's starting to get soft. Hitting the fast food more. And all the weed.

Most nights he feels cooped up in his small apartment, pacing the floor like a man in a cell. His car is nicer than his place and sometimes he just drives around until dawn, sleeping on the side of the road somewhere, or in the parking lot outside the dispensary. The gun range is his only real sense of release, but it just feels like an exhibition game.

The point of this trip is to get out of the penalty box and back in Lemke's good graces. He just needs to not go around the bend again. He told himself he only brought the speed along in case of an emergency. To stay focused and alert if he had to work all night. Then he took a blast before heading out.

Going north past Stockton, he's hovering around ninety, Sepultura cranking. The arsenal is secured in the trunk. He wonders what would happen if he were rear-ended. His mom drove a Pinto when he was a kid and he always worried about the fender bender and the fiery explosion. Did they really do that?

The opposite of going out in a blaze of glory.

He grinds his teeth. Another two-hundred miles to Reno. For the first time he wonders why Reno. You go to Vegas to get married, you go to Reno to get divorced. And Capri doesn't seem like the marrying kind. That detail doesn't add up. They must be up to something else. Some connection up there.

35

GUY LOOKS OUT the passenger window, remembering the shimmering mirages of desert cartoons. He remembers seeing a real roadrunner out here on a camping trip with Amanda. He remembers it didn't look like the one in the cartoons.

This outing came at the right time. He's grateful for the change of scenery. Not that the scenery changes much here. But it's good to be temporarily freed from the grid of Van Nuys. Moving through the avenues and side streets like a sad Pac-Man. Ghosts of disappointment and regret ganging up behind him. This almost qualifies as a vacation.

The past few weeks he's felt late summer boring down on him like a drill, round and round, spiraling into shit. Even in the unshakable California sunshine, Guy still feels the sadness of shifting seasons he remembers from growing up in Massachusetts.

Here there's no looming darkness and cold, no dragging the tarp over the pool after Labor Day, but summertime still holds a strong sway. Something to make the most of. Now it's almost over and he's foggy on the fun parts.

How can something suck and still feel like it's going by too fast?

May to August was mostly missing Amanda. Losing cases. Gaining weight. He didn't get to the beach once. Better afternoons he'd shimmy out of his court suit and loaf in a pool float at the Red Roof Inn in Panorama City. There's a bar and grill called Tom Foolery's off the lobby. The daytime manager is a former DUI client who gives Guy free margaritas and nachos and the pass key for the pool area. Sometimes he bobs alongside a traveling salesman, but he usually has it to himself.

He'll have to go back to real life eventually but for now he's just trying to relax. Trying to enjoy Harry's company. Trying not to worry about whether the rent checks on his apartment and office are going to clear. He needs to get rid of the office. It pretty much functions as a storage space these days anyway. He takes his meetings at the American Legion Post 815 on Reedley and Roscoe. It's quiet and gives clients the impression he's a veteran. It also has decent BBQ.

When he ditches the office, he can finally unload his old man's teak desk and leather furniture, pretty much the only part of his inheritance he hasn't already burned through. He's been considering pawning some or all of it for months.

It's been a slow year and money is tight. He's been living check to check, cashing the checks at the check-cashing place. He wriggled out of the looptyloop of the payday loan system, but his credit is tanked. The Discover card is still in circulation, on the life support of minimum payments, but the interest rate is so high it's like buying everything twice. Money orders are reserved for when nothing else can be trusted.

Guy fixes his eyes on the horizon.

"Those mountains never seem to get any closer. Even though we're going seventy straight toward them."

189 \ ZIG ZAG

"They'll be behind us before you know it," Harry says.

"What do we do then?"

"We go on down the road."

MORE MILES FALL away in silence. Harry takes a gulp of water and the cheap plastic bottle collapses like an accordion in his hand. "Buddy Holly die?" he says.

"What?"

"I need some drivin' music."

Guy reaches in the back for the boot box that houses Harry's cassettes. He sets it on his lap and selects *The Gilded Palace Of Sin* by the Flying Burrito Brothers.

The tape is wound to the beginning of side two. The soft twang of "Wheels" scores the desert scenery, getting Harry thinking about the drive out to L.A. with Nederhoffer in '72.

They'd been playing around Austin and the surrounding areas for a couple years by then. When they decided to move to L.A., they pieced together a mini tour of Texas, New Mexico, and Arizona to make some money on the way out.

Harry and Nederhoffer barrel-assed through the Southwest, strung out and sideways, passing joints and tequila bottles between them, the same Burritos tape on the deck, talking about California, where they could sleep out every night.

Thinking about it now, Harry isn't sure if it was the drugs or just being young and dumb that let them live with such abandon. Or what kind of luck or fate it was that took Nederhoffer out in his early twenties and let Harry live to limp through his late sixties.

Sometimes he wonders how things might be if Chris was still around and some version of a music career had panned out for them. They had the lifestyle down, that's for sure. As far as talent, who knew.

Despite Nederhoffer's ambitions, Harry knew they weren't going to be Willie and Waylon. But he didn't give a shit. They probably would have had as much fun kicking it out in a bar band on the weekends.

But things went the way they did. Harry did what he could.

When Harry planned the drive back to Texas for Christmas, the idea was to talk Chris down and get him back home for a bit. When they found him in the Tropicana a couple nights before they were supposed to leave, Harry thought he'd cancel the trip.

He ended up heading out solo but only made it as far as the Arizona border. He couldn't bring himself to leave California. It weirded him out that Nederhoffer's body was also in transit to the same destination, in some refrigerated truck on the same highways he was driving on. He had visions of the truck passing him in the night.

There was no reason to attend the funeral and be frowned upon and blamed by the holy Nederhoffers on high. Harry got a room in Needles and had to go to three liquor stores before he could find a decent bottle of tequila. He spent Christmas Eve and Christmas alone, watching TV on a motel bed with the AC on high, drinking and smoking cigarettes, Camels back then, before heading back to L.A.

Some people go cold turkey when a friend O.D.s but Harry found himself going harder in the months after. Defiance. Tempting fate. Or a way of plowing through the grief.

He eventually went softball, adrift on a lazy river of weed and psychedelics, but the amount of pills and powders he's consumed over the years dwarfs the shallow pool in the spoon that took Nederhoffer down. He romanticizes him like a fallen gunslinger, but the loss cut deep and cast a long shadow. He's still riding with the ghost.

The tape ends and Harry wants to hear something else.

"What kind of sounds you like?"

"Hip-hop mostly," Guy says. "West Coast. Some hyphy shit. You like hip-hop?"

"An ex-sweetheart of mine from Houston turned me on to a guy called Devin the Dude. He's pretty good. Reefer-smokin' music. I generally keep it country, though."

"I don't listen to much country. I like Garth Brooks."

"You know what they say about Garth, don't you?"

"No, what's that?"

"He did for country music what pantyhose did for finger-fuckin.'"

36

THE **SILVER LEGACY** Resort Casino has five bars and lounges onsite. Frankie Valli and the Four Seasons are playing the main ballroom and George Lopez is in the comedy club.

Carvell sets himself up in a Deluxe King smoking room. He calls Rick to check in and give him his coordinates. Then he takes a shower and stretches out bareass on the California King, smoking a Black & Mild Wood Tip and planning his evening, trying to keep things level.

First stop is the Blender Bar, where he polishes off a 48oz. Party Barge Margarita before heading over to the Rum Bullions Island Bar, serving specialty rums from around the world, for a flaming Kava Kava cocktail.

The Kava Kava is served Scorpion Bowl style, meant for two or more people, but Carvell's security uniform gives him an air of authority and the bartender lets it slide.

He's pretty oiled up by the time he decides to get to work. Carvell prides himself on having high tolerances for both pain and intoxicants. Train hard and party hard. He doesn't get fucked up every day. Usually chills with a couple Guinness Extra Stouts and a fat pre-roll, watches Steve Harvey on the *Feud*. Tonight he feels bulletproof.

First order of business is to get the lay of the land and ask around.
He passes through the Biggest Little City In The World arch and walks
a few blocks to the Chapel of the Bells. They do drive-thru weddings
there, but there's no line at the window, just a small gathering at the
outside gazebo. Older looking crowd.

Inside, it looks more like a funeral parlor than a wedding chapel.
It reminds him of when his friend Mickey's grandmother died and he
had to go to pay his respects the way Catholics do it, with the body
right there in the room.

He grabs a fistful of mints from the dish on his way out.

If Capri and Ted are in town with money to burn, they'll be in the
casinos. Carvell makes the rounds. He plays the nickel slots, some
roulette, then hits the tables. At Circus Circus, he has a run-in with a
blackjack dealer and gets ejected from the casino. After security escorts
him out, he finds his way to the employee parking area in the Circus
Circus garage, planning to lie in wait until that fucker comes out after
his shift. After a half-hour of waiting around, he cools down a bit and
heads back to the Rum Bullions for another Kava Kava. It's been a
long day with a long drive. He'll take the rest of the night to blow off
some steam and get started in earnest tomorrow.

The Rum Bullions is a rowdy spot. Customers chant as Carvell
slurps the bowl of booze up his straw. Two women join him and ask if
he needs some help. Carvell promptly orders another, along with three
Jell-O shots served in souvenir syringes. There's another close huddle
on the next round and Carvell looks at one girl then the other.

"Either of you guys want a blast?"

He lets them assume he's talking about coke.

A HUNDRED AND eight degrees and a roadside Smokey The Bear sign has the fire danger level set to Very High.

The Olds is on the verge of overheating, the needle diving into the red, and Harry cranks the heat to cool the engine. Hot air from the vent floods the car, mixing with the dead-ass breeze.

"Smokey the Bear wears a hat and pants, a belt even," Guy says. "How come he doesn't have a shirt on?"

"The real question is why is he carrying a shovel?"

Big box stores and fast-food chains have crowded pockets of the Twentynine Palms Highway since Harry was last down here. There are billboards for legal pot. Billboards for high desert housing developments. But the spaces between remain unchanged. Junk shops and crystal stands. Jackrabbits darting around in traffic, vultures feasting on the ones who didn't make it.

They pass the Joshua Tree Inn where they charge a premium to stay in the room where Gram Parsons died. It makes Harry flash on Nederhoffer again, dying alone at the Tropicana, unknown and unsung.

A mile or two more and they decide to not court breakdown any longer. There's a flock of Harleys in the lot of the Safari Motor Inn and Harry warns Guy to pull around them slow.

The air conditioning is on in the room, but you can hear it more than you can feel it. Harry pours a bucket of ice in the bathroom sink and sets the tequila bottle there to cool. He sits at the edge of one of the beds, his bare feet on the dirty tile. Someone has carved a circular design into the center of the ceiling fan, like a hypnosis wheel, to give it the appearance of turning faster. It isn't fooling anyone.

He goes to check out the swimming pool but it's filled with bikers.

Hulking longhairs with topless women propped on their shoulders, having chicken fights. Everyone is rummed up and rowdy, smeared in tattoos. Loud music blares from somewhere and the pool water looks like cloudy Midori. He was going to cuff his pants and put his feet in but he decides to take a cold shower instead.

The night drags and the temperature doesn't drop a degree. Harry and Guy lie in glazed silence, sweating out beer and tequila as fast as they're drinking it. They watch the credits roll on an episode of *Bonanza* through a cloud of smoke. The TV is locked at a frustrating angle that offers neither of them a direct view.

Harry's phone buzzes on the nightstand. Elmer.

"How goes the turkey hunt?"

Harry looks over at Guy. Flat on his back. A beer can planted on his chest.

"I'd say we're in lukewarm pursuit."

"Well look alive," Elmer says. "We got a bite on the line."

Elmer informs Harry that Capri and Ted have surfaced at the High Desert Wellness dispensary outside Barstow, toward Baker. The clerk recognized them from the Wanted poster.

He mentions that part twice.

"These kids haven't the foggiest idea what they're doing. They waltz in there with a smile and a shoeshine like my guy is going to buy up their stock sight unseen. They're carrying coals to Newcastle. It's a buyers' market. Where are you guys?"

"Joshua Tree."

"What're you doing all the way down there?"

"You steered us this way, remember?"

"Fella says there's gold in the valley and you go to the valley?"

"What?"

"Not me. I go to the mountain."

That torques Harry.

"But we're supposed to listen to you now?"

"Don't get your tail up. We're on the same side here."

"You're sure this information is good?"

"You can hang your Open Road on it. How soon can you be there?"

Harry sighs. "We'll head out first thing in the morning."

"I'll see if my guy can set something up for tomorrow. Check back in when you're in the vicinity."

Harry hangs up and Guy props himself on an elbow.

"Where we headed?"

"North," Harry says.

"North usually means cooler."

"It can."

"I could leave right now," Guy says.

Harry stares at the slow spiral in the hub of the ceiling fan and feels the reverberations of the bikers' music coming through the walls.

"Let's hitch up the reindeer," he says.

VAPE CLOUDS FOG the room, compounding the shabby swelter of the Value Inn.

Capri and Ted strip to their underwear and go outside for a night swim. The water is warm and the pool lights tint everything purple. They float on their backs and watch the clouds blur the stars.

When the rain comes, they submarine themselves, re-emerging in the shallow end and diving back under. Ted watches Capri surface. Purple light swirling around her. Her hair slicked back and makeup gone. Nipples visible through the mesh of her bra.

There's a low flash of lightning. They face each other, treading water, and he tells her about a picture he saw one time where lightning turned the water in a bathtub black. She spooks like it's a ghost story and they run back to the room holding towels over their heads. The rain looks like movie rain.

They get dressed and walk next door to a bar called the Mouse Trap. Beerlight neon oil-slicks the wet parking lot. The place is mostly empty. They drink kamikaze shots and pitchers of beer. Play Big Buck Hunter and shoot pool.

Two guys in gas station uniforms put quarters on the table. They eye Capri and make comments to each other. Ted gets the feeling she likes it, even encourages it, the way she bends over to line up a shot. It makes him mad but it also turns him on.

Capri gets more quarters from the bartender and cups them in her hands on her way to the cigarette machine. Ted hangs back with his cue, watching the gas station guys watch her. She comes back complaining all they had for menthols were Salems.

The guys challenge them to a game and Capri runs the table for three straight. It's like Ted isn't even there. He's relieved when the last-call lights come up and it's time to go back to the room. There are two tallboys left in the minifridge. They shotgun them in the shower and lob the empty cans over the curtain rod.

They get started in the shower and move to the bed. Ted tries to hold off finishing, but he never can, even when he's drunk. He passes out for a while then wakes up parched an hour later. He gets a cup of water and realizes Capri isn't in the room.

He goes to the window and parts the heavy curtains. Capri is out in the parking lot, pacing and smoking in the neon half-light. She's talking to somebody on the phone.

37

RICK IS WITH Margo, one of his usual escorts, in their usual room at the El Cortez Motel, around back where the limo can't be seen from the street. Rick doesn't like girls knowing where he lives. Let them in the Devlin Arms and they start casing the joint. Come back the next night with their boyfriend and take the 70-inch TV.

The muscle relaxer she gave him is kicking in, mixing with the juniper bloom of the second gin and tonic. He lies on his back. Talking and talking. Not caring if she's bored or not. His dime, his time. Not unlike a therapist if you choose to look at it that way. Rick chooses to look at it that way.

She gets up to refill their drinks. He watches her sashay across the room. Her long legs like sharp scissors, her ass perfectly bisected by the flossy g-string he makes her keep on the whole time, along with her heels.

She comes back to bed and rubs up against him. He's usually good for two rounds if he remembers to take the Viagra on an empty stomach and take it slow with the gin. But his mind is elsewhere. On his mounting pile of bills, on his two alimonies, on the latest threatening e-mail from Sun Surety, on the two hundred he spent on Margo, on the fifty he spent on the room, on the five grand the security guy from the dispensary mentioned.

Need to check in with him.

Make sure he's on track. Make sure he hasn't killed anyone.

GUY STARTS UP the Olds and pulls out of the parking lot of the Safari Motor Inn. It's just past eleven, but everything is so quiet on the Twentynine Palms Highway it feels like three in the morning.

Harry lights a mondo torpedo and reclines the passenger seat a few degrees. He takes a couple deep hits before stubbing it out in the center console and tilting his hat down. A minute later he's out.

Guy drives through the night. He can only see what's immediately visible in the high beams, except for sudden seconds when dry lightning pops off in the distance like an old camera flash, the horizon lighting up and going dark.

Harry's joint is sitting there doing nothing in the center console. Guy sees no harm in sparking it up. Just a hit or two to help the time pass.

Soon the wind picks up, swaying the car. Smoke fogs the car like dry ice and Guy feels like he's at the wheel of a ship. The kind you see on the wall at beach restaurants. The lightning flashes double in frequency and wattage. If there's any rain, it's evaporating before it reaches the ground. Guy's mind drifts to pressure systems. How storms form.

Semis appear out of nowhere and roar past. He has images of spooked animals running in front of the car. An hour passes. Another. A sign appears in the distance.

ARIZONA. THE GRAND CANYON STATE WELCOMES YOU.

It occurs to him he's been driving in the wrong direction for some time.

He pulls over.

Luckily Harry is still in a deep sleep. He talked yesterday about how being a passenger in motion lulls him. How he's always wanted to have his bed rigged up to rock like a train. Guy hopes he can get this train moving in the right direction without Harry realizing how far off-track he's gotten them.

He finds Barstow on the roadmap and sets a northward course to meet the 40 in Needles. It's been years since he travelled without GPS and his phone is running too low to use the one on there.

Headed north, on a desolate stretch outside a town called Desert Hills, the headlights pan across a swerve of road and Guy sees a woman and child hitchhiking.

He passes them by, trying to make up time, but feels a pang of guilt when he looks in the rearview and sees them huddled together. It looks like the rain may start again.

He pulls over and they come running to the car. It's an Indian woman with her young daughter. They got stranded in Lake Havasu and are trying to get back to Peach Springs, outside the Hualapai Reservation. It's more than an hour out of the way but Guy figures he's gone this far, he may as well help the lady out. The girl looks lost and scared and who knows who else is going to come by.

"Okay, hop in. But you've got to keep quiet. My partner here is asleep."

The woman and her daughter doze off in the back. Guy would give anything to sleep right now, but he tries to make the best of it. In daylight, this may have been an interesting drive, up old Route 66, but at night there's nothing to see. At least he seems to have outrun the rain.

Harry shifts in his seat and Guy is afraid he's going to wake up. It'd be hard to explain the hitchhikers on top of everything else. But he just turns over on his right side.

Guy drops the woman and her daughter off without incident. She says he looks tired, but Guy politely declines her offer of hospitality and says he'll stop for a coffee. She thanks him again and he drives on.

Things start to go sideways two hours later, somewhere around the Mojave National Preserve. There's a rumble of bowling ball thunder and the rain comes roaring back in sheets. Lightning strikes low and the road flickers and warps like a filmstrip. Guy sees double, then triple, then things turn kaleidoscopic for extended seconds. He stops for gas and thinks it might be a good idea to take a short power nap and clear his head. He fills the tank and parks in the outskirts of a Chevron lot.

When Guy opens his eyes an hour later, Harry is sitting upright. Groggy. His face a blank slate without his tinted glasses.

"Where the Christ are we?"

Guy straightens up. "Outside Barstow."

The rain has stopped but it's still dark out. Harry squints at the time on his phone.

"How far outside Barstow?"

"A ways. I took a wrong turn."

Guy steps out to take a piss. When he comes back, Harry is finishing the joint from the center console. He stubs it out without a word, puts his hat over his eyes and goes back to sleep.

FUZZY PROPS A cinderblock in front of the door to air out the bar. The AC is on the fritz again, just a couple floor fans blowing the smoke around.

He stands outside beneath the awning. The pavement hisses under the cars going by on Oxnard, none of them carrying a potential customer. Rain parachutes through the streetlamp glow. Everything feels slowed by the humidity.

He's thinking about closing early when he sees Rick's limo idling at the corner stoplight. He prays he's only passing by, then the blinker flashes. Fuzzy goes back inside, turns a Collins glass right-side-up and unholsters the bottle of Gilbey's from the rack.

"I'm not saying I condone it." Rick stirs his third nightcap. "I'm saying I understand it."

"O.J., you mean?"

"O.J. Any of those Petersons. It's a good thing my last name isn't Peterson. Who knows what I'd be capable of."

Fuzzy shakes his head. He has issues with his ex-wife, but he doesn't want to kill her.

"I'd get caught," Rick says. "I've shot my mouth off about it too much in barrooms. If she died in a plane crash, they'd check and see if I was out at LAX tinkering with the craft. And they'd be right. They'd have you under the lights, Fuzzard. You'd crumble, you'd crack."

Fuzzy tunes him out. Polishes pint glasses. Ponders his own predicaments.

She had a drinking problem. And it was me. That's how Fuzzy nutshells his own divorce. It plays well in the bar and prevents people from prying.

When Peggy left him, he felt like an abandoned dog. Those days, if he opened the Grotto at all, it wasn't unusual to find Fuzzy in his bathrobe, serving himself more than the customers.

When he finally moved out of the back room of the Grotto and into the efficiency on Victory, Peggy came over and showed him how to make his favorite meals, leaving him handwritten recipes and instructions that were easy to follow. She bought him a set of pots and pans. Tupperware. She also left an album full of photos of her and Ted. All the things he missed out on over the years.

He's cleaned up his act since then. Other than Irish whiskey at Christmastime he hasn't had anything stronger than a bottle of Budweiser in nine years. Peggy moved in with the landscaper in Agoura Hills and let him have the house back. He did his best to mend his relationship with Ted. For whatever good that's doing him now.

Still, he hasn't taken a woman to bed in ages. And the last one, Gloria, was nothing to strut around about. A courthouse attorney leathered by blended malts. Runs in her stockings. Lipstick on her teeth. Unbecoming in every way.

The choppers of "Goodnight Saigon" thud out of the jukebox speakers and Rick puts forth the opinion that the song really captures what it felt like to be there.

"Billy Joel wasn't even in Vietnam."

"Neither was I," Rick says.

"Bunch of bullshit."

"Is Jimmy Buffett a pirate?"

Rick has him there.

In the Grotto's karaoke days, "A Pirate Looks At Forty" was Fuzzy's big closer. There's a photograph by the register, Fuzzy bronzed and smiling at the Full Moon Saloon in Key West, posing with an urn containing the ashes of Phil Clark, the legendary bartender who inspired the song.

Fuzzy mostly stopped listening to Jimmy Buffett after the *Floridays* album, and completely after *Banana Wind*, but the lifestyle still appeals to him. He and Peggy used to talk about when Ted went off to college, back when that was still a possibility. The plan was to sell the Grotto and the house on Costello and buy a condo in Marina Del Rey. Everything taken care of. No mowing lawns. No repairs. Fuzzy imagined himself with a mustache and suntan, captaining a small pleasure craft on day trips to Catalina, cracking an imported beer with a bottle opener shaped like a mermaid.

He remembers them talking about it on that Key West trip, huddled around the horseshoe bar at the Full Moon, not wanting to go home.

The Marina Del Rey dream kept them going for years. Until there was just the here and now and the only remaining fantasies were escape strategies. Getting out while there was still time to start over.

Ted never went anywhere, college or otherwise. He was an albatross around her neck and now he's an albatross around his. But at least Ted's got time on his side. Fuzzy may feel like a man before a firing squad, trying to stretch his last cigarette, but he holds onto a shred of hope that his only son hasn't gone too far wrong to turn around. He still imagines a future for him somewhere, with an upstanding woman if he can find one.

Fuzzy sees no great romance in his own future. He can't be bothered with the spruce-up that would be required. And he can't imagine the kind of woman who'd settle for him as-is. Maybe he'll end up like old Phil Clark, in an urn above the register. He's been behind this bar so long, he's starting to feel like a man who can't survive on the outside.

He's afraid if he sells the place he'll be like Ron over at Lucky Pierre's. Perched like a sad eagle on a stool in the place he used to own. At least behind the stick Fuzzy has some purpose, some authority.

"Alright." Rick siphons the last of his last gin. "Time to turn momma's picture to the wall."

Fuzzy follows him out. He watches the limo weave onto Oxnard and stands there a minute before he pulls the gate down and locks up.

A police helicopter hovers low. Sounds like that shitty Billy Joel song. The spotlight sweeps the lot, rubbernecking around the neighborhood.

Goodnight Van Nuys.

THE ROAD
TO CALICO

38

DAYBREAK FINDS THE Olds busted flat in a ditch on the side of a desert highway.

The blow-out woke Harry out of a deep sleep. He suspects it may have roused Guy out of a drifting slumber as well. He grabs his dimmers from the glovebox and takes a second to orient himself. There are no markers in sight.

Guy is already out of the car, standing in the middle of the empty blacktop.

"We hit a horseshoe!"

This only adds to Harry's disorientation. He feels drugged. By something stronger than the weed he's been smoking. Strange dreams last night in the car.

He looks at his phone. 5:45 a.m. They left Joshua Tree just past eleven. That leaves a lot of time unaccounted for. And he still doesn't know how far they are from Barstow.

He hoists himself out of the car, one boot in front of the other, and takes a 360-degree look around. The tire is beyond flat, shredded to ribbons, and there's no spare in the trunk. Not that it matters. The rim is completely bent. The Olds looks anchored.

"You over-inflated the tires," Harry says.

Guy points at four horseshoes scattered in the road.

"I don't know what they're doing there."

Harry calls for a tow.

Guy eventually stops repeating "horseshoe" and "I can't believe this" and the two of them lapse into a moody silence.

Being yoked to Guy, even for this limited stretch, has worn Harry down. Whatever Guy was doing behind the wheel, he could've killed them both. Harry leans against the bumper and calms his nerves with the day's inaugural Tareyton.

After three more cigarettes and forty-five minutes that feels like six hours, a tow finally arrives. Guy squeezes in between Harry and the driver, a blue-jowled knight of the road, and they have the Olds hauled to the closest garage. Turns out they're only about ten miles outside of Barstow. A town called Yermo.

A fifties diner is the only thing open for breakfast. A waitress in a pink uniform seats them in a pink booth. The paper placemat is a grid of local business ads, mostly service and repair. Guy eyes the refrigerated pie case and Harry sits preoccupied, rolling his lucky marble back and forth.

"What's that?"

"My lucky marble."

"Can I hold it?"

"No."

"Is it heavy?"

"Does it look heavy?"

"I thought marble was heavy."

"Marbles ain't made of marble."

"Then why are they called marbles?"

The waitress arrives and Harry feels bullied into ordering his break-fast combo, the Big Bopper, by name, despite his best effort to just point at it.

Guy points to a card clipped to his menu. The card features a horn of plenty and promotes the house special: a full Thanksgiving dinner, with all the trimmings, 24 hours a day, 365 days a year.

"I'm going to go for it," he says.

The waitress takes the order and scoops both menus off the table.

"Thanksgiving dinner?" Harry says. "It's seven o'clock in the morn-ing. In August."

"I drove all night."

"Why is that, by the way? That should've been a straight shot. Three hours max. We're hours off course."

"I took a wrong turn."

Harry decides to drop it. He's too hungry to argue. There's a Select-O-Matic jukebox at the table, two plays for a quarter, and he flips through the selections.

Guy leans in for a look.

"Did the Chipmunks only do Christmas music?"

Harry keeps flipping. "There's an album of Beatles covers."

He lands on a card featuring two Statler Brothers songs, "Flowers On The Wall" and "I'll Go To My Grave Loving You." He plays them both.

Guy's first course arrives, a flat iceberg salad on a cold glass plate, pre-dressed with watery ranch. A basket of rolls follows, three for the two of them. They each help themselves to one then Guy lunges for the last before Harry can object. He shoves it in his mouth unbuttered.

"We can get more rolls." Harry says. "You didn't have to bear-claw that one."

"I didn't bear-claw it."

"You bear-clawed it."

Guy chews the roll in a cow-like manner that makes Harry want to take a swing at him. "Tell me what really happened, Guy."

"Out there on the road, you mean?"

"Out there on the road."

"God's honest truth, I was driving along and hit a horseshoe." Guy wipes his mouth with a napkin. "Blew out the tire."

"Before that."

"I told you. Wrong turn. Maybe a couple wrong turns."

Harry narrows his eyes.

"Was there an Indian woman in the car with us last night?"

Guy nods solemnly.

Harry contemplates this, looking out the diner window, hesitant to pursue it any further.

The turkey comes and Harry has to admit it looks pretty good. The mashed potatoes have that volcano effect he likes, the gravy cratered in the center. He wishes he'd ordered that instead. The Big Bopper is a big disappointment. The pancakes, country ham, and hash browns are the same dull color.

Guy gets talking about old Donleavy family Thanksgivings. The feast, the football, the flop in the recliner. He confesses he ate last Thanksgiving dinner alone at the Norm's on Sherman Way. It's a lonely image, Guy at the counter with the other solitaires, empty stools between them. It's sadder to eat alone in a diner than to drink alone in a bar. Especially on Thanksgiving.

The waitress arrives with the check. Harry looks it over and raises his eyebrows.

"What'd we do, break a window?"

He passes it over to Guy.

"You're payin' for this one."

39

THE MECHANIC STANDS behind the register, craggy in a dark blue jumpsuit. He says his name's Bernard and points to a tag on the jumpsuit that proves it. He has an oversized flyswatter in his hand and a struck-dumb expression on his face.

"Funny thing," he says. "You hitting a horseshoe like that."

"Funny thing." Harry leans against the counter. "So when we good to hit the trail?"

"That's the shit of it. I had her up on the lift and I ran into some trub-trub."

Harry mentions what he remembers Beryl saying about the torque converter.

"I don't know about all that. I do know the wheel come off."

"What do you mean it *come off*?"

"What I said. I was fixing the tire and the wheel come right off. Something's broke."

He slams the flyswatter on the counter.

"Dang it. I got fly trouble."

"Listen, we're tryin' to make tracks here," Harry says. "What are we lookin' at?"

"It's my first priority. I'll work through the night if I have to."

Guy turns to Harry. "What do you think?"

"You'll have it first thing tomorrow at the latest." Bernard raises his hand. "Honest Injun."

"I saw a bar a couple miles back," Guy says.

"They got good Budweiser there," Bernard says.

Harry sighs. "What time's first thing?"

"Roundabout eight a.m. And here—" Bernard removes a card from a display by the register. "Check in over at the Bluebird Motel, half-mile or so down the road. Fifteen percent off if you give 'em my name."

"Okay, Bernie. Good enough. Listen, we may want to tool around a bit. My insurance covers a rental. Can you help me with that?"

Bernard scratches at a scab that looks like a strip of bacon taped to his arm.

"I ain't got rent-a-cars exactly."

Behind the garage, a few skinny horses are milling around in a fenced enclosure. Other than a gutted pick-up there are no cars to be seen. Bernard approaches the gate and one of the horses hobbles over to greet him.

"Happy to saddle up a couple palominos for you. Not a bad mode of transport if you're staying local."

Harry took a horseback tour of Monument Valley with a Navajo guide a few years ago. Most of what he remembered from riding as a kid came back. He's not opposed to cowboying around for a day. He looks at Guy.

"Any experience in horsemanship, Counselor?"

"Only at birthday parties."

"Recently?"

Guy shakes his head no.

Bernard says to Harry, "You handle yourself on a steed or you playing dress-up with the boots and hat?"

The jab rankles him.

"Grab the saddles, Bernie."

Bernard picks up on Guy's panic.

"How about your pal here?"

"He'll survive."

Bernard heads back to the stable and Harry tells Guy to be cool. They just need to get themselves over to the motel, maybe down to that bar.

"Can't we take a cab or something?"

"You see any cabs around here?"

Bernard returns with two saddled nags falling in line behind him. Harry approaches the brown one and runs his hand down its muzzle.

"At least you don't have to break these babies," Bernard says. "Someone done that a long time ago."

CAPRI AND TED sleep past checkout and pay for another night at the Value Inn. They hit the new vaporizer and walk over to the Mouse Trap for a late breakfast. Chicken fried steak with white gravy, eggs, hash browns. No sign of the gas station attendants.

The OJs turn to screwdrivers and they go from refreshed and rejuvenated to drunk and drowsy. Another blast furnace day. They hide out in the air-conditioned dark of the bar as long as they can. Then out by the pool, fading fast under a flimsy table umbrella.

'What are you reading?"

Capri looks up from her phone and improvises an answer.

"Interesting study of serial killers. There's a triad of behaviors that signal the likelihood of someone growing up to be a serial killer. Bedwetting, hurting animals, and starting fires. I only knew about the animals."

"I wonder what bedwetting has to do with it."

"Apparently it can be indicative of psychological issues stemming from sexual abuse or neglect." She lights a cigarette. "There's also fecal hoarding."

The bullshit explanation seems to satisfy him. She scrolls through her last few messages from Jamey. He's getting impatient. She texts him back, telling him everything is coming together. She'll have an update soon.

Her phone rings as she's holding it. It's the guy from the dispensary. Gerry. She'd entered the number off the business card so she'd know it was him when he called.

"This is Capri," she says.

"You need a license to drive a horse?" Guy says.

"Uh-uh. Don't need to fill 'em up with gas, either."

Harry and Guy canter down the dusty road. Past Stagg's Worm Farm. Past the site of the original Del Taco stand. Past a dumpster with a welcome mat in front of it.

The road runs along a railroad track where old Union Pacific train cars look stranded.

Slanted shacks hide behind bulwarks of corrugated metal. More than one have bobtail trucks in the driveway. Not quite a CinemaScope panorama, but Harry likes the idea of himself on horseback. A tall-in-the-saddle western hero riding into town on the trail of two fugitives.

The Bluebird Motel is at the far end of the strip. Harry helps Guy down and they hitch the horses to a post near a rock garden where an old woman is pressure-washing graffiti off a cactus. Outside the front office, someone has strung a chain of empty Tecate cans on a short pinyon pine, like an alcoholic Christmas tree.

The man who comes to the desk could be Bernard's double. He introduces himself as Francis. When Harry hands him Bernard's business card, Francis looks like he's never seen it before.

"One room or two?"

"One room, two beds," Harry says.

There's a key on every hook and no cars in the lot, but there's a lot of quiet deliberation as Francis decides what room to give them. It's Guy's turn to pay so Harry leaves him to it and walks across the street to the general store.

After procuring supplies, Harry sits on a bench outside the store, next to a Gatorade bottle half-full of dip spit. The town feels blown-through. A frantic woman stands on the side of the road gesturing to nonexistent traffic. A black dog limps by. Harry watches him make slow concentric circles in the dust, strategizing, like he's about to take the most important piss of his life.

He fills out a postcard to Ruby. There's nothing postcard worthy about Yermo, but the store had a couple for the Calico Ghost Town, a tourist attraction up the road. Harry picked one with a picture of Hank's Hotel, a ramshackle relic, and he writes Ruby that he's found a new place to dwell. He drops the postcard in a mailbox that looks like an abandoned vessel of correspondence.

When Harry gets back to the room, the air is thick with pot smoke and Guy is lying on his belly at the foot of his bed, laughing at a broad Spanish-language comedy on the TV. He's stripped to his boxers and the room smells like wide open ass.

Harry looks in the bathroom and finds a dead match floating over Conestoga wagon tracks in the toilet bowl. No dust on the plunger with him around. Whatever it is that comes out of Guy appears to be more like manure than anything human.

Harry lights the roach Guy left in the ashtray and rifles through the

219 \ ZIG ZAG

bag from the store.

The AC is kicking in. Harry regrets not packing his poncho. It'd be nice to take a couple tokes, hop in the shower, and stretch out on the bed in the cool room. But no poncho. It's a little skimpy for male company anyway. A robe would be ideal, but this isn't the kind of place that has them hanging in the closet.

In 1984, the one time he actually spent the night there, Harry stole a robe from the Chateau Marmont. It was plush, inches-thick, and Harry liked to swan around in it, bareass underneath. It made him feel like an emperor. He ruined it with a cigarette burn years ago and he still misses it.

"I got you somethin', Guy." Harry sails a straw cowboy hat across the room. "You're going to need one of these."

Guy squeezes the hat down on his head. It fits like a glove. A very tight glove.

Harry's looking at the channel numbers taped to the remote when his phone rings. Elmer.

"Pieces are moving on the board. You guys in the vicinity?"

"We're in Yermo, not far from—"

"Calico. I know where it is."

"Calico?" Harry was going to say Barstow.

"Calico Ghost Town. Had a big heyday during the silver rush. Walter Knott, of Knott's Berry Farm, turned it into a tourist attraction in the fifties. It's seen better days, but who hasn't."

"Right. I saw the postcards."

Harry mutes the TV while Elmer runs down the latest developments.

"My guy Gerry, from High Desert Wellness, is stalling the culprits. Told them he needed time to get some cash together. They're prepared to sell the whole dang lot of it. Dunces. He's supposed to call me back in a few hours. Wanted to get my sights on where you are. Figured Barstow. Why Yermo?"

"We hit a horseshoe."

"I don't follow."

"We hit a horseshoe in the road here and dinged up the tire. Car's in the shop 'til tomorrow."

"I have a guy works for Enterprise. Get you a deal on a rental."

"We've got a couple horses."

"Cut the monkeyshines. We need to figure this out."

"No monkeyin'. As of now, we're on horseback."

"So I'm trying to get our ducks in a row and you're out there gallivanting around, behaving as a cowboy?"

"Tell us where we need to be and when. We'll get there."

There's a silence on the line.

"Elmy?"

"I'm thinking a second here. This may work if I can finagle it."

"Finagle what?"

"I've been trying to set things up so the deal goes down at High Desert, but my guy's being extra careful. Belt and suspenders."

"It isn't a legal outfit?"

"It is. That's why the caution flag is out, A.J. Foyt. As a legal concern, they need to go through the proper channels, distribution-wise."

"And these ain't the proper channels."

"Not even close. This place just opened and the local law would love nothing more than to shut him down on a technicality. He doesn't need to invite scrutiny."

"So what's the finagle?"

"Well, I didn't think of it 'til Calico came up, but maybe we can shift operations."

"To Calico?"

"My pal Willy, the Calico Cat, operates out of memorabilia shop up there. Strictly a distribution hub, but..." Harry's listening but Elmer is talking more to himself, thinking out loud. "Deal like this...make it look like a standard pick-up...no police presence to speak of... puny security force..."

Elmer snaps back into direct conversation.

"Let me circle the wagons. Sit tight."

The line goes dead.

Guy is sitting up in bed now, eating a banana. He looks at the sticker on the peel. "Chiquita makes a good banana."

"You sound like Elmer."

"What'd he have to say?"

Harry tells Guy what Elmer had to say.

Guy searches Calico on his phone and pulls up a video on YouTube.

A drone shot lowers over an Old West mining town and a bed of canned saloon piano underscores peppy podunk narration, encouraging visitors to set aside a whole day for activities including playing checkers and relaxing in a rocking chair. A striped-cap coot engineers a choo-choo at three miles an hour through a rocky mountain pass.

Calico's main drag appears on the screen in a slow pan and Harry tells Guy to pause it. "Can you blow that up?"

Guy expands the frozen image to full screen. Willy's Western Memorabilia sits right next door to a blacksmith's shop. Looks open for business.

Half-hour later, Elmer calls and says he's got green lights all the way down the line. The deal is to go down at noon tomorrow. Harry and Guy should get there an hour early and be ready and waiting.

Harry hangs up and his phone buzzes again. Ruby's lap steel ringtone this time.

"Buenos dias from a lonely room, baby," he says. "Let me guess. You need help with the puzzle."

Sundays, Harry and Ruby do the *L.A. Times* crossword together, usually over a couple Bloody Marys at the Grotto, but she's getting a late start this morning.

"I haven't done it either," Harry says.

He fills her in on recent events—the bum steer south, the horseshoe, the horses, the detour to Calico. "Looks like line dancin' will have to wait. But we should be headed home sometime tomorrow night. I love you, darlin'."

Harry hangs up and takes the last sip out of his Tecate can. He shakes the empty.

"You said you saw a barroom a couple miles back?"

Guy says that he did.

RICK IS ACROSS the bar telling a Rick joke.

He pauses a second before the big punchline.

"The guy says, 'I got a brown house. I want to see what it'd look like with pink shutters.'"

Ruby sits with her Bloody Mary and her crossword, trying to drown him out. It's weird being at the Grotto without Harry but she misses him after the phone call and wants to keep up their usual routine.

It's the first Sunday they've been apart in months. It's usually a day of recovery from their boozy weekend and an evening of preparation for the week ahead. Harry makes breakfast and after coming home from the Grotto they nap or sink into the couch and watch bad TV.

Late afternoon they hit Ralph's. Ruby likes to make sure Harry has healthy food for the week. Left to his own vices and devices, dinner is a sleeve of Ritz, a jar of Skippy, and a six-pack. She bought him a smoothie maker, but he mostly uses it to blend up his tequila slushies.

If she's feeling generous, she'll press his shirts and do his laundry properly, separating the colors. When Harry does a load, he throws everything in there at once. That's why his whites are dingy.

Here comes Rick, no surprise. He slithers up to her, Sunday casual in a floral shirt and baggy cargo shorts. He pulls the celery stalk out of his drink and takes a bite.

"Sounds like Harry's having quite a time out there on the road."

Fuzzy is always polite, always a gentleman, but Rick seems incapable of not being an asshole. Ruby continues with the puzzle. The best way to deal with Rick is to ignore him, but today he won't be dissuaded.

He leans in to look at the puzzle and Ruby guards it with her arm like he's trying to cheat off her test. He continues on unfazed. The Grotto is quiet and there's no one else for him to bother.

"Last time I talked to him, his portly barrister sidekick was getting his dicky sticky in a Reno poon palace." Rick puts his hands up. "Don't kill the messenger. Just sayin'. When the cat's away, the mouse do play."

Ruby rolls her eyes. Fuck this guy. She ought to come out and say it. Harry wouldn't be mad. He'd probably high-five her. And Rick has no clue what he's talking about.

"What are you talking about, Reno? I just talked to him. He's not anywhere near Reno."

"That's not what I heard."

She tries to resist, but she can't pass up the chance to make Rick look stupid.

"Well, you heard it wrong. He's in some place called Calico as a matter of fact."

"Calico?"

Rick looks taken aback and Ruby realizes maybe she said something she shouldn't have. "Maybe it wasn't Calico," she says. "Maybe it was Calexico. I can't remember."

It's too late to backtrack.

"*Calico*," Rick says again.

41

"**M**R. KING."

A bellman from the Silver Legacy Resort Casino has been dispatched to check on the guest in Suite 1330. A few insistent knocks, then the "Mr. King" again, a tone of emergency this time.

Carvell's eyes slit. The room phone is off the hook on the nightstand. He gets up and wraps a blanket around himself. "King here," he says, standing at the door but not opening it.

The bellman identifies himself and Carvell opens the door enough for him to slip the message under the latch. Rick apparently contacted the desk. Carvell plugs in his phone and boots it up. Alerts for missed calls and texts stack on the screen. Shit.

He turns on a lamp and opens the blackout curtains. Sunshine. Looks at the phone again. Almost noon. He tries to orient himself.

The girl in the bed rolls over. Paulette? She looks older in the light. The other girl, can't remember her name, is in the fetal position on the floor, half-wrapped in a bedsheet. He looks around the room. Guns scattered everywhere. He must've been showing off last night. Lucky it wasn't the cops at the door.

Carvell pieces together what happened after he got back to the Rum

Bullions. By the time he realized the two girls were hookers on the make and not just being friendly, it was too late. He hit the ATM and took out eight hundred. The three of them blew through the rest of the speed and had to downgrade, sending out for Adderall around 4 a.m. The lowlife who delivered it to the room was some guy the girls knew. He tried to hang around and party but Carvell wasn't having it. That was when he brought the guns out, he remembers now. That got the guy out of there.

He runs the shower while he sits on the bowl and calls Rick. The news isn't good. Rick tells him to get moving and hangs up on him. Asshole. He dreads the thought of another long drive. Where the fuck is Calico anyway?

He steps out of his boxers, unwraps a plastic cup and chugs water to dull the raw burn in his throat. The mirror fogs over. He reaches into the shower, waving his hand under the spray before stepping in.

The water pummels his back, firehose pressure, better than home, and he leans his head against the wall. Booze and chemicals emanate from his pores. Things have gotten out of hand again. Time to rein it in. He runs his hand over his stomach. Chub beginning to envelop him. A gut. And a fleshy face now. Not defined like it used to be. It makes him look younger and older at the same time.

He holds his head under the blast. In the military it was pushups and cold showers first thing. Start the day with a cannon shot. Now it's all he can do to stay standing. He wants to sit on the floor and let the water run off him like a jetty but he's afraid he won't get up. The maid will find him hours from now, puckered and comatose. Ten-counted.

He manages a lather with the tiny tile of soap then gets to work with the mini shampoos and conditioners. His body is coming back to life but his head is clogged and heavy. He rockets crust-caked nostrils. The bluish residue hits the white floor like a paintball blast, fading in color as it sluices toward the drain.

A towel half-wrapped around him, he ushers the girls out of the room and sits on the bed collecting his thoughts. He pulls up the map on his phone. Another straight shot, another seven hours. He jots the broad strokes on resort stationery with a resort pen.

There's enough dust left on the room service menu to scrape together two thin blue lines.

CAPRI SAYS TO Ted, "The guy told me they never do buys at the dispensary. They do all their intake at a distribution facility in Calico."

Ted winces into the sun and thinks maybe he'll go for a swim. It's so hot he can't think straight. "Where's Calico?"

"Like twenty minutes from here. Some kind of ghost town."

"Seems like a weird place to do a deal."

"Could be why they want to do the deal there."

Capri types something into her phone. Is it Jamey she keeps texting? Is that who she was talking to last night? Ted is afraid what she'll do if he asks. He's not even sure he wants to know.

"They said noon tomorrow," Capri says. "That gives us plenty of time to figure out a game plan."

That makes Ted nervous.

"The game plan is to sell the stuff, right?"

"Right."

"You sure it's not a trap?"

"A trap by who? These people are hicks."

"Hicks have guns."

"So do we."

A mother and daughter come out to the pool area. Time to head back to the room.

They take cold showers and get dressed. Gerry from the dispensary told her to have the product packed in plastic storage containers so they find a Walmart and buy some plastic storage containers.

The sun is finally defusing but the heat still feels other-planetary. The air-conditioning in the car is better than air-conditioning in the motel so they drive around and smoke. Let things simmer.

Coming up on exit 194, there's an eighty-foot-tall ice cream sundae in the distance. Ted is so high he thinks it's a mirage. Then Capri sees it too. Towering over a rest stop that looks like a desert mission. A vista of gas pumps and charging stations. An asphalt sea. The sign says Eddie World.

Ted hits the blinker.

They wander the bright emporium. A vast food court harbors a maze of islands with volcanic candy mountains. Wax cola bottles, Atomic Fireballs, Red Hot Dollars. Rock candies that look like hard drugs. All wrapped in stickered Ziplocs. There are bigger bags with endless variations on popcorn and less popular displays devoted to jerkies, mixed nuts, and dried fruits.

Capri gets an iced coffee and Ted goes through each item on a gummy breakfast buffet: gummy waffle with a gummy pad of butter, gummy egg over easy, two strips of gummy bacon. She gets Sour Patch Peaches and a bag of Bit O' Honeys. He gets chocolate-covered pretzels coated with Reese's Pieces and a bag of green gumballs molded to look like tennis balls. There's a Sugar Daddy pop the size of a canoe paddle behind the register and Ted thinks about how badly he'd like to bend Capri over and spank her with it.

They sit and smoke in a far corner of the lot. The giant ice cream sundae is all lit up now and the grid of gas pumps glows like a power plant. They're not ready to leave this small pulse of civilization and go back to the isolation of the desert and the motel. They watch cars and trucks funnel down the exit ramp into the parking lot. People stretching and smoking and going inside to piss. Coming back out with bags of candy and cups of coffee.

Capri says they should get gas before they leave.

WILLY'S WESTERN MEMORABILIA is located at 7 Main Street, ten paces from the entrance to Downtown Calico. Like the radio ad says.

It hasn't always been a front. For years, Willy limped along like everyone else, surviving on tourist plankton. His nephew talked him into this set-up in 2008 when things were going south. It's a shipshape operation, serving a decent-sized market between Barstow and Baker. He works with people he trusts and there's nothing unusual about pieces of furniture being picked up and delivered at his loading dock. The same cheap antiques stuffed with contraband crossing and re-crossing the desert again and again.

Store transactions are cash only. There's an ATM built into a cigar store Indian shell. The extra cash flow has allowed Willy to broaden his inventory to include more authentic western artifacts, antiques, and historical documents. The online business is starting to pick up, which means more clean money coming through. They're even getting into some gold trading.

The front of the shop features the usual cultural flotsam. Made in China cowboy hats and Indian drums. Cheapo lassos. Knockoff Navajo blankets. A singing buck head on the wall. More expensive items are displayed in the back, along with an air-brushed Remington mural and a waxwork of Wild Bill Hickok jailed in a glass case.

The very back is where the real business takes place.

It's the night before the deal and Willy's nervous. This transaction is outside of normal proceedings. He stays out of the day-to-day, but tomorrow he will handle the deal himself, as a favor to his friend Elmer.

The exchange will happen at the same time as the High Noon In Calico show, when everyone will be on the main drag watching the performance. The product will be placed in shipping containers in the trunk of the car. The sellers will back up to the loading dock where the containers will be unloaded by Willy's men, supervised by Willy.

The inventory will be evaluated and, assuming all is on the up-and-up, Willy will excuse himself to go into his office for the cash. That's when the bondsman will step in and take over. For his part, Willy will take a ten percent cut of the inventory and get a discount rate on Elmer's Eatables for a period of one year.

Elmer had called again that afternoon, in fact. He assured Willy the bondsman and the barrister were good eggs who would handle things with no fanfare. Then he reminded Willy to keep his eyes peeled for his Stetson. "My wife gave me that hat," he said.

42

"SEE AMERICA BY horse," Harry says.

He and Guy are moving down the road at a slow trot, headed to the Sombrero Room. Harry fixes his attention on the horizon, humming the opening bars of "Wanderin' Star."

They continue on, stoned in the saddle, Harry's head bobbing metronomically to the clap of the hooves. He can feel the horse's labored movements beneath him. He figures the horses are probably twenty-five years old and thinks about how far they've come only to end up here, trudging through the heat. But he could say the same thing about him and Guy.

"Pretty amazing how Elmer knew exactly where you were from," Guy says.

"Almost to the town."

"I've never been there."

"Del Rio?"

"Texas."

"If you ain't been to Texas, you ain't been to Del Rio."

"What was it like growing up down there?"

"You ever seen *The Last Picture Show*?"

"No."

"It was a little like that."

Guy adjusts his hat.

"You ever think you'd go back?"

"Shit, I'd go back to Texas in a second if I thought I could break even." Harry stole that line from Guy Clark and he likes saying it, even if it isn't true. "I think Mexico's the plan long-term, though."

"To live?"

"Gone for good. Chuck it all. Not that there's much to chuck. I need to sell Ruby on the idea."

They don't have to do it right away, just have it as a plan. Something to look forward to. Scope out a coastal town where they can live cheap. He can see himself on a white beach with blue water. Fresh fish. Chickee umbrellas. Palm trees that don't look diseased. Finally kick the Tareytons and just have a big cigar at night. Live to a hundred like George Burns.

It'd be nice to be somewhere a few years behind. Spin off in another orbit.

The older he gets, the older he gets. Sometimes he worries Ruby's too young for the sunset ride. Things feel permanent with her, but they've felt permanent before. He doesn't want her to get sick of his routine. They usually do. Like he's a phase they go through. Then they go find someone nothing like him and he looks around for someone exactly like them.

He doesn't know how many fresh starts he has left in him. It hadn't dawned on him until fairly recently that he never thought to change the routine, only the women. Which eventually became another part of the routine. Ruby was a highlight, though, coming along at a time when he was feeling wrung-out and wasted, older than Abraham. She feels like a winning hand. Like he can walk away from the table and feel like he's coming out way ahead.

"They say Mexico's nice." Guy struggles with the horse's bridle, the cheap cowboy hat jammed on his head. "I've never been there."

"You'd fit right in."

"Margaritas and senoritas."

"Livin' on refried dreams."

Harry remembers the last time he and Ruby were down there together, drinking Coronas in the clear surf and dropping the limes in the water, watching swarms of silver fish chew them to the rinds.

They hitch the horses outside the bar. Harry wants to have a smoke before they go in. He lights a Tareyton and Guy tells him the charcoal smell reminds him of his dad.

Guy's old man got Harry started on the Tareytons. Terry was always trying to quit and every day he'd abandon a near-full pack at the bar. He tried to return them the first couple times, but Terry waved them away.

Harry couldn't afford to turn down free smokes, especially in those days, and he started taking to them. Finally made the switch from his Camels.

"Can I get one?"

Harry hands him the pack, along with a box of Elmer's matches. Guy gets it lit and takes a halted drag.

"How was he to work with?" Guy says.

"Terry?"

"Yeah. Was he hard on you?"

"I fucked up a bit but nothin' too bad. Usually blew over after a couple Heinekens."

"He liked Heineken because JFK drank it."

"He mentioned that once or twice."

"I miss him sometimes, but I started missing him before he was even gone. He was off the last couple years."

Harry remembers. Terry was a man unmoored in retirement. Floundering. Distant.

"After he stopped workin', it seemed like he was either drunk or he was over in Ireland," Harry says. "Or he was over in Ireland and he was drunk."

"Always drinking those airplane-sized bottles of whiskey. Tullamore Dew. We found them everywhere after he died."

"Imagine that," Harry says. "A bottle of whiskey the size of an airplane."

"You ever miss your dad?"

"Things remind me of him. My lucky marble. A shirt I bought the other day. Some movies."

"What was his name?"

"Harry."

"You're a junior?"

"I'm Harry Samuel and he was Harry William. Maybe he thought he'd give himself some plausible deniability." Harry crushes the cigarette under his boot. "He liked Irish whiskey too."

"You like Irish whiskey, Harry?"

"I know what it tastes like."

The Sombrero Room doesn't have Tullamore Dew. The only Irish on hand is Powers, which has been a fair-weather friend to Harry at best, but they decide to put their oars in the water anyway.

Guy looks solemnly into his double shot.

"There's no man bigger than this small glass."

Harry raises his. "You've got to swim before you fly."

"To Terry."

"Terry."

"And Harry."

"Harry."

They clink them and drink them.

"We should keep to beer after this," Harry says. "Big day tomorrow."

"Heinekens."

"Like JFK used to drink."

The Sombrero Room is Harry's kind of place. Pitch dark in the afternoon. Functioning cigarette machine. Betty the bartender is a honkytonk Madonna. Our Lady Of Denim Cutoffs And Red Cowboy Boots.

There's a country outfit onstage. The singer does an old Gary Mule Deer bit, dropping his guitar pick in the sound hole during the chorus of "Ring Of Fire." They finish that one out and start in on "Uncle John's Band."

"I followed the Grateful Dead for a while," Harry says.

"Yeah?"

"Never caught up to 'em, though."

"What do you mean?"

The hours disappear into the day-drunk ether. They order jalapeno poppers. Harry steps outside to feed and water the horses. Bernard loaded them up on hay at the garage earlier, but Harry gets some apples and carrots from the bar kitchen.

The bartenders are changing over and Harry offers to settle up with Betty before she goes so they can give her a tip. He watches the night man sign in at the register. Little peacock of a guy with a Marty Stuart haircut. Harry elbows Guy. "Look at this plastic saddle motherfucker."

"Hey, Hoss," Harry says.

Little Marty Stuart duckwalks over. "Another round?"

Guy says he'll have one more.

Harry indicates he'd like another.

"Never say, 'One more' to a bartender," Harry says. "Gives 'em somethin' to trip you up. We're havin' several more."

After several more, any notion of keeping things moderate and staying sharp for tomorrow has gone out the window. The idea was to have a couple afternoon belts and knock out early. Now they're still swinging in the later rounds.

Harry's better angels argue that each drink jeopardizes tomorrow's mission. That they should salvage what's left of the night and get back to the room. It's only a couple miles, but considering their condition, making the trip on horseback seems daunting. His devils tell him the night is too far gone to be redeemed. Ride it out. Face the music in the morning.

He compromises, downgrading from doubles to singles on the next round, but it hardly matters. Harry's drunker than who-shot-John and Guy is gutterball plastered, twenty minutes into another meandering tale of courtroom defeat.

"So he's banging his little judge hammer," Guy says, laughing. "Order in the court, order in the court."

"His gavel?"

"Right. His gavel."

"Don't you have to pass an exam to do what you do?"

"The bar."

"Right. The bar."

Harry checks his phone. Almost midnight. He counts on his fingers, calculating the hours of sleep still available to them. They don't need to be in Calico until eleven. So even if they're up another hour, they could get a solid six hours and get to the garage when it opens at eight.

He gets the bartender's attention, his finger making a slow, lopsided circle over the empties. The bartender tells them they drank every bottle of Heineken in the place.

"Guinness might not be a bad idea," Guy says.

Harry looks down the bar. The Guinness is on the same tap line as the rest of the beers, a bad sign, but they order two.

The pints come back faster than they should. They let them settle a second, then raise them and sip them.

"It ain't St. James Gate," Harry says. "But sturdy enough to keep the whiskey company."

Guy nods in agreement.

Half-hour later the lights come up and the bartender makes his way back around.

"Last call. You guys want another?"

"I'll do this again." Harry slides his sudsy pint glass forward. "I'll have a little shotski too." He pinches his thumb and forefinger in the air and squints at it. "Just enough to fill a hen's ear."

The bartender turns to Guy, impatient. "What'll it be?"

Harry elbows him. "Why don't you have one of them Foghorn Leghorns?"

"Fog Cutter?"

"A Fog Cutter!" Harry says. "Close it out in style."

The bartender sighs. "What's in it?"

Guy leans over the bar. "Let's see. Rum, gin..."

43

BEHIND THE MOTEL, Ted hunches in trunklight, digging the stash from the gutter of the spare. He hands the bales of weed to Capri and she stacks them in the plastic containers.

Once that's done they consider the Mouse Trap but don't feel like getting drunk again. There's a menu in the room for a Chinese place that delivers so they order in.

Capri picks at her food in silence, eyes locked on the TV. It's unsettling how quiet she's being about everything. All Ted wants is to be reassured tomorrow will go smoothly and everything will shake out okay after. It's a conversation that calms him like a bedtime story.

Whenever he brings anything up, she says they've already been over it. That the plan is in place. She says it's bad luck to talk about it, but he knows she's just dodging.

After dinner they smoke and eat their bags of candy in bed. Flipping from channel to channel. Capri passes out early but Ted can't sleep. He packs a bowl of Acapulco Gold and goes outside.

Stretched out on a deck chair next to the pool, looking at the sky, Ted tries to calm his racing thoughts. Out here the light is lighter and the dark is darker. Last night in the rain, the stars came on one at a time, pushing through the cloud cover. Tonight they look like stripper glitter.

The pool looks different too. Stagnant. The purple light a bruise on the surface.

He can't shake the feeling that they're coming to the end of something. Like it's the last night of vacation and everything is already packed up for the morning departure. They won't be going home after tomorrow, but they'll be going somewhere.

Where? And why won't she talk about it?

He tries not to worry about that. Or about the idea of Harry potentially being on their trail. Or Carvell. The Jamey thing is eating him, though. And anytime he asks, he's the asshole. The jealous bastard. There's no way to win there.

Ted blazes another bowl. Capri is right. Where they go, and how far, depends on tomorrow. How much money they make. Everything rides on that. If it goes right, they'll unload almost their entire haul—close to fifty-thousand, she says—and have enough left to smoke for a year. That's enough to get them started anywhere.

He's considered a few long-term options. One idea is to go to Vegas. Stay in a motel with a weekly rate and see what opportunities come their way. Capri could be a tradeshow model and he could get a job at a casino. Or he can work construction. That pays good money and something is always being torn down and rebuilt out there.

Maybe Vegas is too close. Where else is there? He's from California and she's from Arizona, so nowhere cold. Florida? Capri likes Disneyland but she's never been to Disney World. They could go there. Then down to Miami.

A CAR VEERS wide to avoid Harry and Guy as they canter in the direction of the Bluebird Motel.

Dizzied by the taillight blur, Harry leans over and pukes off the side of his horse. He wipes his mouth and takes a cautious look around, steadying himself with the saddle horn. He knows a guy who got a DUI on horseback in Chatsworth leaving the Cowboy Palace. They also hit him with an animal neglect charge for putting the horse in harm's way.

Lost the license. Lost the horse.

Guy isn't in much better shape. Chin on chest, he tilts dangerously to the left before snapping awake and righting himself. It was no easy task mounting these ponies outside the bar. Don't need him falling off now.

"Hang on, Counselor. We're only a mile out."

"I can't go on."

"Could be less than a mile."

"I can't see."

"Well, a horse ain't got no high beams." Harry points to the sky. "We've got to go by the light of the moon."

"I need to stop."

Guy performs a sloppy dismount and hits the ground hard. Three attempts and he finally hoists himself up, using the horse to keep his balance. He gestures toward the shrubs and sagebrush. "I say we set up camp and get started fresh in the morning."

"Set up camp?" Another car hurtles past. "We're in the midst of civilization."

"You go then. I'll catch up to you tomorrow."

Harry gives this serious consideration, but his conscience won't let him leave Guy to the elements. "Wouldn't want the Comanche to get you, pal. Tell you what, I'll double back to that gas station and get some supplies."

Guy is already staggering into the darkness, dragging the horse by its bridle.

Harry guides his horse toward the beacon of the ampm. He nudges the nag to a near-gallop and feels the wind sober him a bit. He always feels like a million after he throws up.

Outside the store two strung-out kids on a parking block look at him like he's been beamed in from another century.

Entering the convenience store is like walking into direct sunlight. Harry's dimmers dim. Cherry slush swirls in the mixer, revved up like a washing machine. He procures a few sundries and grabs a couple packets of travel aspirins from the rack.

Returning, he half-expects to find his partner face down in the sand, his horse gone. He's surprised to find Guy has constructed a capable makeshift campsite. His horse is tied to a short tree. He's got a bright fire going.

Harry hitches his horse next to Guy's and sets a six-pack of Tecate on the ground. "You got us pretty well arranged, Counselor. How'd you manage it?"

He lobs Guy a beer and misses him by a mile.

"I was a Boy Scout." Guy roots around in the dark for the can. He cracks it open and laps the foam off the mouth.

"Got a couple taquitos off the roller. Some of these too." Harry shakes a bag of Haribo Twin Cherries. "Looks like a goddamn slot machine, don't it?"

GUY JABS A stick in his taquito and browns it over the fire. He threw up while Harry was gone and it stopped the spins. It'll be good to get something in his stomach to soak up the rest of the whiskey while he sleeps.

He washes down his taquito with another lap of beer. "You underestimated me."

Harry lies on his side and lights a cigarette. He throws the dead match into the flame. "Meanin'?"

"The campsite."

"You going to milk this? I told you, you got us well arranged."

"*Well arranged.*"

"Bein' underestimated is a good thing, Guy. Like Columbo. Let them think you're a little slow, a little behind. It puts their guard down." Harry cracks his can. "Sometimes with me, I don't know if it's an act."

"Amanda always told me I was lazy," Guy says. "Terry too."

"More harm in this world has been done by the ambitious than the lazy. The great villains of history were all self-starters. There's nobility in doing nothin'." Harry struggles to his feet. "I've got to water the cactus."

He steps into the darkness then weaves back into the reach of the firelight.

"Maybe I should have been a park ranger or something," Guy says. "Out here my skills are valued. If I wasn't here, you'd be out of luck."

"If you weren't here, I'd be back at the motel." Harry stretches out on the ground. "We need to get back first thing. I don't want to miss the continental breakfast."

"Why do they call it a continental breakfast?"

"Means it's free."

Guy lies flat on his back.

Except for the odd car or eighteen-wheeler chugging past, it's quiet and peaceful. Whenever he and Amanda came camping out here, they talked about how they could stay forever, just the two of them. He remembers when they rented the homesteader's cabin with the hot tub. Drinking prosecco under a planetarium sky. That hike when they saw the sidewinder snake. Guy picking her up and carrying her out feeling heroic.

This is the first time he's been able to remember something like that without getting too sad about it. It makes him think he may be moving out of that period into something better. Not like the false starts of the past, where it was only weeks or days before he'd fall into the old routines again. Beached on the couch, overserving himself, sweatpants pulled up over his belly. He wants to try for real this time.

Guy stares at the sky, lost in the stars, drifting off. Under that vast expanse, forty doesn't seem so old. May not even be the halfway point. Terry made it past 80. A lot of that stuff is genetic.

The spins come on again and he closes his eyes. His dreams, when he remembers them, are usually just tweaked versions of whatever happened during the day. Like each event plants a seed that blossoms and tangles into strange shapes in his mind at night. It feels like one world rubbing up against another.

44

WAKING UNDER THE pointed dome of a rented teepee, Carvell regrets not following through on an impulse he had earlier.

Passing through Carson City, he considered the possibility of turning east on Route 50, America's loneliest highway, and disappearing into the void of Utah. Become a cop in some unincorporated town. Build a compound, start a sex cult.

The card on the nightstand reminds him he's at the Olancha RV Park and Motel. He remembers thinking it was a joke when the guy told him the only room they had left was a teepee. He checks his phone. 8:00 a.m. A good ten hours of sleep. He needed it.

There are more missed calls and texts from Rick. Asshole. The bum steer to Reno is on him. If he catches up with Capri and Ted, and that's doubtful at this point, he isn't going to give Rick a dime of whatever he recovers.

He checks the map. Calico is only two hours south. He's already come this far. May as well follow the trail to the end. Maybe the intel is good this time. If not, he'll be back in Van Nuys by this afternoon.

In a Texaco bathroom he crushes what's left of his Adderall on the toilet tank and dustpans it into the empty prescription bottle. That way he can do the pen cap dip-and-scoop while he drives. No more hammering out gravelly lines on the dash. Breakfast is two sausage biscuits and two hash brown patties from a McDonald's drive thru. The syrupy fizz of the Coke is rejuvenating.

An hour-and-a-half in, he sees signs for Las Vegas and Needles and thinks the Las Vegas Needles would be a good name for a metal band. When he turns east, the landscape flattens and the road feels like an endless runway, the Crosstour taxiing indefinitely. On a barren stretch not far from Calico something is scattered in his path and his combat reflexes kick in. Situational awareness.

The car swerves and skids then straightens out.

"Fucking horseshoes in the road," he says.

"I TAKE COMPLETE responsibility, you understand, but there's nothing I can do." Bernard is flustered. "Part is en route from Victorville as we speak. I can have you up and running this afternoon."

"Too late, Bernie," Harry says. "We need to be movin' now."

They're already behind schedule. The blame for that lies squarely on Guy. He's the one who set up camp in the desert last night. Who insisted on stopping at the ampm for his Bud Clamato hangover cure this morning. Who delayed their departure another twenty minutes barricading himself in the bathroom taking a shit that sounded like a shotgun suicide.

Bernard puts his hands up. "I'm at a loss here."

Elmer's instructions were clear. Get to town at eleven, an hour before the deal is to take place. It's just after ten now. Calico is only a few miles away but that's a lot longer by horse than it is by car.

"How about you?" Harry says. "You have a car?"

"Right outside."

Bernard points out the shop window at a rusted husk on blocks. It's surrounded by a moat of shattered glass and has been stripped of everything, even its paint

"It's like they say about the cobbler," Bernard says. "He ain't even got his own pair of shoes."

Harry turns to Guy. "Time to get back in the saddle, partner."

Guy is defiant. "Not me."

"Don't act like I dragged you along. I told you at the outset I wanted to go it alone."

"I didn't know we'd be riding horses."

"You think I did?"

"My back is killing me. I'm never getting on that horse again."

"The horse will be happy to hear that."

"Fuck you, Harry. If you want to go it alone so bad, you can do it now. I'm going back to the room."

"Suit yourself."

OUTSIDE THE PASSENGER window, the scenery seems to run on a loop. Everything dead and tan and dry. Capri wants to drop a match and set fire to all of it.

Ted adjusts his hands on the wheel. "So where are we going after this?"

Capri feels a tinge of sadness knowing there will be no after this. Not for them. "Let's focus on making sure this goes over," she says, unable to look Ted in the eye.

It's weird to think about never seeing him again but there are lots of people she's never seen again. People she knew longer than Ted.

She survived. Most of them survived.

There is one person she will see again. Even though she swore she never would.

Jamey got to town yesterday. He checked into a motel not far from where they were staying. He texted her a few times trying to change her mind about today.

Jamey doesn't like the Calico plan. Too many chances for things to go wrong. Last night he said they should make a break for it. Load the weed in his trunk and aim the car toward Florida.

She told him no, the plan was set. Up to him if he was in or out.

It's easier to be in control with Ted than it is with Jamey. She needs to stick to her guns and not let him take over. He can have a bigger role in the Florida deal with his uncle. Until then, this is her show.

She hasn't decided what will happen after that. If she and Jamey continue down the road together, try Miami for a while, or if he's just the next stepping-stone on her way across the river. Part of her regrets involving him at all.

She went to bed early last night but didn't sleep well. When she woke up at one a.m., Ted was gone. She thought he might've gotten jumpy and run out on her but then she saw him sitting out by the pool.

"How about a cruise?" Ted says. "The Bahamas or somewhere. Some of them have casinos. And a pool. A pool on a boat."

"It's a ship, not a boat."

"What's the difference?"

"You can put a boat on a ship. You can't put a ship on a boat."

One of her mother's boyfriends, a Navy man from San Diego, taught her that.

They drive by the Half Moon Motel, where Jamey is staying, and she sees a Honda with Arizona plates parked in front of Room Six. It makes her nervous knowing he's on the other side of that door. That these are the final moments of being able to change course.

"Let's do this one straight-up," Ted says.

"Whatever."

"I'm serious. Let's not do another Elmer thing here. We sell the stuff and go. Deal?"

"As long as they're cool, I'll be cool."

Another Elmer thing is exactly what she has in mind. When the buyers take out their money, she'll take out her gun. Then Jamey will appear. Element of surprise. He'll hold his gun on them while she grabs the weed back, plus all the money they have. Ted will probably hightail as soon as the guns come out. Either way, she and Jamey will be out of there before Ted even knows what happened.

Then, go to Florida in style. With a chunk of change plus the merchandise. The deal with Jamey's uncle will be the third time she's sold this same score. Like the joke her mother used to make about the whore. You sell it and you still got it.

"How about Miami?" Ted says.

That stops her for a second. There's no way he knows. He never could've played it cool and casual like this. The second he got wind of it he would've freaked.

"Miami?" she says.

"As somewhere to go after this. It's warm. There's cool clubs and beaches. We could get ourselves set up down there."

"Florida is a shithole," she says. "I'd never fucking live there."

HARRY RIDES ON alone, cantering north on Calico Road.

The sun climbs higher in the sky, hotter by the second. The campfire smell from last night is clinging to him. The hangover is hanging on too. Hopefully he sweats it out.

It's quiet on the trail without Guy. He hums the riff to "1983... (A Merman I Should Turn To Be)," the thirteen-minute psychedelic crown jewel of *Electric Ladyland*. Another old road trip staple and time machine back to the acid days. Nederhoffer stoned in the passenger seat, eyes closed, lost in the ebbtide. The two of them singing *straight ahead* along with Jimi, aiming the car toward the frontier and imagining the year 1983 way off in the future.

He's not worried about backup. It's likely Ted will surrender and go quietly. The owning-the-Grotto thing is bullshit. He'll never collect on that. He's a renter, not an owner. The bar tab is the real collateral. He's thrown some money at it over the years but even the ballpark figure is considerable. Deliver on this and he'll be sitting pretty on barstool mountain for some time. Maybe forever. Better than owning the place.

Approaching the 15 overpass, Harry feels a presence behind him. Someone on his trail. He halts his horse on the shoulder, beneath a stationary wind turbine, and turns to look. A horseman approaches in the distance. The horse has the demeanor of a whipped mule. The rider looks worse for wear as well.

Guy sulks in the saddle, scowling under the brim of the cheap souvenir cowboy hat that seems to draw instead of deflect the sun. It looks like he has half a mind to Frisbee it into the desert. But he showed up. Give him that.

Coming up on Harry, Guy has trouble halting his horse.

"Don't pull the reins so hard, just tighten your grip," Harry says. "Squeeze your legs. There you go."

They stare each other down a second.

"Decided to ride along?"

"Wouldn't want the Comanche to get you," Guy says.

Harry grins.

"Let's ride."

CAPRI AND TED pull off the 15 and head north on Calico Road.

The old tourist signs remind Capri of another one of her mother's ex-boyfriends, a western history buff named Fritz who wore safari jackets and smelled like bug spray. He took them on a trip to Tombstone one time. Her mom met him through a dating site in a period when she was sober and working an office job.

Capri remembers a conservative cut and color, talk of nursing school, but it wasn't long until she was back picking up housecleaning jobs during the day and cocktailing at night in bars polluted with degenerate men. Fritz was boring. His accent wasn't sexy or exotic. It just made him sound overly serious. He was good to her mother and made some fatherly efforts with her but the two of them were too far gone to be redeemed by Fritz.

Ted pulls wide around two men on horseback, passing them on the left.

"Look at these assholes," Capri says. She leans over the center console and drops a hard palm on the horn. Ted looks intently in the rearview and mouths something to himself.

"What?" Capri says.

Ted says it's nothing, but he looks worried. His nerves must be eating him.

It'll all be over soon.

IT'S A LONG straight stretch beyond the overpass. Heat waves shimmer off the asphalt. Billboard skeletons stand like scarecrows in a moonscape.

A car weaves past, the driver leaning heavy on the horn. It sounds like a freight train to Harry but the horses don't have the energy to spook.

"How you feelin', Counselor?" Harry says.

"I'm tired but I'm awake."

"I'm awake but I'm tired."

"I still feel drunk," Guy says.

"We were visited by spirits last night."

"That's it for me," Guy says. "No more heavy drinking for a while. I need to taper down. I might do sober October in the fall."

"That's ambitious."

Harry rolls up his sleeves and double-checks that his holster isn't visible on his belt. As a man who normally tucks in, he feels unfinished with the long tails of his new Rancher hanging out. It's compounded by the fact that he bought the shirt because it was the same kind his father used to wear. H.W. Robatore never went untucked.

253 \ Zig Zag

"Today's the big day, Counselor. No more dilly-dallyin'. Are you ready?"

"I'm ready," Guy says.

"Man and mouse."

The half-assed pep talk is as much for himself as it is for Guy. Harry just wants to go home. His living room is an oasis in the visible distance. A postcard seascape. WISH YOU WERE HERE embroidered into the couch cushions.

"Man and mouse," Guy says.

They make decent time in the final mile. Up ahead, CALICO is written on the mountainside in giant letters. Guy points it out to Harry.

"That's where we're goin'," Harry says.

"What happens when we get them? How are we going to bring them back?"

"We commandeer their vehicle."

"What about the horses?"

"They can ride in the trunk."

Approaching Calico, they pass a shabby covered wagon and a tall wooden sign featuring a prospector leaning on a shovel and pointing up the hill. The prospector is riddled with bullet holes. More rotted-out wooden signs are staggered down the road, meant to build excitement as you get closer.

TAKE AN HISTORIC TOUR.

EXPERIENCE AN OLD WEST ADVENTURE.

COME UP THE HILL AND STEP BACK IN TIME.

HORSE OPERA

45

FROM HIS VANTAGE point on the ridge, Carvell can see Calico laid out in its entirety. The Boot Hill Cemetery to the west, the old Silver King mine to the east. Behind him, steep rocky cliffs climb toward the big *CALICO* lettering stenciled on the mountaintop.

This may have been a town once, but it isn't now. He's never heard of a town that charges an eight dollar admission fee. The plan was to check in somewhere, but Hank's Hotel is only an exterior. A cowboy movie set. Like the fake stagecoach stand and the fake blacksmith's shop and pretty much everything else on the wide main drag leading up to the hill he's standing on.

Whoever spun Rick's arrow this way got bad information.

Tourists peer in the windows of the old church just below him on the hill. Others pose for photos in front of the Glass House, made of thousands of empty bottles glinting in the sun. Carvell mops his brow. He's sweating through his uniform, still winded from the short hike up here.

A whistle sounds. He watches a train round the bend and pull into the station. A wooden sign advertises a five dollar tour and he decides it's easier to get the lay of the land that way.

Walking toward the depot he sees the 15 freeway in the distance and imagines he'll be driving west on it soon enough. Then back to Lemke, hat in hand. Another fuck-up on his record.

He boards the train with four other passengers and walks to the rear car, setting his shoulder bag on the seat beside him. Inside the bag is a bottle of water, two energy bars, a steel-plated Valkyrie vest, and a CZ Scorpion EVO3 sub-gun with three clips of ammunition.

The Scorpion is a light 9mm piece, five pounds, with a folding stock that allows it to function as a pistol or rifle. Could probably take out the whole town with it.

The conductor sits catatonic at the controls while a voiceover recording does the tour guiding. Two characters, Hard Rock Harris and Harriet, give a hokey history lesson with *Hee Haw* music cues punctuating the jokes. Carvell and the other riders learn about the silver rush, the boom and bust, the fates of the early Chinamen.

The train rumbles past old silver mines dug out like snake holes in the mineral-stained mountainside. The swirls of colors gave the town its name. "As purdy as a gal's calico skirt," Hard Rock Harris says in a bucktooth drawl.

Throughout the tour, Carvell eyes potential escape routes, hideouts, and positions of advantage. He does this everywhere he goes. Locates all entrances and exits. Every area of higher ground. He notes the bell tower on the town hall. The second-story balcony over the saloon.

The train labors through the final tunnel and comes to a raspy stop. The conductor removes his striped cap and sets it out for tips, reminding everybody not to miss the High Noon In Calico show coming up.

Back on the dusty drag, an empty Coke can blows by like a tumbleweed. The Calico House Restaurant looks real enough and open for business. Carvell decides he deserves a second breakfast before the three-hour drive home.

That's when he sees Capri and Ted on the other side of the street.

THE WOMAN AT the ticket booth waves Harry and Guy around the line of cars and says the performers for the High Noon In Calico show are to report to the lot next to the train depot. Harry gives an affirmative nod and they canter past. He was worried about a hold-up with the horses, so that's a break.

He checks his phone. Almost eleven-thirty. Behind schedule but not too late.

Climbing the hill past the RVs and tour buses on the outskirts of the lot, it already feels like peak midafternoon heat. They ride on through the main parking area where families with young kids are exiting their vehicles and swarming the entrance.

The open space next to the train depot looks like an old studio back-lot. Saloon girls sweating in frilly dresses, capgun cowboys twirling their pistols, a mustachioed bandito X-ed out in bullet belts. There's a square-jawed man on a white horse who appears to be the star of the show. He wears a Halloween sheriff's badge and bright silver Roy Rogers spurs.

Harry and Guy continue on toward Willy's Western Memorabilia.

On the main drag, Harry is struck by how inauthentic everything looks. Calico evokes a 1980s theme park more than an 1880s frontier town. Morricone Muzak blares over the PA speakers as cheap props are wheeled out and more actors half-heartedly play their roles. Three outlaws in dusters, a toothless old prospector cast from the local drunk tank, an undertaker hammering a wooden casket.

In front of the Calico House Restaurant, a low-rent Lash Larue bullwhips the dust to the delight of a group of kids sitting in rocking chairs on the porch. A man in a long-billed cap snaps a photo of Harry and Guy. A tourist thinking they're a tourist attraction.

"Let's veer off here and stay out of sight," Harry says, feeling like a jackass. "Willy's is just ahead but we're cuttin' it close."

THE LAST TEXT Capri got from Jamey, twenty minutes ago, said he was ten minutes out, which means he must be here somewhere.

She and Ted are checking out Willy's Western Memorabilia, where the deal is set to go down. It's an ordinary gift shop. Cowboy and Indian crap, cactus candy, pouches of chocolate coins. An animated mannequin in a shaggy mustache and scarecrow outfit plays guitar with a slow hand, his mouth moving out of sync with his lines.

Here's a song about an old cowboy whose ridin' days are behind him.

"Let's get out of here," Capri says.

Outside she sneaks a look at her phone. A text from Jamey. He's here. Having a drink in the Calico Saloon. She thinks of an excuse to sneak away.

"Gerry said to call when we got to town, but he didn't say there's no service here." She holds her phone to the sky like she's trying to catch reception. "Maybe it's better over there."

She crosses the street toward the Calico Saloon.

Ted calls to her, pointing at his phone. "I've got three bars. Wait a minute."

Capri keeps walking, picking up her pace to cross ahead of an oncoming herd of skinny cows being led through town by cowboys on horses. The cowboys are whooping and hollering like you see in movies.

A runty guy in red long-johns staggers through the swinging doors. He waves a bottle around, hamming it up. Capri brushes past him.

It's dim and cool inside the saloon. Wanted posters on the wall. A green velvet poker table. She sees Jamey as soon as she walks in. Sitting at the bar with a bottle of beer.

Jamey stands out in the small crowd of tourists. He has his back to the door and hasn't seen her yet. She feels a drop in her stomach. The rush of trouble. He looks broader in the shoulders, bulkier, with a thicker neck. All muscle, though. Not an ounce of fat.

She sees him notice her in the mirror. He turns around. His face looks older, more weathered, but better looking. There's a harder edge to him she thinks is hot. The high and tight haircut is new. So is the neck tat. He sits with his legs apart looking her up and down. The same hungry eye-fuck as always.

She catches him flex a little when he flashes that coyote smile.

"Hey, babe," he says.

"You ready?" She keeps it all business. This isn't a romantic rendez-vous. Not yet. She looks over her shoulder. "I need to get out of here. Just making sure you're good to go."

"You sure you want to do this?"

She doesn't acknowledge that.

"I just checked out the store," she says. "It looks like you'll be able to walk right through to the back. If you run into trouble, that's what the gun is for. You have it?"

Jamey nods toward his belt.

"Okay, good," she says. "Did you park where I told you to?"

Jamey gives her a weary look.

"Did you fucking park where I told you to?"

"I parked out back," he says. "By the loading dock. Like you said."

"Good."

Capri checks over her shoulder again.

"What, is your boyfriend coming?" Jamey cranes his neck. "I want to get a look at this loser."

Capri is surprised to feel a spark of defensiveness. An instinct to stand up for Ted even as she's about to betray him. "Just be where I told you to be when I told you to be there," she says. "And be ready to shoot your way out if things go bad."

HARRY AND GUY turn down an alley that leads to the lot behind the storefronts.

Harry is clear on the instructions. Come around to the loading dock and wait by the rear entrance until Willy gives the signal. At noon Ted and the girl will back up to the dock like a routine delivery.

Once everyone's inside, the fugitives will be apprehended, quick and discreet as possible. Elmer hammered home the fact that Willy wants no trouble and is only doing this as a personal favor to him. And that he wants his Stetson back.

Harry's not sure what Ted's driving but the plan is to take it. Drive back to the garage and pick up the car. Let Bernard arrange to retrieve the ponies. Assuming it isn't stolen, Guy can drive their car back to

Van Nuys and he can take Ted in the Olds.

He hasn't decided what to do with the girl yet. It might be better for everyone if she turns tail and runs. Harry's only objective is to bring Ted back and stand him before the judge. Protect his investment. If all goes as planned, they could be out of here by twelve-thirty. He may make it home in time to see Ruby before she leaves.

They're coming up behind Willy's. There's no attempt at period detail back here. Concrete loading docks with truck bumpers, trash-compacting dumpsters, a parking lot filled with dust-covered beaters. One car stands out among the rest. A tricked-out Honda Crosstour with a Keyes plate frame and a big red Semper Fi sticker.

It looks familiar. Harry leans in to take a squint at it.

There's a stack of *Soldier of Fortune* magazines on the passenger seat, crowned by a military watch cap.

Carvell.

It hadn't occurred to him until now that Big Smoke may have sent out their own search party. Probably why they downplayed the robbery to the cops. Wanted to handle it internally.

This could complicate things.

46

I N THE MEN'S Room of the Calico Saloon, Carvell peers through a crack in the door, watching the bartender watch Capri. The same dog-at-the-door look guys at the dispensary give her.

She's talking to some dude sitting there having a beer. Looks like an ex-con. She must've left Ted outside. He notices a bulge in the waistband of her skimpy denim shorts. She's carrying.

What kind of game is she playing here? And where's the weed at?

When he first spotted Capri and Ted on the other side of the street, they were too busy looking at their phones to notice him standing there. He ducked into the saloon to get out of sight and stood watching from the window, plotting his next move.

Then she started walking right toward the place.

He debates whether to apprehend her now or tail her until she leads him to Ted and the merchandise. Even if she pulls out that popgun, it's no match for what he's carrying.

The bartender looks like a putz. He won't be a problem. And what kind of fight could these tourists possibly put up? Most of them aren't even American. Fucking Canadian maple leaves all over their backpacks. Like that's something to be proud of.

Just do it now. Get this shit over with.

Carvell goes into a toilet stall and dumps the rest of the Adderall out on the tank. Four thick blue rails disappear up his nose in four seconds. The bulletproof feeling is back but he still straps on the body armor. He also grabs his phony badge. That and the uniform should suffice if anyone asks any questions.

The Scorpion is ready to go. He holds it down by his side, on the pistol setting, and exits the stall. He cracks the door again. Capri is still standing there talking to the ex-con. Once he gets her alone and gets the weed back he'll put a hurt on her.

If he does this job right, with a balance of force and restraint, plus full recovery of the merchandise, it will go a long way with Lemke. He'll be back in action. He takes a breath and steps through the door. He locks eyes with Capri and watches the recognition and surprise register on her face.

Then a look of rage.

Carvell holds up his badge, identifies himself as law enforcement, and asks if she wants to do this the easy way or the hard way. He nods in the direction of his weapon and watches her hand closely to make sure she's not reaching for hers.

Turns out he watches too closely. He doesn't notice the skillethead ex-con pulling out his piece until it's too late. Before Carvell can blink, they both have guns up.

The tourists in the bar go into full panic. Carvell upends a poker table and dives behind it in a tight shoulder-roll.

APPROACHING THE LOADING dock, Guy spots an old man in a straw hat with a toothpick jumping in his mouth. "That must be Willy," he says.

Harry tips his brim and Willy gives them the go sign.

Then they hear what sounds like a gunshot followed by another gunshot.

At first Guy thinks it might be the wild west show starting up. But something about it doesn't sound right. The look on Willy's face confirms it.

Two more shots ring out, followed by a staccato blast of gunfire.

"That's semi-automatic," Harry says.

The horses are riled and the air is pierced by the sound of more shots and people running and screaming. Willy bolts inside as Harry reins in his horse and unholsters his gun. "Stay out of sight, Guy. Looks like things aren't going according to plan."

Harry takes off at a full gallop and Guy's horse jerks around, making that sneezy whinnying sound. Guy sits there a second feeling useless. If Harry had any faith in him, he would've given him a gun to carry. But here he slumps on the sidelines.

He keeps talking about making a change. Here's a chance to stop being a tagalong. Ditch the defeatist thinking. Show up and fight. That's what Amanda used to tell him when he was bracing himself for another skewering in court. You walk in thinking like a loser, looking like a loser, guess what, you're going to lose.

It'll be over before it even begins.

Thirty seconds go by without another shot. Guy grabs the reins on his horse, gives himself one last kick in the ass, and gets moving.

Rounding the corner, he sees tourists ducking in entryways, trying to get a look at what's happening in the street. Cowboy actors on horseback make a run for the parking lot, their toy guns useless against the threat of real bullets.

Harry is fast approaching the Calico Saloon where Ted is darting back and forth on the sidewalk out front, eyes wide, like a squirrel with a truck coming toward it.

A guy and girl crash through the saloon doors and walk back-to-back, guns up, slowly making their way toward an alley leading to the rear parking lot. They're almost there when the shooting starts up again, this time from the second-story balcony above the saloon. It's a man in uniform but there's no way that's a cop.

The couple races away from the gunfire and toward Guy.

When Guy yanks the reins to dart right, he hears a sharp screech like rusty train wheels braking. His horse lurches forward and collapses underneath him. Then he feels a sudden, searing pain. A branding iron driven through his gut. He tries to breathe but it's like there's a vacuum in his throat.

He looks down and his shirt is black with blood.

CAPRI AND JAMEY crouch behind the telegraph office.

Windows shatter and wooden planks split and splinter around them. It's a glorified phone booth and Capri knows it's a matter of seconds before the whole thing collapses in on itself.

Jamey glances around the corner between shots.

"Who the fuck is this guy?"

"The security guard from the dispensary."

Capri can feel the plan crumbling in her hands. She tries to rein in her panic.

"Isn't your boyfriend the one who robbed the place? Why is this guy only shooting at us?"

"Probably because we shot him," Capri says. "Aim for the head next time."

She points to a small church halfway up the hill. The idea is to get there, gather themselves another second, then bolt down the other side toward the train station. From there it's a straight shot to the parking lot.

If they don't make it back to the car before Ted does, it's all over.

The only thing standing between them and the church is a house on the hill that looks to be made entirely of glass bottles. It reflects the sun at strange intense angles. Capri hopes it has a blinding effect that can buy them an extra second.

They make a break for it.

When they sprint past the glass house, bullets pinging the sand and gravel around them, it sounds like a cement mixer crashing through a jewelry store window. Capri feels a sharp pain in her lower back. She's not sure if it's a bullet or a shard of glass.

No time to stop and look.

They make it to the church and zero in on the most direct path to the parking lot. Capri winces in pain and Jamey tells her the gash on her back looks serious. He takes off his shirt and wraps it around her waist. Blood soaks right through. She raises her gun and squeezes off a shot in frustration.

"C'mon, babe," Jamey says. "All that's left is to get down that hill. You can lay down in my car and I'll unload the shit from yours. Give me the keys."

"I don't have the keys."

"What do you mean you don't have the keys? How do you not have the keys?"

"He drove! I was going to get them when we unloaded the trunk."

"Jesus Christ," Jamey says.

"You can't break into a car? Shoot the fucking trunk open."

Jamey gives her a look he's given her before. A look like she's the stupidest piece of shit he's ever seen. Like she's never gotten anything right in her life.

"I knew you'd fuck this up," he says.

Her mouth is dry but she manages to hawk up enough to spit in his face. He grabs her by the wrist and drags her toward him.

"What the fuck is wrong with you?" he says. "Are you trying to get us both killed?"

She bites down hard on his forearm and rakes her nails across his bare chest.

Then he hits her. Open hand, no fist. But hard. She reels from the force of it, even though she was expecting it, baiting him to do it. She tastes blood on her lip and looks at him standing there, that condescending look still smeared all over his face, like he's expecting her to apologize for something.

Over Jamey's shoulder, she sees Ted running up the hill toward the mining tunnels. She screams out to him but he's too far off to hear.

"You trying to fuck me now?" Jamey says, his mouth crooked, his eyes lit up with anger. "You think he's going to save your ass?"

Jamey raises his gun and takes aim at Ted just as Carvell's shooting kicks back into gear.

Capri uses all her strength to shove Jamey out into the spray.

CARVELL PEERS THROUGH the Cyclops scope at the body on the hill.

It looked like they were trying to make a break for it, but then it was just the dude lunging out from behind the church, directly into the line of fire. He caught three or four shots, snaking around like a cut powerline, before falling flat on his back on the hill.

One down.

He can't believe he let the two of them get the jump on him like that in the saloon. The body armor protected him, but he was hit twice. Probably why his aim was off and he took down that fat fuck on the horse. Still, he's pretty sure he tagged Capri when he blew that glass pagoda or whatever the fuck to smithereens.

He puts the Scorpion on the three-shot setting and trains it back on the church.

When he opens fire this time, he shifts into a new gear. The reins are cut and he's in the control of something outside himself. He peels off more and more shots, shells popcorning over his shoulder as he burns through the rest of the thirty-round magazine.

Under his body armor, Carvell can feel bruises blooming on his shoulder and side. The Adderall effects are waning. There's none left but it doesn't matter. If he manages to shoot his way out of here, he'll be sailing on enough adrenaline to rob a CVS.

He snaps in a fresh clip and Capri finally shows herself. It looks like she's going through the dead guy's pockets. Picking the bones before running off and leaving him there. Cold.

Carvell chops the bolt release as Capri approaches the brink of the hill. He has a clear bead on her when shots are fired from below and a sharp stab in his side spins him around.

Down in the street, a man on a horse is holding a gun. It takes a second to make out the gaunt face under the hat. Carvell levels his weapon unsteadily, trying to line up a killshot.

Harry squeezes the trigger again.

TED RACES THROUGH a mining tunnel looking for a shortcut to the other side of the mountain.

His heart sledgehammers in his chest when the tunnel dead-ends at a staged digging site. Car crash dummies in overalls lean on pickaxes and a hand-painted sign threatens all claim jumpers with death by hanging. A rusty mine cart sits stranded on dead rails. Ted imagines an Indiana Jones escape before turning around and running back the way he came.

Collapsed skeletons and boxes of dynamite lurk in the shadows. A kid wouldn't even find this shit scary under normal circumstances but right now it only adds to Ted's terror. The tunnel forks and he heads left without thinking.

He finds an exit and passes a family cowering by the turnstile. A mother and father shield a boy in a wheelchair. Ted raises his hands to show he's not carrying anything but his car keys.

Outside he bolts past the saddle shed toward the train depot.

There's more gunfire and he stops for half a second to look. It's hard to see in the sun but it looks like there's a dead body on the hill.

At the train depot he jumps the turnstile and sprints out on the railroad bridge. The bridge runs through a tunnel and comes out over an incline that slants down to the rear parking lot. It's a six-foot drop, with a steep landing, but it looks like the only way down.

He hears an automated voice in the distance. A train is halted just beyond the tunnel. An old man in a conductor's uniform says something into a walkie-talkie and the three or four passengers duck for cover as more gunfire rings out from the street.

Ted jumps off a rounded corner of the track and lands in a gravelly slide that tears up his palms and forearms. His right ankle feels fucked but nothing too bad.

He reaches the lot where they parked the Yaris and nearly collapses with relief when he sees it there. He manages to get his hands to stop shaking enough to unlock the door and get it going.

There's a frantic scene in the main parking lot. Ted leans on the horn. He pulls around the line of cars backed up at the exit and speeds out via the entry lane.

The check engine light blinks on.

HARRY LOWERS HIS gun and steps out of the saddle. Carvell is sprawled in a heap on the sidewalk in front of the saloon, strings cut, ten feet below the broken balcony rail.

Harry has never shot and killed a man before. A couple pheasants. A whitetail dove one time. But never a man. It's not something he set out to do, but in this case, it was the only course of action. He watches Carvell convulse, a weak eruption of blood from his mouth. There's a small measure of satisfaction in leaving him there to die.

Guy isn't faring much better unfortunately. Gutshot and bleeding out. Harry kneels beside him. There's nothing he or anyone else can do to stop it. The poor bastard is a goner.

Why in the hell didn't he stay put like he was told?

Willy comes running out of the store and covers Guy with a Navajo blanket. Guy frees his arm from underneath. He gestures to Harry, trying to tell him something.

"It's okay, buddy," Harry says. "Just keep quiet. Hang on. We've got someone comin'."

Guy tries with more urgency, gesturing to his pocket this time, but Harry still can't understand.

Marvin. Marvel. He finally gets it.

"My lucky marble."

Guy nods. Harry removes the marble from his pocket and places it in Guy's open palm. Guy's hand clasps around it tight. He doesn't have the strength to speak but there's a grateful look in his eyes. Harry covers him up to his neck in the blanket and stays with him there. It's only a minute or two before his eyes go wide and then he's gone.

There's no sign of Ted. When Harry came riding down the street, Ted was standing right there in front of the saloon. He thought he'd grab him easy. Then the shooting started again. Carvell on the balcony like a belltower wingnut. Looks like the girl got away too.

Harry climbs to his feet and wipes the dust off his knee. He apologizes to Willy and gives his word that he won't mention his name. Willy walks back toward his store as the sirens get closer. Ambulances and police cruisers arriving. A firetruck.

Harry lights a Tareyton and kneels back down next to Guy. He lifts the blanket and sees Guy's fist clenched over his heart. Harry pries the marble out of his hand and puts it back in his pocket. His father gave

him that marble and he intends to be buried with it. It's not going in
the ground with Guy.

47

BY THE TIME Capri drags herself to the parking lot, the Yaris is gone. Which means everything is gone. The weed, the money, the shit she had in her bag. Everything.

It hits her like an attack of vertigo. She can't believe she was dumb enough to think Ted might be dumb enough to be waiting there for her.

The ground tilts and she clutches her lower back. She's still got Jamey's shirt bandaging her wound, but it's soaked through and keeps sliding down over her waist. She needs to get somewhere and patch herself up.

Jamey's car keys have been in her hand since she snagged them off his belt. It was only seconds after he was killed but he looked very dead. She was also able to grab his wallet and phone. His gun was thrown too far to risk going for. She still has hers but there's only a couple bullets left.

Hopefully she won't have to part with any more of them today.

She hits the key fob until a Honda with Arizona plates lights up. The one she saw in front of the motel this morning. She lowers herself into the driver's seat. The car has been roasting in the sun and it's unbearable inside.

She starts it up and leaves the door open for a second while the AC kicks in. Blood beads down her back and pools on the seat. She pats down her pockets and realizes she left her cigarettes in the Yaris. Another kick in the teeth.

A waving man walks intently in her direction. He looks like he wants to help her, not apprehend her, but she doesn't want anything to do with it.

She guns it past the do-gooder, nearly clipping him, then around the caravan of cars backed up in the main lot. After clearing the exit, she barrels down the hill on the shoulder of the road. Two ambulances and a cop car streak past in the opposite direction.

She throws Jamey's phone out the window and it smashes in the street. The best move would be to get on the freeway and speed as far away as possible but her back needs attention. She feels like she could pass out.

The sun through the windshield is blinding. She leans hard on the wheel trying to keep the car straight and swerves into the parking lot of the first motel she sees. The lot is mostly empty. She sits and collects herself. Jamey's duffel bag is on the passenger seat and she finds an oversized hoodie to throw on over her bloody clothes.

Capri hands over Jamey's credit card to the man at the desk.

"He checked out," the man says.

Capri looks at the sign above the counter. THE HALF MOON MOTEL. The place Jamey stayed last night. She comes up with a quick line about how she's Jamey's wife and she just got to town. They'd like to stay one more night.

The man looks suspicious, but he swipes the card anyway.

"You're in luck," he says. "Room Six is still available."

She'd prefer a different room, and a different motel, but she needs to get herself fixed up right now. He hands her the receipt and a key with a numbered plastic tag. The same one Jamey had in his hand only a couple hours ago.

When she gets to the room she leans against the wall and stands in the emptiness a second, listening to the air-conditioner hum. The room has been cleaned and turned over. No indication Jamey just spent the last night of his life there. She drops his bag on the bed and staggers to the liquor store across the street.

The liquor store clerk is a rangy desert rat with a prison pussy goatee. He gives her the once-over twice as she buys two packs of Camel Crushes and a handle of the cheapest vodka they have.

Back in the room she strips down and examines herself in the bathroom mirror. There are tiny pieces of glass in her wound. Brutal pain but not as bad as a bullet. She drenches a bath towel in vodka then takes a double shot and lights a cigarette.

It stings like a bitch when she presses the towel down. She deep-drags on the cigarette and stubs it out on her wrist. It calms her for a second. A pain to cancel out the other pain.

Wrapped in a clean towel, she sits at the edge of the bed and slides Jamey's duffel bag toward her. It only takes a second to find what she's looking for. An orange prescription bottle. Percs.

She takes three and starts calling Ted.

THE BARSTOW SHERIFF'S Station is a low concrete fortress they keep air-conditioned like a meat locker. Harry sits at a table in a glassed-in office talking to a deputy named Nunez.

Nunez is a trim guy, about fifty, with long hair for a cop. Wearing the short-sleeve tan uniform shirt with the green pants. He takes Harry's statement in a rapid shorthand.

"Let's back up a second. You and Mr. Donleavy were on horseback why?"

"We broke down in Yermo. My car's at Bernard's Garage at present. You can check with him. He lent us the ponies."

"In lieu of a rental car?"

"Somethin' like that."

"And you arrived just as the shooting was taking place?"

"Right before."

"And, for the record, the reason you were in Calico?"

Harry is careful not to implicate Willy in any of this.

"I was told they were comin' there as a rendezvous point, to sell some of the stuff they picked up in the original robbery."

"Who told you this?"

He leaves Elmer out of it as well.

"A guy who works for me spoke to someone else they robbed. They got wind of it from some other dealer they knew. It was the only lead I had, so I followed it."

"You think they were pulling something similar here?"

"I think the girl was double-crossing him, my client, this time. She was the planner behind this. My guy is no innocent, but this whole scheme, half-baked as it is, is beyond him."

"You think he was just along for the ride?"

"I don't see him cookin' all this up. She worked at the dispensary he robbed, back in Van Nuys. Put him up to it, I imagine. Probably would have ditched him sooner if they didn't end up going on the run."

"Nothing on the other guy?"

"The one she ditched him for?"

Nunez nods.

"No idea," Harry says. "He didn't make it too far."

"He did not. No wallet but we recovered a gun near the body so we should get an ID once we pull the prints. You're sure your guy went home?"

"I'm hopin' he did. I'm going home either way."

"Not on horseback, I hope."

"Car ought to be ready now."

Nunez leans back.

"As far as Mr. Donleavy is concerned, we reached a sister in Massachusetts. She connected us with the mother. They're arranging to have the body sent back there. I'm sorry again."

"Thanks."

"If you think of anything else, give me a call." Nunez taps his business card and pushes it across the table. "Meanwhile, we've got an all-points out on your client. You don't remember what he was driving?"

"Not a clue."

Nunez shifts a stack of paper on the table and sighs heavily, the sun slanting through the blinds behind him. He sucks some iced coffee up his straw.

"And nothing on Mr. King other than that he worked security at the dispensary?"

"That was the extent of our relationship. I had no idea he was out here after them too."

"Well he wasn't taking in the sights. He was armed to the teeth. Not that it did him much good. If it's any ease on your conscience, it probably wasn't your shot that killed him. He was wearing pretty substantial body armor and we found what looks like three different bullet fragments in it. Of course it was the fall that ultimately did him in."

Harry forces a tight smile. "I'm just happy to have been a part of it."

"I understand." Nunez opens a manila folder. "I may need to call you to follow up on some details, but your account of things checks out with what everybody else has told us. We're still trying to get a sense of King's movements before this morning, though. From what we found in the car it appears he came down from Reno."

A coin drops when Harry hears Reno. Only one person who could've pointed Carvell in that direction.

Nunez continues. "Receipt from the Silver Legacy Resort Casino. A motel in Olancha. Some gas receipts. Looks like he was keeping track of expenses. A few of these cards were in with the papers. You're bail bonds, this mean anything to you?"

Harry knows what's on the card before Nunez tosses it on the table. GOLD KEY BAIL BONDS. Gold on black with a glamour shot of Rick holding the keys to a giant pair of handcuffs.

The slippery shitheel. How the Christ did he get connected with Carvell? And who told him about Calico? Why would he even get involved?

He considers telling Nunez to dig into Rick Devlin further, that he may be the key to this whole thing, then he decides against it. He'll handle it on his own.

"Never heard of him," Harry says. "Can I take one of those, though? Maybe it'll rattle somethin' loose."

Nunez slides one of Rick's cards across the table. Harry puts it in his shirt pocket.

TED'S PHONE BUZZES and jumps on the passenger seat.

He knows it's her. And he knows she's only calling because she wants the weed and the money. It's got nothing to do with him.

It probably never did.

Freeway traffic is mostly trucks. Blocking his sightline as he checks for blue lights in the rearview. The reality of the situation lifts for seconds at a time, but he can't escape it for long.

He flashes on the gunfire. Everything turning to shit in a matter of seconds. Harry and Carvell closing in. Then Capri running off with Jamey.

He barely remembers the rest. The panic in the tunnel and the run to the car then he was free. All he can think about is how long she'd been planning to fuck him over. From the beginning?

It's lonely in the car without her. He smokes the Camel Crushes she left behind. The cigarettes remind him of her, the sharp minty flavor, and there's a momentary calm in snapping the glass capsule to release the menthol.

He wonders how she got away. Where she's calling from. Is she still with Jamey? Are they in some motel room planning to lure him back there and rob him? What happened to Harry?

At the High Desert Truck Stop, Ted buys a 5-Hour Energy Drink and another pack of Camel Crushes then gets back on the road.

He tries to find some satisfaction in the fact that he's finally doing the right thing. Going home and facing the music. After he stashes the weed, he'll drive the Yaris out to Panorama City somewhere and leave the keys in it. Wipe it down and take the bus home.

Maybe they'll never nail him on that.

It'd be cool if he could stay out in Malibu with Max for a couple days, put the feelers out for what's happening in Van Nuys before he starts showing his face around, but Capri fucked that up too. Max will probably never speak to him again.

Once everything's settled, he'll call Bobby up in Santa Cruz and see if he can crash there for a while. New girls, new beaches, new surroundings. Sell off the weed a little at a time to keep himself afloat.

There's no future for anyone in Van Nuys. Especially him.

For the first time since this all started, he has a clear direction. Westward. Homeward.

There's just one more thing he needs to do.

48

ELMER IS ON the mend.

The eyepatch is no longer necessary, just BluBlocker wraparounds during peak daytime hours. He's steadier on his feet but still feels the absence of his hat. He's wearing another Stetson for the time being, a straw Airway Breezer, but it's not a sufficient replacement.

The Stetson website has his old model, the Buffalo Silver Mine, available for purchase. He's looked at it several times, even selected the size and color and put it in the checkout cart, but he hasn't been able to pull the trigger.

Now he's being targeted by pop-up ads. As a businessman, he appreciates the marketing angle. Behavioral tracking, they call it. Look at an item on a site and they follow you around the net for a while, tugging at your coat about it. But it's a sad reminder and he finds himself spending less time online on account of it.

He's currently reading a book on the minimalist lifestyle. Eliminating unnecessary clutter in one's home and mind. He plans to donate the lion's share of his business books, each stamped with his personal insignia, to the local library and reduce his wardrobe to wash-and-wear staples.

He's only unloaded a few items at the Goodwill so far but the trailer already feels spartan. He looks around the kitchen. Teakwood table. Pots and pans. Shotgun leaning against the windowsill. He's afraid this new approach may backfire. Set him adrift and make him feel even more alone in the world. But maybe cleaning the slate will be liberating.

Over the weekend he had a long night when he considered giving up the Eatables enterprise altogether. Thinking he may be getting too old, too slow. Everyone has their doubts. Even Christ. Elmer considered it his Gethsemane moment. And he decided to buffalo right through it.

Max is still on thin ice, having sent unscrupulous business his way without proper vetting, but Elmer has decided not to cut him out of the operation. Everybody makes a bad call. You need people you know. That's the important part.

He received a fresh delivery of product from his regular supplier and is back to baking. It feels good to get lost in the work. Shake simmering in butter. Chocolate liquefying over low heat. It keeps his mind occupied. He also has to recoup some of his losses.

Luckily they weren't aware of the second safe in the bedroom when they rolled him. That's where the real money is kept. Plus his savings in the bank, but he doesn't like to touch that.

He's reaching for a block of Kerrygold Irish Butter when he hears the crunch of gravel outside, followed by the animals raising a ruckus.

He looks out the window. It's the kid from the other day. He's getting out of the driver's side and walking around to the back of the car. Where's the girl? Elmer feels fear in the pit of his stomach. The kid appears to be rummaging in the trunk now.

Elmer reaches for the shotgun next to the open window and slowly lowers himself down on one knee. He removes his hat, slides the
BluBlockers up on his bald head, and peers down the barrel with his
good eye.

He waits for the kid to come around the side of the car again.

HARRY'S HORSE HAD been stabled at a farm outside Calico while Harry
dealt with things at the station. The farmer has a truck with a horse
trailer and he offers to give Harry a ride back to Bernard's garage. He's
also arranged for Guy's horse to be burned or buried or whatever they
do. Harry doesn't want the details. He called Bernard to fill him in and
to tell him he was coming by to get the car whether it was ready or
not.

When Harry gets dropped off at the garage, he returns his horse to
the fenced-in area out back. Standing there on his last legs, the horse
reminds Harry of Zippy Chippy, the famous racehorse who never won
a race. King of the last-place finish. People used to come from miles
around to see him lose. Retired with a 0-100 record but made his
mark. Harry runs his hand along the horse's dull coat and flat forehead. He says his goodbyes and thanks him before heading inside to
pick up the Olds.

From outside the office door, Harry overhears Bernard having a conversation with a customer. "They say a horseshoe in the road is lucky,"
Bernard says.

"Lucky for you maybe," a man's voice says. "I need a new goddamn
tire."

Harry peers in the doorway. The man at the counter appears flustered, put out.

"Tires? We got tires." Bernard gestures with his flyswatter, indicating the tires. "Looks like there may be some trouble with the wheel. Won't know 'til we get her up on the lift."

Harry watches Bernard run down the rest of the spiel.

"Tell you what, check in over at the Bluebird while I get this taken care of." Bernard hands the man the motel's business card. "Half-mile or so down the road from here. Fifteen percent off if you give 'em my name."

Harry steps inside and walks to the counter. Bernard looks sheepish handing over the car keys.

"You're somethin' else," Harry says.

Bernard shrugs and hands him the bill. Harry looks at it then back at Bernard. He makes no reach for his wallet.

"That's gratis," Bernard says. "Just wanted you to see the itemization."

"What a gent."

Harry gets it. Life in a highway town. Some people put up a billboard. Some people scatter horseshoes in the road. Have to get them to stop somehow. But he's not falling for it.

"I'm sorry about the horse," Harry says.

"He had a lot of miles under the hoof," Bernard says. "Your friend okay?"

"He didn't make it either."

Harry knocks on the counter and leaves Bernard standing there.

When he stops at the motel to grab the bags, Harry sees the stranded traveler from the garage trudging toward the front desk entrance, wheeling a wobbly suitcase in the dust behind him. He must've forgone the horse rental package.

Harry stops for gas before getting on the Mojave Freeway. This is the tank that will take him home. No more desert gas stations. No more motel beds. He watches trucks barrel west. Soon the Olds will be among them. He's going home empty-handed but at least he's going home.

His phone buzzes in his pocket. He looks at the screen.

Elmer.

49

"WHAT WAS THE thinkin' here?" Harry says.

"May have been a little quick on the trigger."

Harry stands with a solemn Elmer. A bedside vigil in the guest room of the doublewide. Ted looks borderline comatose, his arm suspended in a makeshift sheet-sling.

Elmer had summoned Harry to the compound with the news that Ted had shown up there. Only after several minutes of hemming and hawing did Elmer reveal he'd shot him on sight.

"You're lucky you didn't kill him."

"It was only buckshot."

"Still."

"I didn't know what the hell to think. He comes rolling up my driveway, how do I know he's not coming back to finish what he started? I had to defend the ponderosa."

He lifts his hat and wipes a sheen of sweat off his bald head.

"Looks like you got your Stetson back," Harry says.

Elmer nods, chastened.

"It appears now the boy came here trying to make things right. I found the money and product they robbed me of stacked neatly in the trunk. My Stetson resting on top like the star on a Christmas tree. But by then I'd already nipped him."

Ted jerks and twitches on the bed.

"Boy dreams like a dog," Elmer says

"I ought to get him to a hospital."

"I don't think that's necessary. They'd have to report something like this. I've got him fixed up." Elmer inspects the dressing of the wound. "And he's not feeling any pain. I melted down some of my chocolates into a cocoa. Powerhouse indica with a high CBD level. He's out like a bulb."

"Stuff must be pretty strong."

"I gave the same concoction to my wife in her final days. She died in that bed."

Ted drifts into consciousness and Elmer tells him not to make any sudden movements.

"I feel fucked up," Ted says.

"I nipped you on the shoulder. You spooked me." Elmer grabs the mug of cocoa off the nightstand and hands it to him. "Drink some more of this."

Ted drinks from the mug, holding it cautiously with both hands. He sets it back on the stand and looks up bleary-eyed.

"Harry? What are you doing here?"

"What do you think I'm doin' here? I'm takin' you back to Van Nuys."

"I don't think I can move."

"I'll wait."

"We ought to let him sit a bit," Elmer says.

Harry says he needs to make a couple calls. Elmer tells him he's at liberty to do so.

Sitting in Elmer's porch rocker, Harry calls Ruby to let her know how everything went.

She's shocked and upset when she hears about Guy, but grateful Harry got out okay. He leaves out the part about having to shoot Carvell, that's a longer conversation, and says he'll fill her in on the rest later, hopefully in person if he can get on the road soon enough. She says she'll wait as long as she can, but she has to get home before it's too late. She can't afford to take another day off.

He calls Fuzzy next, telling him he'll be coming back with Ted sometime tonight. When Harry mentions Calico, Fuzzy says he saw something on the news about it but no names were mentioned and he didn't put two and two together. Harry tells him about Guy but doesn't mention Rick's involvement. Fuzzy seems preoccupied. Sounds like the Grotto is busy.

Harry lights a cigarette and lets out a deep exhale. He looks around at the barren landscape. Sometimes he can imagine himself as an old prospector, off the grid, living out the rest of his days like a lizard baking on a rock. He started his life in the Texas desert, maybe he'll end his days in this one. But for now he's had his fill of the internal stare-downs that confront you out here. The way the desert plays tricks on your mind. It's like that feeling when you think you see a person you recognize, then you remember that person is dead.

He'll want to leave Van Nuys as soon as he gets there, but for the moment he's relieved to be headed back.

When Harry steps back inside, Elmer is tidying up the kitchen.

"You hungry? I can cook us up some rations."

"Ostrich lay a couple fresh ones this morning?"

"There are other items on the menu."

"I don't have much of an appetite," Harry says.

"Good enough. How about a belt?"

"There's an idea."

Harry takes a seat at the kitchen table and Elmer produces a bottle of George T. Stagg bourbon. "I think this qualifies as an occasion," he says, pouring them two, neat, in heavy crystal tumblers. "I'm sorry about your pal the lawyer."

They raise their glasses and tap them on the table before taking the first sip.

"What's the plan with the Toyota the kid's driving?"

"My guess is it's stolen," Harry says.

"That's not the end of the world."

Harry looks at him.

"I know someone who could take care of it is all I'm saying."

"Your network?"

"Something like that. How's four grand?"

"You got that kind of money lyin' around?"

"I got the cash, you got the barrelhead?"

Harry agrees to the terms.

"While we're negotiating, you happen to have any idea how much inventory the kid has left? I retrieved my hat and product, along with my cash, but there's plenty more."

Doesn't seem to be much negotiating happening here, Elmer's the one doing all the wheeling and dealing, but what the hell.

"Let's take a look," Harry says.

Outside the sun is sinking. Late summer dusk. Harry's lenses adjust to the golden light. Elmer watches it like a magic trick. "There goes that tint again."

The Yaris is unlocked. Harry lifts the rubber containers out of the trunk and Elmer sets the bales on the hood and sizes them up. Harry's no good at that kind of ballparking so he believes Elmer when he tells him there must be close to thirty pounds there.

"It may take me a while," Harry says. "But I believe I can smoke it."

Elmer grins.

"How about twenty-five grand for the lot? I'll bump it up to a clean thirty, including the car. That's a bulk rate. You could sell it off a little at a time and make more but you're no dealer."

Harry makes a face like he's considering it but it's just for show. He doesn't seem to have much choice in the matter. He's not about to be peddling dime bags on the boulevard.

"I'll bet you a white hat you ain't going to get a better fell-swoop offer than that. Not to mention, I greased the wheels here. To say the least of it."

"Hang onto your hat, Elmy. You just got it back."

Harry roots through the pile and sets aside two sizable bundles of the Acapulco Gold, enough to keep him and Ruby good and toasted for months.

"I'll hang onto these for safekeeping. Deal still good?"

They shake on it and Harry helps Elmer haul the containers inside and stack them in his utility closet. Back at the kitchen table, Elmer doles out two more short pours of Stagg to commemorate the deal.

"Looks like there's still a few miles left on the shoe-leather approach," Elmer says, holding up his glass. "Tracked 'em down the old-fashioned way."

Harry raises his glass to meet Elmer's. "When we were kids, the science fiction movies were set in the times we're livin' in right now. Now here we are and what's the big change? Our phones?"

Elmer shrugs. "It's all a smoke and pony show anyway."

They tap them on the table and drink them down.

An hour later Elmer checks Ted's vitals and declares that he is lucid and mobile enough for highway travel. They walk Ted outside and Elmer helps Harry get him situated in the passenger seat.

Elmer hands over a bag of chocolates and reaches out to shake Harry's hand.

"Thanks again for what you done for me," he says.

Harry returns a firm shake. "Good luck, pal."

He climbs behind the wheel and sets his hat on the dashboard next to the dancing hula girls. The Olds starts up like new.

Halfway down the long driveway, they pass Elmer's dog, a stern heeler, strutting up the hill toward the trailer. In the rearview Harry watches Elmer kneel down and scoop the dog into his arms.

EVEN WITH THE vodka and pills, Capri can't seem to wind herself down. She nods off and snaps awake seconds later. It's like trying to sleep on a plane that's about to crash.

Normally she'd smoke herself comatose, bowl after bowl until she was in the fetal position, dead to the world, but Jamey didn't have any weed stashed in the bag or the car. She looked everywhere.

So she scoops more watery ice from the bucket and pours more vodka over it. She's lost track of how many pills she's taken but it can't be more than four or five. There are still plenty rattling around in the bottle. She swallows another and hopes this one works. The throbbing in her back will not let up.

She can't remember the last time she took painkillers to actually kill pain.

The room is so smoky she goes outside to smoke. It's getting dark now. She eases herself into a chair that's chained to the wall. Her throat is raw and she winces at the scorch of the menthol when she lights up. She looks down at the rabbit lighter, the one Ted got her, and feels even worse.

She finally gave up calling him. It was nauseating to hear herself begging into his voicemail. Trying to convince him that Jamey ambushed her. That she needed him to come pick her up. They could take the cruise, go to Miami, whatever he wanted. She was convinced she could turn him around if she got to him. But the phone just rang and rang.

She wonders where he's going. He won't get far on his own. Maybe he was right. They should've just sold it off fair. Made enough to start over somewhere together. But that wasn't enough. Nothing ever is.

She flicks her cigarette and watches it skid across the empty lot, kicking up sparks like a busted muffler.

Jamey told her more than once that she was the worst thing that ever happened to him. She's probably the worst thing that ever happened to a few people. Ted too now. She knows that Ted loved her at least, and she may have even loved him, but she can't let herself get too hung up on it. If she thinks about every time she's fucked up and landed back at zero, she'll never get out of this chair.

She steadies herself on the wall, lightheaded from the loss of blood, and guides herself toward the doorway. In the room she stretches out on the bed and tries to lull herself with the white noise, the cool air, the campfire glow of the TV. Nothing. Still wide awake.

She turns over and stares at the water stains on the ceiling. Every siren in the distance makes her think the cops are about to kick down the door. Even with no ID or phone, they'll eventually get a name on Jamey. There are only a few motels in this town. It won't be long before they find his car parked in front of this one.

She needs to get moving.

Vegas is a hundred and fifty miles away. Just over two hours.

She knows that promoter there. Benny Berman. He can probably get her a job as a bottle girl. Or she could dance somewhere for a while if she has to. Whatever hustle she gets going, Vegas will be a good place to stack some cash and plan the next move.

There's one clean towel left in the bathroom. She pours vodka directly on her wound then ties the towel tight and throws on a clean dark shirt over that.

The air outside is almost cool enough to breathe now. She props a pillow from the room in a comfortable position over the dried blood on the driver's seat and gets in. The Half Moon Motel sign switches on, the neon sizzling on the rear windshield as she backs out of her parking spot.

There's no traffic on the 15, no one to follow, just the cone of light from the high beams pointing north. She passes runaway truck ramps and empty rest stops. Jamey's bag is on the passenger seat, filled with

295 \ ZIG ZAG

everything he left behind. His wallet is in the center console. It contains two-hundred and forty dollars plus a Visa and a Discover card.

She wonders where his body is right now. What they'll do with it. Who they'll call. She can't remember who in his family is alive or dead. But none of that matters anymore.

She just needs to get to Vegas in one piece before they cancel his credit cards.

ON THE SONNY Bono Memorial Freeway, leaving the area designated as Other Desert Cities, Harry sips coffee and stares straight ahead. Ted is asleep in the passenger seat, his face pressed against the cold window glass.

A light rain comes on. Harry listens to the tires clicking on the blacktop and hums an old Dave Dudley ballad about raindrops on the windshield and teardrops on the steering wheel. He drives through Morongo, past the outlets and casinos. It's dimming dark and red lights are blinking over the Yucca Valley wind farms.

He lights a cigarette and thinks about all the pinballing around he's done over the years. Mostly through the Southwest and Mexico. Every jagged inch of the Republic of Texas. He thinks about places he's been that he'll never go back to. And places, entire continents, he'll probably never see. Asia. Australia. Antarctica. Africa. He wonders if he'll get back down to New Orleans at some point. He hopes so.

He'll never go back to Calico again. Yermo either.

Every thought lately circles back to bailing on the bail bonds business and escaping Van Nuys. He wishes it was a business he could sell. Everything he owns is rented. And it's not like he has what Elmer calls brand recognition. He leaves, they'll just take the Buckaroo shingle down and hang a FOR RENT sign in its place. The local jailbirds won't care. Even Cal Hensley and Lenny Disco will just call the next name on the list.

He's going home with some money in his pocket, though. That feels good. He'll let Ruby handle it. She's smarter with finances. Always socking something away. The thirty grand would go a lot further in Mexico. He wonders if she'll go for it.

Ted shifts in his seat, half-awake, and takes a long drink from a bottle of water.

"Smoke botherin' you?" Harry says.

"No, I'm fine."

"Good. Because I ain't puttin' it out."

Ted tries to smile but even that looks like it hurts. He leans in, holding his shoulder steady while he adjusts his seat to a more upright position.

"I can't believe he shot me."

"He was within his rights. You're lucky he didn't kill you."

"Yeah," Ted says, looking out the window.

"The girl still callin' you?"

"My phone's dead."

"Probably for the best."

Ted nods.

"Who was the guy she run off with?"

"Her ex-boyfriend. She told me he was trying to hook us up with a buyer but obviously something else was going on. I was too dumb to pick up on it."

"Well it didn't work out for him. He got pretty thoroughly plugged."

That doesn't seem to give Ted any satisfaction.

"What happened to Carvell?"

"I took care of him," Harry says. "You didn't see that part?"

"No. I did see him shoot your friend Guy. That was fucked up."

Guy's death hasn't sunk in yet. Not that Harry expects himself to be suddenly racked with sobs when it does, but he imagines he'll feel something more eventually.

"Was he a good friend of yours?"

"His dad was. And he'd become a friend. We've been through some things, especially these past few days."

Even though he told Guy to stay behind more than once, Harry still feels some responsibility for what happened. Guy wouldn't have been out there if it weren't for him. But by that line of thinking Harry wouldn't have been out there if Ted hadn't committed the robbery and skipped bail. And Ted wouldn't have committed the robbery and skipped bail if it weren't for the girl. You can't start pulling at those strings without everything coming unraveled. A chain of bad decisions and wrong moves led to the events that transpired and there's no going back now to change any of it.

"How old was he?"

"Forty."

"Damn, that's not that old."

Harry's sentimental side leans to thinking of Guy's lost potential. Maybe he was just going through a bad patch and all he needed was some good news, a break, a run of better luck. Seemed like he was determined to turn a corner. But it's easy to give someone the benefit of the doubt after they're dead. You never know. Some things we can change. Others are dyed in the wool, blown in the glass.

"I know it doesn't matter now," Ted says. "But I never planned for things to turn out like they did. Everything got away from us."

"What was the plan?"

"She obviously had other ideas, but my plan was to sell the weed and make enough money to start over somewhere together."

"And leave your old man and me holding the bag."

"I wasn't thinking straight."

"Well you didn't get the money and you didn't get her."

Ted sits with that a second.

"Best-laid plans."

"This was not a case of best-laid plans, Teddy. This was a fuckin' shitshow. People are dead because of your plans. And you could end up that way yourself once the people from Big Smoke hear you're back in town."

Harry watches Ted for a reaction. It looks like his mind is clouding with dark potentialities.

"You need to lay low until your court date. Lemke, the guy who runs Big Smoke, isn't going to forget about this. But I'll talk to him. I've gotten a couple of his associates out before. I can tell him Capri got away and is still out there with his merchandise. Carvell isn't around to tell them any different. I plan to pin that on her too if I can."

"You think I'm going to jail?" Ted says.

"Depends how it goes in court. The fact that Big Smoke kept every-thing hushed up works in your favor there. It'll just be the breaking and entering. But it also means they want to settle this themselves. If they don't buy my line about the girl, you might be better off in jail."

"I was thinking of moving up to Santa Cruz. After my court date, I mean. I have a buddy up there I could stay with."

"I don't care what you do, long as you do it after your court date," Harry says. "For now, you need to lay low. And find a new lawyer."

ONE FOR
THE DITCH

50

WHEN **HARRY WALKS** in the door, it's like he's been away longer than a few days. Ruby is gone and he feels the hollow quiet of coming home to an empty apartment.

Emmylou descends from her perch above the kitchen cabinets and does her tentative two-step bounce to the floor. She follows Harry into the bedroom, climbs on the bed, and rubs against him, tail in the air, while he unpacks his duffel and throws his dirty clothes in the hamper. He'll put the cheeba and the Ranger and the cash in the safe at the office tomorrow but he stashes everything in the closet for now.

Crossing back through the kitchen, he switches on the light and sees the emerald peak of the Tullamore Dew bottle standing tall on the bar cart. He feels a stab of sentimentality.

One for Guy.

His phone buzzes in his pocket as he pours. A text from Manny saying he got an alert about Ted's cell. He says it looks like Ted is back in the area. Thanks, pal.

Harry ignores the text and walks his whiskey down to the mailbox.

The Calico postcard he sent Ruby is slotted inside. He forgot to leave her the box key. He remembers writing to her from that bench in

Yermo, the dog drag-assing in the dust in front of him. It felt strange sending a postcard to his own address. Stranger now receiving it. The rest is mostly junk mail. He doesn't know how he got on the list for the hearing aid deals but he gets something from them almost every day.

It's quiet at the Sylvan Shores this time of night. He has a cigarette on the landing and watches the glow-worm light of his neighbor's TV flicker on the courtyard. Traffic on the 60 got them back later than expected. By the time he pulled off the 101 and coasted down Victory, it was past eleven.

Ted slept most of the last leg. When Harry dropped him home he looked like he was going to keep on sleeping. The last thing he said before going inside was, "I'm not going anywhere."

Harry believed that was true.

He locks the door behind him and sets the mail on the coffee table. Ruby left him a fresh torpedo in the ashtray and he offers a silent, weary thanks for the kindness of the gesture. She's a hell of a good woman. A keeper if he can keep her.

What he really wants is to spark up some of this Acapulco Gold. He grabs his papers out of the candy dish and seals two together, doubling them up to roll a megaphone bomber. One drag and he's on a hot air balloon. Thirty seconds over Tokyo.

He tops off his drink and puts Billy Walker, the Tall Texan, on the turntable.

Stretched on the couch, smoking and thinking, Harry's mind drifts to Billy Walker dying in a car wreck in Fort Deposit, Alabama. On his way back to Nashville after performing a show at an RV park. Seventy-seven years old. What a way to go out.

"Cross The Brazos At Waco" moves into "Down To My Last Ciga-rette" and Harry's thoughts turn to Lee Hazlewood, another one of his favorite singers, at the end.

Lee was sick the last few years of his life and when it looked like he wasn't going to be around much longer, his wife threw him a big birth-day party. He was living in Nevada, not far from Vegas, and people flew in from all over. People he made records with. Famous people. Old friends. Everyone wanted to say their farewells. Share one last Chivas, one last cigarette.

But then he didn't die right away. Another birthday came around. Another. The parties got smaller. He finally died at seventy-eight, Har-ry always keeps track of when old smokers die, and at his last party, when it was really time to say goodbye, only the people that mattered were there. The inner circle.

Harry lights a cigarette and makes a note to add "My Autumn's Done Come," a Hazlewood classic, to his ever-growing funeral playlist.

He's been curating this list for years—"Feel Like Going Home," "My Rifle, My Pony and Me," "Dublin Blues," "Bird On A Wire," "Desper-ados Under The Eaves" and a dozen or so more—usually late at night with a glass of whiskey in front of him and a graveyard of cigarette butts in the ashtray.

It's the closest thing he has to a last will and testament.

He likes to imagine people listening to the songs, heads bowed, qui-etly remembering him. Most of them are people he hopes die before him. So that means he somehow wants to outlive them and be mourn-ed by them.

It's a contradiction he doesn't worry about too much. It's all a roll of the bones. Who knows when he'll have a boozy stumble like William Holden. Or conk out on the couch, the poncho set ablaze by the cherry of a Tareyton. Could be the Tareytons themselves will do it. An X-ray that lights up like a Christmas tree. Or he'll quit and that big yellow school bus will find him.

He imagines a sad sack final act, sweeping up the empties after the party, so broke he's walking around with his pants pockets inside-out. Then it's the hearse at the curb. The slow boat to China. The late great Harry Robatore. A man of means by no means. Bury him in a Nudie suit and be done with it.

His phone buzzes on the table. He hears the familiar lilt of lap steel.

Ruby says on the other end, "I got two fortune cookies. One's cracked and one isn't. Which do I pick?"

"Pick the cracked one. It's tryin' to tell you something."

Harry hears the rumple of cellophane, the static of her cheek pressing the phone against her shoulder.

She reads the fortune aloud.

"*A friend asks only for your time, not your money.*"

"Can I borrow fifty bucks?"

"Funny."

"What's the other one say?"

"I'm not opening it. I hate that they gave me two. That means I ordered enough for two people. I'm not going back to that place."

"There's leeway in Chinese. It's not like you ordered two steak dinners, darlin'. There's sides. Leftovers."

"I still don't like it."

There's a pause on her end and Harry hears the bubbling of the bong. The one he gave her. She says it's like a lamp that unleashes a Harry genie in her house. He loves that thing, but he can't trust himself to have it around. Not without a set of jumper cables next to the couch.

"You're going to get hungry again. Good thing you ordered enough for two."

"Shut up, Harry."

He takes a deep drink, the ice cubes piling on his teeth, and decides it's time to float it by her. "Darlin', how do you feel about goin' down to Mexico?"

"That's a good idea. We need a vacation. I got some time off saved for whenever I want. Maybe we go to Costa Rica instead. Somewhere new. In a couple months when it's not so hot."

"I'm talkin' about goin' down there to live for a while. I made a little chunk on this deal. I could liquidate what there is to liquidate up here. You're always talkin' about how you never get to see your momma. Maybe we stay with her for a while until we get settled. She'd probably like that, right?"

There's a sigh on her end of the line.

"Oh Harry, my rainy day cowboy. You know I think the world of you. I think two worlds of you. But you're crazy, baby."

"What's so crazy?"

"You always talk about moving to Mexico when you're drunk. And you always act like you just thought of it for the first time."

"I'm not drunk."

"I hear the ice in the glass."

"This is my first one. And I've been plannin'—"

"It's okay, baby. You're tired from your trip. We don't have to talk about all of this right now. But you know how hard I worked to move here. To go to school and get this job I have. I send money back there. I can't move back there."

Harry sets his glasses on the coffee table and rubs the indents on the bridge of his nose.

"Don't be melancholy, Harry. I know how you get. Are you sad about Guy?"

"I'm fine. I just miss you. I like when we have somethin' to look forward to."

"Look forward to next weekend. You still need to take me dancing."

"I know. We missed our date."

"We'll go next Sunday."

They always have a good time when they go line dancing at the Cowboy Palace. It's an occasion to get dressed up. Ruby in her red boots. Harry in his tan suit, like Joe Don Baker in *Charley Varrick*.

"I wish we could go right now."

Ruby laughs.

"It's a little late, Harry."

"Too bad you had to leave tonight. I wanted to see you."

"I know but I have to work tomorrow. I already took an extra day."

"Maybe I'll come to you."

"Now?"

"Yeah."

"That's not a good idea, Harry. You should go to bed."

"I want to go to bed with you."

"I'd like that too."

"How about you move in with me?" he says.

"It's every woman's dream to live in Van Nuys."

Harry grins. Even people who live in La Puente look down on Van Nuys.

"You know that joke? First prize: One week in Van Nuys. Second prize: Two weeks in Van Nuys."

Ruby thinks about that a second.

"Oh, I get it," she says.

He wants to kiss her then. But she'd just tell him to trim his mustache. It's gotten shaggy again. He'll have to take care of that before Thursday.

"Do you mean it this time?" Ruby says.

"Mean what?"

"Me and you living together. We've talked about that before too, Harry. I kind of figured if that was going to happen it would have already. You're such a lonely wolf. I thought you didn't want to."

"Of course I want to. I'm the one who brought it up."

"You bring a lot of things up."

"I'm serious. I promise."

"You are mysterious to me sometimes, Harry."

"Well, I'll warn you now. Livin' with me ain't no picnic basket."

"We'll see," she says. "When I go in tomorrow, I'll ask about making a transfer to a hospital in the Valley."

"That's a plan," he says. "You okay? Sounds like your mind is somewhere else."

"I'm good. Just tired. This is a big conversation to be having right now."

"You're right, darlin'. Talk to you tomorrow. I love you."

"I love you too."

"Goodnight."

"Goodnight, Harry."

Most nights when he's alone, Harry falls asleep on the couch, counting cowboys on the screen, and stumbles to bed around four or five when he gets up to take his first piss. *Cheyenne Autumn* is on Encore Westerns but he isn't in the mood. *The Wild Bunch* is on next but he doubts he'll stay up for it. He re-lights the torpedo and pictures him and Guy in opening credit freeze-frame. Then he staggers out to the kitchen for a refill.

The Tullamore bottle is coasting on fumes. He pours the last of it. There were many times over the past few days when he'd have loved a moment like this to himself. To pour a final belt, slip into the poncho, lie on the couch, and let the long day cave in around him. But right now he feels lower than whale shit, as Terry Donleavy used to say. And there's the matter of no whiskey.

He looks at the clock.

There's a higher risk of getting popped on the boulevard so he takes Hazeltine up to Oxnard. Slow and steady. He wasn't expecting to be back in the car so soon. Dead bugs are shellacked on the windshield and desert sand is still in everything.

Stopped at a red light, he lights the filter end of a Tareyton and that noxious smell hits him. He rolls the window all the way down and lights another one, the right way this time.

It's coming up on two. The lights are off at the Grotto but Rick's limo is out front. Fuzzy hasn't closed up yet. Harry looks at himself in the rearview and cuts the ignition.

Giving the limo a slow pass on his way in, he hooks the jagged edge of his office key in a loose spot of vinyl above the wheel well and scrapes it across the custom wrap job. Rick's face splits and peels like a fresh scab. He wishes he had the energy and instrumentation to slash all four tires, but the key job will suffice for now. He steadies himself on the hood and shoves himself toward the entrance.

He gives the locked door a hard rap and hears plodding footsteps then the sliding of the deadbolt. The door opens a crack. Fuzzy looks at him and turns back to the bar. "It's only Harry," he says.

The Grotto at this hour is like a tomb. All the gaudiness gone dark. Beerlights unplugged and cooling. Only the dim yellow lamp over the register. After a long night this after-hours time is a respite, a welcome wind-down when all is now quiet and drinks are now free. But showing up this late in the game, coming in at the end of things, feels all wrong. Harry already regrets coming out.

Fuzzy steps behind the bar. "You doing a Salty?"

"Just a Tullamore."

Harry approaches his stool with balance-beam concentration, but mounting it seems like too much of an endeavor. He leans against the bar. Fuzzy sets the drink in front of him and goes back to counting out the drawer.

"Thought you might've been Dirty Dorrie," Rick says. "She came by earlier trying to make me jealous. Making out with some Samoan-looking guy. She comes over and tells me not to try anything funny because her new boyfriend, the Samoan, carries a gun. Then she laughs and says she's never actually seen him take it out. So, I lean in and I say to her, 'What about his gun?'"

Rick pauses for the big yuk. Harry sips his whiskey and doesn't give it to him.

"What's got you stopping in for a beaker at this time of night?" Rick says. "Keeping pimp's hours?"

"I just got back," Harry says.

"I heard you retrieved young Theodore. Bravo. Where's the portly barrister? Thought he'd be here elbowing in on a free round."

"You didn't tell him, Fuzz?"

Fuzzy closes the register and walks over. He twists the cap off a bottle of Bud.

"Tell him what?"

"About Guy."

"What about him?"

"That he didn't make it."

"Christ, Harry. I didn't think you were serious."

"What do you mean he didn't make it?" Rick says. "He fall in a manhole and get stuck?"

Harry feels his blood pressure spike, a flash of temper, but keeps a measured tone.

"He got shot."

"You're kidding," Rick says.

"Do I look like I'm kiddin'?"

"Oh hell, I'm sorry Harry," Fuzzy says. "Who shot him? The girl?"

"Carvell King." Harry lets the name hang there a second, watching

Rick for a sign of recognition. Rick doesn't hide it well. It takes the starch right out of him. "He works security at the dispensary. Or he did before I shot him."

"What the hell happened out there?" Fuzzy says.

"Ask Rick."

Rick feigns surprise.

"The fuck does this have to do with me?"

"Carvell had one of these on him, for one," Harry says, trying to keep to a level tone as he tosses Rick's business card on the bar. "And he'd come down from Reno."

Fuzzy looks confused. "What's Reno got to do with anything?"

"When Rick called and asked where we were, I lied and told him Reno," Harry says. "I didn't want him doggin' my tracks. Now you can see why."

"Listen, Harry," Rick says. "I'm not going to sit here and play Mickey the Dunce. I had no idea who I was getting involved with. I thought I was doing you a favor. He said the girl was a loose cannon. I thought you could be the one getting killed."

"How much was in it for you?" Harry says.

"What do you mean?"

"You know what I mean. What was your cut?"

"Five grand," Rick says.

Fuzzy shakes his head. "Five lousy grand."

"I'm sorry," Rick says. "I never thought it'd turn out like this."

"You thought it'd turn out with you making a quick couple bucks," Fuzzy says. "Your pal also shot Teddy. He could've got killed too."

"Carvell didn't shoot Ted," Harry says. "That was Elmer."

"Who the hell is Elmer?" Fuzzy says.

"That's a whole other story."

"Jesus," Rick says. "I'm sorry for whatever role I may have played, but this whole thing sounds like a clusterfuck. I can't shoulder all the blame here. Your girlfriend's the one who told me about Calico anyway."

"What?"

"When she was in here on Sunday morning. I said something about you being in Reno and she told me you were in Calico."

"How does that make it her fault? She had no clue what you were up to."

"Still."

"Still nothing. The blame is on you. For Guy anyway," Harry says. "If you hadn't tipped Carvell off, Guy would be sitting here having a drink with us right now."

"So it's not all bad, right Fuzzard?" Rick says. "At least we're spared that."

"What's that supposed to mean?" Fuzzy says.

"I'm just kidding."

"You're a miserable prick," Harry says.

Rick shrugs.

"C'mon, Harry. Look, I'm sorry he's gone, but let's not act like this is a big loss for humanity here. Certainly not for the legal profession." Rick slides his glass forward. "Let's do one more here, Fuzzard. Buy Harry one too."

Without warning, Harry lurches forward and slams Rick in the jaw. It's a cheap shot but he deserves it. Rick topples off his stool and sprawls against the brass rail. Harry almost hits the mat himself. His hand is throbbing like a bastard and his legs are barely holding him up.

It's the kind of move that could have started a barroom brawl if anyone else was in the place. But it's just Fuzzy standing there with his bottle in his hand. He calmly sets it down and comes around to do his proprietary duty.

Harry passes Fuzzy and walks behind the bar. He scoops ice and water in a bucket and plunges his hand in it. A jarring jolt of cold. With his left hand, he adds ice to his glass and reaches for the Tullamore bottle. "You mind?"

Fuzzy shakes his head no.

Harry pours himself a double and watches Fuzzy help Rick to his feet. Besides calling Harry a pussy and a cheapshot artist, Rick doesn't say much on his way out. He seems more concerned with the blood-stains on his Callaway shirt. Fuzzy locks the door behind him and walks back toward the bar. Out in the lot the limo revs up and peels out with a blare of the horn.

Rick's middle-finger farewell.

"Sorry for the fisticuffs, Fuzz. I've had it with him."

"I don't believe in kicking a man when he's down," Fuzzy says. "Or I would've kicked him when he was down. Pour me one of those, will you?"

Fuzzy climbs onto a stool and Harry sets a whiskey in front of him. He hasn't seen Fuzzy on that side of the bar in ages. Even after hours, Fuzzy always protects his territory behind the taps. Outside of the annual Christmas toast, he hasn't had a whiskey with him in a long time, either.

Harry leans on the back bar and puts his boot up on the beer cooler.

"If things had turned out differently, Fuzz. This set-up could've been permanent. You over there, me back here."

"If you owned this place, you'd never see me in here again, Harry."

"Bullshit."

"Probably right. Where the hell am I going to go? I do thank you for bringing Teddy back, though. How is he?"

"He got shot in the shoulder and he got his heart broke but he'll live."

"The girl ran off on him?"

"With another guy. Carvell clipped that guy too. So Ted actually came out on top there. I doubt he'll run off after her again, but we should keep an eye on him."

"Is he looking at time?"

"I doubt it."

"Well, I appreciate it again. Despite everything, I do love the little prick. Pain in the ass that he is. I may be washed ashore but hopefully he can still make a go of things somehow."

"Bring in the bagpipes. It's all over for Fuzzy Ryan."

"I'm almost sixty, Harry. The circus is leaving town. You know that."

"You've still got your golden years ahead of you."

"Looks more like rust to me."

Harry gets it. He's starting to feel phased out himself, but it doesn't bother him too much. He's grown accustomed to the view from behind, from below, from farther and farther away. Maybe that's a dark kindness of growing older. More and more the world becomes a place you mind leaving less and less.

Fuzzy slides his empty glass forward.

"Make yourself useful while you're back there."

Harry stands and sways, a wave rocking the vessel. He steadies himself and pours a refill for Fuzzy and a short one for himself. They raise them in a silent toast.

"I could drink this stuff every day," Fuzzy says, turning the glass in his hand and staring down into it.

"I remember when you did."

"I don't."

"I think that was part of the problem."

"Maybe it was a blessing." Fuzzy looks at the clock. "You think we could get some blow?"

Harry laughs.

"I haven't done coke in years. I wouldn't even know who to call."

"We need to get the party crowd back in here," Fuzzy says. "I've been thinking about getting the karaoke going again."

"Thanks for the warning."

"It's been gone long enough now that I think I can endure it. Friday and Saturday nights only."

"The machine still work?"

Fuzzy looks like the question hadn't occurred to him and Harry immediately wishes he hadn't asked it. "Let's see," he says. He downs the rest of his drink and heads back to the storage closet.

Harry can hear him rummaging around in there. He looks at the clock. Even factoring in bar time, it's almost three. No part of him wants to turn on the house lights and help Fuzzy futz around with that machine.

A few minutes later, Fuzzy wheels out a cart with an amplifier and microphone kit on it. The big binders full of song selections are stacked on the top. He backs the cart up to the old karaoke area and plugs everything in.

The machine comes to life in a blast of static then quiets down. Fuzzy does a mic check and comes in clear. "I'm not going to do the whole set-up," he says into the microphone. "But it looks like everything still works."

Harry lights a cigarette and watches Fuzzy boot up the computer and scroll through the song selections. He looks around behind the bar to see if there's anything he can do to cut the power.

"Pour me a short one will you, Harry? I'm going to do one number before we go."

Harry brings him the drink and slides into a booth with a view of the stage.

"You know any Irish songs?"

"I'm not singing fucking 'Danny Boy' for you, lad."

Fuzzy punches a button and the opening harmonica of Jimmy Buffett's "A Pirate Looks At Forty" rings tinny through the small amp. There's no screen to display the lyrics but Fuzzy doesn't need it. He knows this one by heart.

Standing there in his baggy guayabera, illuminated by the rainbow lightboard of the monitor, Fuzzy could be a shipwrecked salt in some Florida tiki lounge. He sings the song like a man overboard, treading water, about to go down three times and come up twice.

Harry thinks Fuzzy's interpretation adds nuance to the song because he's singing from the weary point of view of a man looking back at forty, not ahead. It reminds him of the "My Way" renditions a certain breed of broken-down barfly always performs at karaoke. Sung in such a way that it's not hard to guess that doing things their way probably involved failed marriages, jail time, more than a few regrets.

When the song ends, Fuzzy shuts down the machine and pulls the plug. There's a new color in his complexion that's from something other than the whiskey. It's the most alive Harry has seen him in a couple years. He can almost make out young Fuzzy from the old days somewhere in there. The barroom lothario with the Panama hat and the long skinny cigars.

He grabs Harry by the shoulder and leads him toward the bar. "Let's paddle to shore," he says.

Fuzzy assumes his post behind the mahogany and pours out two more short ones. He leaves the bottle, which Harry takes as a bad sign.

"You sure you can't get any blow?" Fuzzy laughs. "Fuck, can you imagine? One toot and I'd keel over dead."

"We could have your wake right here."

"Put my ashes above the register."

"I guess this could qualify as a wake for Guy," Harry says.

"As good an excuse as any."

Guy came from a Catholic family so Harry figures they'll probably have a service back east. He'll get the widow Donleavy's number and put in a condolence call. Maybe she'll fly him out for it. Terry left her plenty of money.

"The night before he got shot, we tied one on like this." Harry is blackjacked by the realization that he's talking about last night. Feels like days ago. No wonder he's barely standing. "We put a sizable dent in a whiskey bottle. Powers, unfortunately. Place didn't have Tullamore."

"Powers is poison," Fuzzy says. "I don't even stock the stuff."

They do the obligatory toasts and Harry shares another story or two from the road. He says how Guy had grown on him over the course of the trip. "He reminded me a little of Andy Devine," he says.

"Andy Devine used to be the honorary mayor of Van Nuys."

"You mention that every time his name comes up."

"Believe it or not, his name doesn't come up that often," Fuzzy says. "Unless I'm talking to you. Fortunately I've managed to make it this far on just the one anecdote."

Eventually the conversation drifts back to themselves and their own triumphs and sorrows. Which is what most wakes end up being about anyways. An occasion to drink too much and say the things you really mean for once.

Harry lights a cigarette, his hand still killing him. He's surprised when Fuzzy asks for one. He must really be looped. He hasn't had a cigarette since the nineties. That's what the cigars were about.

Harry struggles to shake one of the last Tareytons out of the pack to give him. Fuzzy gets it lit. Even after years away he smokes like a pro.

"What were those long skinny cigars you used to smoke?" Harry says.

"Lanceros. I'm thinking of taking them up again."

He says it like a New Year's resolution.

"Why'd you give them up?"

"Cigars are celebratory. I didn't feel like I had anything to celebrate anymore. You don't uncork a bottle of champagne when you're sitting home alone on New Year's."

Harry nods toward his glass. "Usually you're drinkin' this."

"It's delicious, isn't it? Let me enjoy one more. It's a long four months until Christmas."

"This has to be the last one."

Fuzzy checks the clock. "I already missed the *Feud*."

Harry is trying to maintain but his head feels like a caved-in jack o'lantern. His thoughts are strobing and guttering, going dark. Too late has ticked into too early and it feels like the worst of both.

There was a time when a second wind could come on strong and a night like this could still take flight. Tonight isn't it. Even if Fuzzy scored some blow. Harry needs to sleep.

They don't say much over the final two. They drink them slow, sobering somehow, until it's time to go. Outside Harry waits while Fuzzy pulls the gate down over the door.

A hazy San Fernando Valley sunrise is creeping up. They talk about going somewhere for breakfast but decide against it. Fuzzy puts his hand on Harry's shoulder and walks him to the Olds.

"Time to rowdy on down, old buddy."

"It's okay with me," Harry says. "I've got nothin' today."

Author Bio

J.D. O'Brien was educated by nuns and holds a degree from the Jack Dempsey Bartending School in New York City. He edited the comedy zine *Flop Sweat* and his writing has appeared in *Arthur Magazine, Dazed and Confused, McSweeney's,* and elsewhere. His essay on Chevy Chase was anthologized in *The Lowbrow Reader Reader*, published by Drag City Books. He has worked as a bartender, cold caller, dishwasher, and Strand Bookstore employee. After stints in New York City, Los Angeles, and Portland, Oregon, he returned to his home of western Massachusetts. He has a dog named Lefty. This is his first novel.